HOLLYWOOD FOREVER

HOLLYWOOD FOREVER

CHRISTOPHER HERZ

amazonpublishing

The characters and events portrayed in this book are fictitious. Any similarity to real persons, living or dead, is coincidental and not intended by the author.

Text copyright © 2012 Christopher Herz
All rights reserved.
Printed in the United States of America.
No part of this book may be reproduced, or stored in a retrieval system, or transmitted in any form or by any means, electronic, mechanical, photocopying, recording, or otherwise, without express written permission of the publisher.

Published by Amazon Publishing
P.O. Box 400818
Las Vegas, NV 89140

ISBN-13: 9781612187037
ISBN-10: 161218703X
Library of Congress Control Number: 2012946019

This one's for Mingus.

CHAPTER 1

Costumes

The woman at the Department of Motor Vehicles, Hollywood Division, didn't need to believe a word she was telling me. When you work that side of protective glass, you just repeat what you've been trained to say.

To that point, I hadn't been trained to say a thing. Had I known then what went into such training—how many Saturday classes this woman must have needed to sit through; how many different levels of supervisors had gone over the same presentations about "proper procedure"; how she'd learned to wear comfortable shoes instead of ones that made her smile while she passed by a reflection—had I taken a breath and thought about those things, I might have been a bit cooler in my current situation.

No doubt I must have looked a little ridiculous with my costume starting to show through my normal clothes. Time was moving away from me, and if I didn't do something to speed things up with this woman, I'd lose my spot on Hollywood Boulevard to the other Superman—the one who *really* looked like Superman.

"I'm telling you," I pleaded with her, "my insurance company closed down without me knowing it. When the cop pulled me over, I handed him what I *thought* were the proper papers. Please don't tell me I broke the law!"

"Mister," she said, stepping a little closer to the bulletproof glass that supported her freedom to speak as she wished, "California law clearly states: All drivers must have, and carry with them, valid, up-to-date insurance. That is the *law*. There is no debating the law."

She looked over my shoulder at the clock on the wall behind me, shifting her eyes to her mobile phone when she realized the clock didn't work.

"It's a *must* that I drive." I had raised my voice, making the common mistake of thinking that saying the same beliefs louder, and with more passion, would change the mind of the person in power. "I've got auditions. Parts out there are waiting for me. You wouldn't want to take away someone's ability to drive, especially in Los Angeles, would you? Clearly you see how important this is."

"All drivers must have, and carry with them, proper insurance. That is the law," she repeated, not changing her delivery of the line she had just given me. "There are other people who need help. Next!"

"I *had* insurance," I said, fumbling with my backpack to find my evidence. "I can show you the canceled checks. Look, here's a package of them. Proof!"

I waved them at her, but her attention again went to her phone, which never left her hand throughout the conversation.

I spun around, thinking that perhaps my fellow DMV-waiters, sitting there hunched in chairs not meant to be hunched in for too long, would join me in solidarity. "For three years I haven't missed a payment," I said, louder still so that the waiters could hear me. "I did what I was supposed to do. I followed the law. You all followed the law! We all follow the law, don't we? What right do they have to take a day away from you by making you wait in line for punishment? This is America, after all—when's the last time you saw us obey anyone else's rules when we want something? Are there any Americans here?"

Everyone continued waiting without any response, without seeming to pay a second's attention to the starting-to-sweat man who was pleading for his driving life. They were all completely absorbed in their own phones, waiting to see if a mailbox icon would flash some notification that someone out there was thinking of them.

"It's not our policy to check if you've paid for insurance," the lady behind the glass said to my back. "We just check to see that you have it. You've been driving without insurance for four months now."

I turned back around. "Well that means I paid for nothing then, doesn't it? Nothing! Why don't you go after the insurance company that kept cashing checks after they shut down? Who, may I ask, is responsible for that?"

"Mister, I suggest you keep your voice down, or I will be forced to notify security. Neither of us wants that, do we?"

I studied her movements as I would study myself in the mirror before reading for a part, trying to find a flaw in her character. "I've got to say, I think you might actually want that just a little bit—just a little. See the corner of your mouth? You're licking the inside of your lips at the chance to have me thrown out of here. Your insides are moving. I've studied a long time to understand how people move on the inside."

She didn't like that one. Her heavy finger moved toward some secret button underneath the counter.

I tried to isolate my thoughts like those people in self-help books tell you to: *Are you really angry? Are you sure? Isn't that anger just a thought? Do you know if it's real? Nothing is there but your thoughts. Laugh at your thoughts.* Those words flashed across my mind like an LED ticker screen.

"Look," I said, lowering my voice, "I know you can't move outside of those lines you read when someone like me is standing on the other side of a person like you, but I need to know how long it's going to be before I can drive again. Would you at least be able to tell me that?"

She sighed, tapped a few keys on her antiquated computer with the hand that wasn't holding her phone, and squinted at the results on the screen. Before giving me an answer, she made eyes at the one headphone-wearing clerk moving behind her as he put another stack of papers in a basket that had held millions of the same.

"The penalty for driving without insurance is a six-month license suspension," she said. "Come back then. You'll pay a fine of two hundred and fifty dollars and be required to retake the written portion of the driving test. Next!"

"Fine," I said, resigned to figuring out how to get around Los Angeles without a car. I'd already started to convince myself I could use it as motivation for a future part dealing with some down-on-his-luck character. "If I pay you now, can I go and get my car out of the impound lot today?"

Reluctantly, her fingers started typing again. "I'm sorry, mister, but you won't be able to get the car out of impound until you pay the fine and retake the written portion of the driving test."

She hit a few more of the keys on her computer, ending with a firm push down on the return button. As the printer started doing its job, she looked again at the clock on the wall behind me and then down again at her phone when she realized, again, that the wall clock didn't work.

I turned to see how the people waiting in the rows of chairs behind me were reacting to the injustice being done before them, but they just went on clutching their tickets bearing the numbers denoting how close they were to being called to a window of their own. Nine out of ten of them had their phones out—playing Words with Friends, no doubt, or posting their thoughts on Twitter: *OMG this guy is #FREAKINGOUT @DMV!*

A screen above flashed, "E 88," and a woman with two kids spinning around her as if they were orbiting moons walked up to a window.

The woman behind the counter tore off my printout and slid it under the glass between us.

"I'll pay the whole two hundred and fifty now," I said. "Can I pay with a card?"

"No, mister, I'm afraid you've misunderstood. There is a fifty-five-dollar-per-day fee for holding your car in the impound lot."

"Fine. So that makes the total three hundred and five dollars, correct?" I said, translating the deleted numbers in my head into the kind of food I'd be able to buy and how much almost-expiring milk and juice I'd have to consume from the ninety-nine-cent store.

"No, mister. We're not going to be able to release your car until you pay the fine, provide proof of insurance, and retake the written portion of the driving test. Our policy dictates that we cannot let the car out of impound until you have a valid license. Your suspension will end in six months. The amount owed after that time will be eight thousand five hundred and eighty dollars. We don't charge for Sundays, which gives you twenty-four free days. If you'd like to pay the entire balance today, you can avoid interest."

She looked at the clock behind me again.

"What the hell do you keep looking at that clock for?" I said, perhaps a bit too loud, knowing the funds I had (and didn't have) in my account. "I paid my insurance! I did what I was supposed to do. Now you're telling me I need to pay you to keep my car in the impound lot and pay a fine for something that I didn't even do in the first place. This is insanity! Have a heart. You can see what happened here, right? I've proven it to you with the canceled checks. Use your brain and give me a break, please! I need my car. I'm asking you to be human."

"The policy is that the car must be kept in the impound lot until you have a valid license and proof of insurance. Is there anything else I can help you with?"

I was trembling at the absurdity, but the realization that she was answering from some script eased the last bit of fight right on out of me. Hell, she was no different than I was. She had a mom as well. Maybe hers, like mine, had just been laid off by the latest round of California cutbacks that had sent teachers shuffling out to early forced retirement without the health benefits or pensions they had been promised. They never mentioned that in their commercials to get people to come to California to ski or sun or play, but then again, commercials don't use real people to trick real people.

She was real, though, this woman behind the glass. The people sitting in the chairs were real, but the sad truth was that none of them wanted to be here—not the people working or the people waiting. How can you hope for reason in a place where nobody wants to be?

Unable to find sanity on the other side of the glass, I turned again to those who were in my position, figuring I might be able to swing popular opinion and change how things were done. Falling back on my training, I tried to think of which modern political heroes I could draw inspiration from—which speeches I'd heard that had genuinely caused me to change the way I thought—but there were none.

Searching deeper, I landed on Victor Laszlo in *Casablanca*. Hell, he'd been able to persuade Humphrey Bogart to make Ingrid Bergman leave Bogart for the sake of defeating Germany. What better pool of desire to tap into to inspire some action at the Department of Motor Vehicles?

I'd given this plenty of thought. Laszlo's desire was not so much the freedom of Europe. No, I believe his desire was equal for Ingrid Bergman—to be with her without all of those people. To have her in a New York apartment, watching her naked body walk freely around, perhaps searching for something to cover herself with when she passed by an open window. As he faced off with Bogart, he was dreaming about laying Ingrid down on the living room floor and reaching slowly up her dress until his hand discovered that she was without panties, allowing him to run his fingers over the top of her recently created trim, then, led by his thumbs, pressing on toward the point where her thighs ended. She'd let him know where to move next simply by her heartbeat and the slightest of shifts in her waist, and he'd respond by taking the tips of her nipples into his lips, inhaling slightly, and biting down so there was only a hint of pain backed up by his tender motion toward her. He'd hold on to the thought of how one of the cheeks of her behind would feel resting perfectly in his hand as he clutched it before letting his pinky fingers curl up and slowly move over her, before making the final move inside after so long on the run.

That was plenty enough to fight the Nazis for, if you ask me. I had someone whom I fantasized about being with as well. An Ingrid of my own I saw from time to time, walking through my life back where I lived. She'd stayed in my thoughts from the first moment I saw her, which is different from most interactions with women here. Those had all just been daydreaming car crushes or stand-in-line romances. I always looked for the perfect words to say to her, but there were never perfect words, so I stayed silent.

For me, unresolved passion is the only emptiness that's real.

"All it takes is one person to follow me, and then another will follow you!" I pleaded with the crowd, snapping back to my very real present, though slightly aroused from my drift. "How many times are you all going to let these people treat us like this? You know what's waiting for you behind these windows, but you just accept it. How many people like this have you been forced to deal with in your life? I say stop going up to the windows! Close down the windows! Refuse to accept what they're telling you and see what happens. Do you think they have the power to act on any of those threatening letters you get in the mail? They can't possibly enforce their laws if we all rise up against them. Hell, this is America right here—the home of the rise-up! We are revolutionary by nature, yet that nature is slowly being diluted by bowing down to processes your brain knows are wrong yet your heart can't act on. What are you going to do about it? Today could be your day of action. Of change! At the very least, it could be the day you walk about of the DMV with a bit of dignity. Who's for dignity? Who's for sanity?"

There were no bands playing, people cheering, or hands rising up in solidarity. The only movement came from the security guard, who had inched a little closer but tried to look as if he wasn't overly concerned. Nobody moved from their seats or answered until numbers were called. Perhaps I should have been yelling out numbers instead of using words. Looking down, I saw that I'd managed to stay aroused, anyway, with the passion of my speech.

I looked back at the LED ticker in my brain, and the calming, internal messages I'd been practicing in hopes of cultivating a quiet mind had all disappeared. Being Zen in Hollywood is a difficult task.

"What are you going to tell yourselves when you look in the mirror?" I yelled, now completely over the line and headed for jail time and more fines I couldn't pay if I didn't stop. I had no intention of practicing deep breathing or going into a downward-facing dog to breathe into the space my asana had created. All the faces of the people at the DMV blended into a *Last Supper*-type picture.

"I'm going to ask once you to leave," the security guard said. "After that, I'm not going to think about asking anything and just do my job. I've done my job very well all over the world—you can believe that." His short-sleeved shirt revealed not only bulging muscles but bold-font tattoos: *Somalia, Iraq, Afghanistan.* Each one was listed with a box containing a check mark.

"No," I said. "I wouldn't want anyone here doing their job. It might be disastrous for the whole operation."

"I understand you and agree with you to some extent," he said. "But my personal feelings will not stop me from doing my job."

Today was not my day for victory. Best to let the crazies have it and keep them on their side of the window while I headed out to the sun-flooded streets of late-summer Hollywood.

Once I was outside, the air-conditioned insanity of the DMV didn't seem all that bad. I could see why those who had jobs there stayed behind the glass.

My cell phone went off. Mom. No time to talk—not even for a quick one. It's tough for me, having that ability to connect always at my hip, because it causes my train of thought to deviate from the task of the moment. She'd been pretty broken up since getting that notice that the youth of the state would no longer be in need of her services. You might have missed it on the evening news, because they needed to run another story about how baseball teams were tossing out half a billion dollars on a few players. It's okay that you missed it—it's hard to sell commercial spots on stories about education—but you might want to think about that later on in the broadcast when they run the story of the teenager who got busted for robbery when he should've been in school.

I've told you already that, at that point, I was a part-time superhero, right? The costume I had on at the DMV—the one under my real clothes—that was for one of my temporary day jobs. I had planned on changing in the DMV bathroom, but due to my recent ejection and the fact that there were no longer such things as phone booths for even regular folks to duck into, I needed to find a place that would let me use their bathroom to change. There was a Chinese restaurant near the DMV, but when I went inside, the hostess dropped her smile when I told her I just needed to use the restroom for a moment.

Without a word, she pointed at the sign that read: FOR PAYING CUSTOMERS ONLY.

Before I left, I put one of my last dimes on the Buddha's hands in the fountain, thinking it might buy me some luck. Since it couldn't get you a phone call anymore, even if there had been phone booths left, I figured it was worth a shot.

I walked over to Gower, where the old Mark Twain Hotel stood as the perfect movie set for an old noir picture—but I don't think anyone has ever used it for anything other than exterior shots. A man wearing a Clippers hat and pushing a cart that held various balloons, cotton candy, inflated animals, and a variety of other toys was followed by his wife, who was pushing her own cart, slicing mangos and putting them in a bed of ice she was trying to keep from melting. Though they weren't talking, there was a sense of intimacy in how they kept in step with each other.

As I walked in through the side entrance, which led to the front desk, I ran into a man named CArl, whose nametag was written out exactly like that. CArl had a mobile phone and a touch-screen pad that he kept diverting his attention to.

"Mind if I use your bathroom real quick?" I asked. "I just need to change into my work clothes. You understand, right, man?"

"The bathrooms are for guests or employees only," he mumbled. "You want a job?"

"No."

"You want a room?"

"Can I please use the bathroom for a minute, brother? I'm in a pinch."

"We don't rent out bathrooms and don't rent by the minute, *brother*!" he snarled in his moment of power. Then he snapped my picture and uploaded it to his Facebook page.

Can you believe this guy? Should I let him use the bathroom?

"A room is forty-five dollars, and you can have it for the entire day. Do whatever you like with it. Bring someone back and do what you like with her. Or him, however you like to do what you do."

"Can't you see that I'm in need?"

I saw the comments starting to post on his page under my picture; not one of them thought it would be a good idea to let me use the bathroom. Everyone wanted to be funnier than the last person. Twenty-three comments in a minute, but still no bathroom.

"You might start trending soon." He laughed. "#Bathroomornot?"

He glanced up from his screen and looked me up and down like he was checking for something interesting to read on a webpage.

The top of my Superman costume was coming out of my button-down shirt.

"About to save the world, are we?" he asked, downing half a bag of Skittles. "Well, you know, Spider-Man was just in here and there's web everywhere, or I would have let you in. Go on and get, freak boy, before I call the cops."

Out the door I went, brushing past a mom and dad who looked like they would for sure think twice from here on out about booking hotels on the Internet. Their little girl was swiping through the thousands of songs on her iPod, while her brother played a video game, biting on his tongue as he weaved through obstacle after obstacle.

Back into the sun of Hollywood.

Nobody would let me in their establishment to change and get ready for work, so I turned to the spots that people either walked past or threw their trash away in. Alleys are places most people don't want to believe exist. The fear that gets trapped in those narrow spaces causes either quick walks past or quick glances down—depending on the kind of spectator you are.

Ducking into the alley next to the hotel, I was cool for a moment; perhaps the sunshine couldn't make its way into that narrow space. I changed quickly, feeling a little ridiculous, but you learn to let your ego slip just a bit when you're late for work and your stomach's grinding with the fear of losing money.

I'd managed to get the top layer of clothes into my backpack, but as I was stuffing in my shoes, a school kid holding his mother's hand passed by and pointed at me, shouting, "*Superman!*" The mother, as most good mothers would do, pulled the kid away from the entrance to the alley. It was obvious that her belief in superheroes had faded a long time ago.

Seeing the boy holding his mother's hand reminded me of my mom—of those nights when she'd come home with that plain brown Tito's Tacos box after working her evening shift tutoring at the ESL night school (after spending all day teaching grade school). I didn't know until I started trying to earn money of my own what it took to get that taste.

She was always aching to sleep but never too exhausted to spend her last breath telling me about how fantastic life could be if I made the right choices—and those choices meant not letting anyone define me. "There are no dress rehearsals, Harold Hall," she said, calling me by my full name, as she always did whenever she had something serious to say. "It's all real. Don't waste a minute trying to be someone you're not."

Now, having heard that all my life, you'd think that maybe I'd try to be something other than an actor; but I grew up in Los Angeles, and nothing else seemed to make as much sense as being paid to create reality. I remember our first television set: it was this huge box that had two indented handles on either side that I thought were holes you could climb into to get on TV.

When we used to watch shows together, one of us would have to bang hard against the side of the TV to get things to come in clear. When you're young, you don't think anything of odd things like that. That's just how things work in your house. Then, as you start hanging around at friends' houses or going to parties, you start seeing how you're different. How they have newer things and fuller fridges.

I started to make promises to myself that when I was older my mom would have a good TV, a decent car, and whatever she wanted in the fridge. Perhaps the coupon book would be a little less essential. For me, it was going to mean striking it big. A regular job with decent pay wouldn't be enough. I'd have to go for the big payoff, but that gamble was never too far away. Not in Hollywood. We're all gamblers in some way out here. Our stories may vary a bit as to the *why*, but the end goal is all the same. All of us are racing up that mountain toward that Hollywood sign in hopes that we'll be able to lean up against it and finally rest.

I shook my head awake from that memory, stuffed the rest of my regular clothes in my backpack, and headed up to Hollywood Boulevard dressed as the best Superman I could be—trying like hell to keep the bottom of my cape off the sidewalk.

Now don't feel sorry for me—I'm no different from anyone else who's late to work and fearing what a possible loss of income could mean.

Regardless of how good of shape you're in, you can't help but sweat when walking multiple blocks anywhere in Hollywood. The city planners must have wanted to test folks and make sure they had what it took not to go insane here. There's no other reason they'd put so many damn palm trees all over the place, eliminating all but the barest possibility of shade. You have to push through it, though, same as you would out East locked inside a subway car—because you need to make rent.

It's not healthy to question your existence while wearing a superhero costume in ninety-degree heat on your way up to Hollywood Boulevard. I thought about going back down to Sunset Boulevard, which was only a block away. That's where the 24 Hour Fitness sports club I belong to is located. A quick shower and costume adjustment would have made sense, but my delay at the DMV had already allowed the other superheroes to gather and begin collecting money.

I had gotten a lifetime membership to 24 Hour Fitness for doing a commercial for them when they were just starting out, and usually I used it as a place to duck into and either work out or clean up. You have to stay clean and lean at all times here; you never know who's going to be watching. You'll notice that people here are waiting to be watched.

On this day, though, there was no time to get clean. I passed by Sunset this time—but still couldn't help my mind from drawing in memories of the Cinerama dome right next to the gym, where I'd seen my first movie, *Peggy Sue Got Married*, in 1986 with my grandmother. I remember loving how she traveled through time and knew her future already. I saw me and my grandmother, her blue scarf around her head that I thought made her look like a strange Little Red Riding Hood, disappearing through the doors of the refurbished theater. Memories are not illusions for me; they can creep through and hug me at any moment, especially when I retrace steps I took in a city I grew up in.

My stomach's growl silenced that memory with the reality of hunger. After the sun went down, I thought, I could head to In-N-Out and grab myself a cheeseburger animal-style. That would be my reward, though. Now was time for work. I pushed west down Hollywood Boulevard, sweat dripping from my face onto the pink stars that had somehow avoided the fate of other pieces of cement in Los Angeles—cracking or just being dissolved by the sun. Maybe it was the people who were cracking and dissolving in search of the big win.

Now, this little strip of Hollywood Boulevard was still relatively untouched by progress and all of the new construction and evictions that come with it. Change to me wasn't that big of a deal. I'd seen the hookers swept away and cruising pushed down to West Hollywood on Sunset.

Hollywood Boulevard was changing a bit, with actors and actresses getting work in the world of interactive advertising, where touch screens were being fixed to the sides of buildings. Mini-movies to sell products were attracting even more people from those roads that reached out to America.

I'd been on a few auditions for those but hadn't gotten the parts—never the right look. You have to tell yourself that, at some point, you'll have the look that someone out there wants for an interactive 7-Eleven ad where pedestrians can push the buttons and create their perfect drink and then upload the recipe right there to a Facebook page.

I made a ½ Sprite, ¼ cherry Coke, ¼ orange soda and named it Pop Speed Supreme!

It made me even thirstier watching that. What the hell was I doing standing there playing with a screen and watching someone else perform a role I didn't get? I knew this much at least: never peek over your neighbors' fence to see what's on their barbecue. Some people went crazy here thinking things like that—you'd see a commercial or movie that you auditioned for and see someone who looked a bit like you with the part you didn't get. You have to be patient—your role is going to come to you. I told myself things like that, dragging myself up Hollywood Boulevard to make enough to eat.

Now, there were a few of the Hollywood holdouts who didn't like the progress that was taking place. Small shop owners had their rents raised and were either forced to pay or forced out. This had attracted a bunch of the Occupy protestors who had been making waves downtown over rich people controlling poor people, as if it were something new. I had watched on several occasions a few of the marchers come up from Hollywood Boulevard from my office building window just a few blocks down. I understood their concerns but was always too busy looking for a job to join them.

Their latest issue was with the cameras that the police were putting in at each intersection—supposedly to stop traffic accidents, though in all my years on Hollywood Boulevard, I thought drivers had been pretty mellow and pedestrians had kept to the red light system for fear of getting a jaywalking ticket and ending up in that downtown courtroom madness that sucks away your time, money, and mental stability. The DMV was an island getaway compared to what took place down there. The Occupy people thought the cameras were a way of keeping an eye on everyone—of watching what they were doing during their ever-increasing marches.

Whatever it was, there were more and more protests at each little thing the city tried to do. I guess the citizens of Hollywood were finally realizing that they were Americans and could protest what they deemed to be the wrongful spending of their money. I wished some of these folks had been at the DMV with me. We'd have gotten something done that way.

I couldn't hold that thought, though, because I was trying to get to work before the other Superman got there and made his presence known to those getting off the tour buses. Tourists were the lifeblood of the city. After all, if there's nobody watching entertainment, there's no difference between what we do and what folks are thrown into asylums for.

It was tough gathering all the thoughts in my head and focusing on the task ahead, which was still six blocks away. When's the last time you held a thought in your head while you were trying to get to work?

I continued down Hollywood Boulevard, trying to manage holding my cape and clearing sweat from my face simultaneously. Little things like a clean cape bottom can make a difference when you're trying to make some little kid believe you have supernatural powers while convincing his parents to open up their wallet to pay you for the illusion.

Two Suits for $99! First five minutes of palm reading free. Ten T-shirts for $5. Five T-shirts for $10. Pipes and rock 'n' roll! Burritos. Pizza. Burgers. These were probably the final days for all these little shops staying open late, and their owners not seeing their kids because they wanted them to go to college so perhaps they could take over the store and do better than they did. Even Frederick's of Hollywood and all of the interesting people pulling up in their rides and dashing in for a last-minute, must-have piece of lingerie that ranged from soft-core cute to cuffs and prods.

I knew I was getting closer as the indies and gutter punk travelers gave way to Foot Locker, McDonald's, and the rest of approaching progress that was determined to clean up this piece of the world. We never asked for it, mind you. It just got served. Got to eat it, though. You could starve, but most just eat it. Don't be ashamed: we're all human.

The end of the old world up on Hollywood Boulevard was marked by the newly constructed cathedral, a shopping center all done up in fake Egyptian opulence—The Pharaoh Center, I called it—complete with two giant elephants at the top and an enormous arch with phony hieroglyphics to give the appearance of royalty. If you made your way to the back of the first level, the Hollywood sign was just far enough off that it still looked magical. I'd walked around in there a few times handing out flyers for stores when they opened, always eyeing the sign and believing that eventually I would be part of its definition.

Next to the mall, they had erected the Kodak Theater to host the Academy Awards. Perhaps they should have just held it at the Roosevelt Hotel across the street, which would have saved them the trouble of recreating glamour that had been created by those who spent their time carving originals instead of cutting along dotted lines and copying ideas onto tracing paper.

Everything was so much cleaner now; there was no doubt about that. My mom used to drive me home down Hollywood Boulevard from my grandmother's apartment, which was converted from an old hotel (The Knickerbocker, I believe), where she lived in a small studio and saved everything in aluminum foil and stuffed it inside of her fridge. I don't think she ever reheated it, though, because when she passed, we spent most of the day cleaning out her leftovers. Can't take it with you, I guess, but people who lived through the Depression never threw anything away. We'd drive home down Hollywood Boulevard—my mom smoking her Kent Golden Light 100s from the stress of being both a mom and a daughter—and we'd pass the hookers, and my mom would say, "Look, Harold, all the ladies are going out for the night."

I drifted into a quick memory, remembering their legs and all of them looking at me in the car—that old gray Toyota Tercel—with the radio tuned to the oldies station— KEARTH 101. Those ladies' legs were the first pieces of skin I associated with sexuality, so it only makes sense that all these years later I go for the part of the leg I wished I could've seen more of. I faintly remember us pulling over right down on Hollywood Boulevard the day the news came over the radio that Marvin Gaye's father had shot him. For me, those stars on the sidewalk never seemed as clean after that.

Time flipped forward again.

Same street—me hovering over thirty years of age, scrambling to my Superman job. I'd done a few commercials and once served a cup of coffee in a sitcom that I can't tell you about because I signed a contract saying I couldn't claim to have been cast in the show because I hadn't been paid for it.

Finally arrived in front of Grauman's Chinese Theatre, which had been redone to make it look as if it had never been touched, and just as I thought, there were multiple superheroes out there posing for pictures with tourists and then asking them for money once their kids were looking at images on the camera's tiny screen. There were both Spider-Men (regular suit and black suit), a guy dressed like Barney, one guy with giant wings on his back who was ripped and had in blue contact lenses that made him appear to have no whites in his eyes, and an Elvis and Marilyn who worked together because they were dating and trying to buy a house in the Valley and be normal so they could get away from the madness (though there is so much porno produced in the Valley I'm not sure it's the right kind of getting away). My eyes finally settled on the other Superman.

Now, this guy looked much more like Superman than I did. He had the hair with the little squiggly thing coming down in front of his face and muscles that pushed through his costume. Me, I was lean and had muscles for a normal city. I worked hard to maintain a four out of six-pack and decently cut arms, but my muscles didn't have the mass to push out like something more than human, so I had an extra set underneath to blow up, which I tried to do as I entered the scene.

This job was just one of many temporary positions I held throughout the city, but it was the one I enjoyed the most. I had no boss telling me what to do, and most importantly, it was the only one that involved acting.

There was a sense of dignity to being the second-best-looking Superman on Hollywood Boulevard, and it was a cash business, which helped keep everything going while I tried for the dream.

The other Superman was getting an autograph from a few of the tourist girls who had gotten out of the eye range of their dad, who was checking his fanny pack to see if everything he had put in there when they'd left the hotel was still there. Then I saw him look up. With his tucked-in gold shirt, cargo shorts, and New Balance sneakers with semi-high gray socks, he was for sure *the dad*—who had worked his ass off all year long so he could bring his family out to California, to Los Angeles, to Hollywood, and now he was soaking it all up.

Who knows what his route was to get here?

Sat in some movie theater in his hometown and shook while trying to decide if it was okay to touch the girl he was sitting next to. Found out it was. Drove. Talked. Loved. Made love. Got jobs. Had kids. Lost jobs. Made do. Now out here on a vacation they didn't have time for but knew they had to take it. He was the true star here among all of the posters and maps to movie stars' homes.

That's how I saw him, anyway.

You have to allow yourself to dream it up like that, even in the most stressful of situations. Even if there is a better-looking Superman standing in front of you on Hollywood Boulevard taking the money off your customers. What a crazy, wonderful, mad city it is. There are ghosts all around, from posters of James Dean that come in any color and size to echoes of Bukowski muttering his poetry without being noticed, because it rode on the smog and dirt that fell to the solemn ground.

Happy as I was to be here, I was steamed from having to walk and from losing my car to the insanity of the DMV, not to mention relinquishing customers to a Superman who was better looking than I am. Drove me wild to think that money that belonged to me was actually going into the hands of someone else. I cringed when he stuffed each bill into his red leather boots. I tried to blow up my uninflated muscles, but there was no time. Sweat was coming down my forehead—the bottom of my cape now dirty, of course, from the Hollywood streets. I guess the cleanup effort hadn't reached the actual people yet.

"What the hell is wrong with you?" I yelled as he held up the little girl and placed her on his shoulder so Mom could take a picture destined for the office desk. "You're stealing from me."

He made sure Mom took the picture and held a smile that really did look like a Superman kind of smile. Then he put the girl down slowly, collected the money from Dad, stuck it in his red leather boot, and at last turned calmly to me.

"What strength are you trying to prove?" he said through his smile. "There's plenty here for all of us. Besides, we are *superheroes*. It's all for the people who visit this great city, right?"

When he said *people*, he spread his arms out and motioned toward the crowd, who seemed to think this was all a big show. They applauded and snapped unlimited pictures. Dad and Mom were thrilled that their little girl was in the show, but they were wary enough to welcome her back once he let her down off his huge shoulders.

"I was here long before you," I said, not taking his niceties. "There's no room on Hollywood Boulevard for two

Supermen! Get the hell out of here. Go back to wherever you came from."

Inside my head I knew what I was doing but couldn't stop myself. I was going to take the block from Superman himself! I thought I was, anyhow.

A crowd had gathered around us and made the scene even bigger than it was. People were holding up their phones and no doubt uploading videos and sending out tweets to the universe telling of the absurdity that was happening on the street. I tried a few times to walk away, but I was pushed back into the middle of the circle by the tourists who had finally found themselves some action worth taking pictures of. Dad slapped me on the back and flicked his hands forward, whooshing me on. This was going to make for a better story back home than taking pictures of painted sidewalks.

The other Superman wasn't smiling. His jaw jutted out perfectly. I had seen this guy in the gym. He was there before me and there when I left after my hour-and-a-half set. Should have known better. If you want to succeed in Los Angeles, in Hollywood, working out is as important as breathing. Even the homeless guys are ripped, and the mailmen wear short-sleeved shirts to show off their guns.

A swift fist crashed into the side of my head—at least I think it was my head, because I felt the pain shoot throughout my body. Another was heading right toward my jaw, which I ducked and used his weight against him, unloading a right to his ribs, which gave a little.

Crack.

I equated the sound with victory, but victory is never attained halfway through a fight. The right that I originally ducked came back for me and found the other side of my jaw, followed by one to the eye and a kick to the gut that laid me out right on Michael Jackson's star. Those red leather boots came with some extra smash! The cameras were all clicking away. My eye went inward, and the rest of the world spun. The crowd cheered. Can't be sure which part of my body I fell on first, but it was an epic fall.

I remember him standing over me, and as he spoke, his head alternated from blocking the sun to letting it shine through and blast right into my face. The crowd applauded and reached into their pockets for bills. Dad and Mom's little girl turned around with a look that said she'd never forget the moment. Wasn't Hollywood a great place?

"That's right, kids. Superheroes all work together," the other Superman said. "We thank you and are humbled by your donations, kind citizens. They help to keep all of Hollywood safe."

I was going in and out of consciousness for a bit there but could see everyone handing him bill after bill. Me? I drank a big fist of money-sunshine-Superman cocktail and went to sleep right there on the stars of Hollywood Boulevard.

CHAPTER 2

A First Touch

It sure would have been easier if she'd just been one of the thousands passing through Hollywood, but this woman woke me up each time I saw her, making all previous moments in my life seem empty. Have you never seen a woman like that? Yeah, it would have been easier if she didn't exist, but I'd eliminated easy options long ago.

    She had rented an office in the same building on Hollywood and Cahuenga. I'd seen her many times but never once had the courage to hold eye contact—doing things like closing the door to my little office and hitting my head against the wall for never having anything to say, pretending to check an e-mail on my phone while sharing the elevator with her, or waiting to see which direction she'd turn when we walked out of the building and then turning the other way and wondering what would have happened if I hadn't. Then it was too late. After allowing fear into my heart, it was our unbreakable routine not to speak to each other—only smile awkwardly when we passed by or rode the elevator together.

Usually I would have gone directly back up to my office, but my keys were missing after I'd regained consciousness. I was waiting for someone I recognized from the building to let me in so I could go and knock on the super's door. The manager rarely left the building, but his buzzer didn't work.

The pizza place on the ground floor corner had AC and seemed as good a spot as any to recover. The sun was still out, and I was swelling up all over from my beatdown.

All of the pain from the swelling faded, though, when I saw her walk up to the counter and say hello to everyone, from the dishwasher to the man pounding the dough. She knew all of them by name. The man making the pizzas made sure she got the freshest slice. She was leaning on the counter, rising up and down on one foot while looking around at the rest of the place. We made eye contact, but I just did my usual thing of not being able to hold it, flashing an awkward smile and then looking away. No doubt I phonied up one of those dumb eyebrow raises when you recognize somebody and you're excited to see them.

She kept her gaze on me longer this time, paid for her slice, and then went to sit at her own table, glancing up at me from time to time while furiously highlighting a book. The squeaking from the highlighter was entering my head in a wrong way.

"Nobody ever goes back and reads what they highlighted," I blurted suddenly, trying to not pay attention to how much my head was pounding at the vibration of my own voice. Maybe it was the excessive blows to my head that caused me to finally speak to her.

"I do," she said, looking over and smiling at the pizza man behind the counter, who was giving me a tough look-over.

He nodded at her, letting her know her slice was ready. She walked back to the counter to get her slice, and in that brief moment, I felt her absence. When she sat back down, she had her slice, a Red Bull, and a cup of ice. I wished in my heart that the ice was for me—to cool my cheek—but she squashed that pretty quickly by opening her silver energy drink and pouring it over my wish.

The pizza guy laughed and turned away.

"What are you studying?" I forced myself to ask. "Looks pretty intense—at least you're using that highlighter intensely. No disrespect to your method or anything, but I don't see why one line is more important than another."

She didn't even bother to answer. I stood up to make my way over but was stopped by the pain I realized again I was in. The best I could do was make it to the table in front of her.

"Are you okay?"

"I'm practicing positive thinking," I said. "I was trying to see if I could get you to care."

"I care about my time, and I know that I have five minutes to eat and highlight and three hours to write the rest of this paper." She sat back and sighed, looking at me. "Though, in our race toward completion, we can't just pass by those in need. We have obligations as humans, you know. You look like you should be in a hospital instead of a pizza spot."

"Hospitals are for people with health insurance," I said, exhaling through my nose because my jaw was too sensitive to breathe through.

"Oh, you're one of those. I see. I figured, since you work in the same building as me."

"I live here, actually," I said. "And doesn't you working in the same building as me make you one of 'those' as well?"

"Not at all," she replied, taking her napkin and soaking up some of the grease on top of the pizza. "Just because I'm surrounded by a certain type doesn't mean I need to be one of them."

"And what type is that?"

She just looked at my bruised face and torn-up Superman costume, letting up a slight smile, which I have to say melted what was left of me. Her cheeks rose slightly in the newly formed cradle of her grin. The muscles in her harsh eyes softened for a moment, giving me a glance into her.

"Why don't you just go up and lie down?" she asked. "Assuming you have a couch up there."

"No keys, ma'am," I told her in an over-the-top western accent. "Need to wait for the great Rob Larry to let me in. He usually can't afford more than two drinks, so he'll be coming around shortly. Don't you worry about me."

"I wasn't worried," she said. "Being kind is essential for our own personal well-being." She closed her book and took her slice with her out the door. Her hips looked amazing swinging under her yellow sundress. I watched her go and wished my eyes could have taken in more of her. As it was, I replayed her face—the tall cheekbones jutting out like little hills and her dark eyes resting over them, cool in their blackness and stillness.

I kept her vision in the space she had just filled while I waited for Rob Larry. Fighting to interrupt my hold on her image were the man talking to himself in the corner, the tourists trying to makes sense of their American currency, and the two kids in back with a bottle of something that shouldn't be consumed so early in the day; these were my people of the moment. I guessed I was one of them.

I laughed at how right my mystery girl was about me and then moved as quickly as I could when I saw Rob Larry stumbling around with his great set of keys outside the window. Holding my side, I ambled out to meet him.

"Rob," I said softly, "I lost my keys. Could you help me get into my place?"

"Mr. Hall," he said, slurring slightly. "I believe I can help you there. I am, after all, Rob Larry, building super, at your service whenever it is you need it. Isn't that what all of you think?"

"Sure, Rob. You're the super."

He leaned up against the bricks of our old four-story building, tilting back and forth with the slow-walking movements of the pedestrians outside who never made it to the cover of a postcard. If you've been on one of those tour buses, you've zoomed past our building. If you've eaten at the Popeye's Fried Chicken across the street, you've looked at it but thought nothing of it. If you've bought a magazine or hard-to-find new copy of an Iceberg Slim novel at the magazine stand across the street, you've looked up and spotted it over the corner pizza shop above the golden cover pages. The likelihood is that, while you may have looked at our building, you didn't see it because you were either concentrating on that damn sign in the hills just north of us or on the stars that were all over the sidewalk at your feet. The building hosted a variety of independent businesses: small production agencies, writers working on scripts or novels, photographers, small magazine presses, Internet start-ups, an inventor or two, a few bands that only came in at night, and maybe forty other individuals of the same type, all looking to make something for themselves that didn't exist under the harsh beatdowns of fluorescent lights and office managers.

Then, of course, there was me. I actually lived there, although it was against the rules to be doing so. Lucky for me, the enforcer of the rules was Rob Larry, an ever-increasingly bent gentleman who wore the same clothes all the time: denim shirt with jeans, Hunter S. Thompson shades, and this Yankees cap with a very long bill. Rob had had a photography studio in one of the offices for the last twenty years and eventually became the super so he wouldn't have to pay rent.

I usually showered and changed at the 24 Hour Fitness down on Sunset and Wilcox, where I kept a locker filled with my various uniforms for whatever jobs I happened to have that week, and although I think Rob suspected something was up, he never said a word. Kicking me out would have meant too much paperwork for him. He had managed to work the system just perfectly to get himself a free ride.

The offices on my side of the building all had windows looking out over the hills so you could get a glimpse of the sign and a look down at the boulevard. Rob's office didn't have a window. "No need to look at that thing," he said when I asked him why he didn't want a view of the sign. "I take pictures of what appeals to me and live with them on my wall."

Rob was an odd guy, but that was just fine with me. Only odd people really ever got what I was trying to say, and Hollywood is filled with wonderful weirdos who just want to keep it going for a little bit longer.

Now, I say office building, but I don't want you to get the idea that it was like any of those buildings downtown—no glass slickness or shiny floors. This was a bit of leftover noir from Hollywood's days of defining itself. The lobby was illuminated by one chandelier hanging from the top and one pretty severely scratched-up mirrored wall.

I checked myself in the reflection, but Rob stepped in front of me.

"I'd be careful about looking into mirrors that others looked into," he said. "I used to do that. No more."

Into the old-school elevator that you needed to pull open by its iron gate—it was the same material that they had used to make the gate that covered the front door to the street. (They must have had some left over and didn't want to waste it.) On the ride to the top floor, by habit I pulled out my phone to look like I had something to do.

"Does anything sound strange to you about the elevator?" Rob asked. "I don't need any strange noises."

I shook my head no, ignoring the screeching, only wanting to get inside my office and pass out for a little bit. The door opened on the third floor, and Rob walked out with me. That long green hallway always soothed me—I'm not sure why. It was the oddest color of green and was there when I moved in not too long ago.

"That green?" Rob asked, seeing me admire the paint. "Girl upstairs arranged it. Paid for the whole thing herself. She got some kids from the local high school to paint it—something about teaching through repeating movements. Who knows? It's just paint, right? Here, you pick out your key."

He'd stretched out his huge ring of keys on its expandable wire string but never released the string from his buckle. I fumbled through a few missed guesses, finally found my fit, and handed Rob back his set. I tried my best to keep the door as closed as possible so as not to show him the bed and mini-fridge that might have given away my living there.

"What kind of business do you do again?" he asked, trying to peek in but unable to keep his balance from his two-drink sway.

"I act."

"You don't need an office for something like that."

"Days like today I do."

"Well, I could care less what you do, mind you, as long as you don't disturb my space. Filling out the paperwork is a pain anyways. Don't make me come up here again asking for rent. I'll expect it under my door this time."

He tipped his hat, gave my bruises a quick look, and then waved them off like they were nothing and ambled out to wherever the evening called him. Me, I went to my couch and tried to pass out—but I couldn't turn without pain, and my head was heavy on one side.

It was still kind of light outside, but it was cooler now. That much I felt with the breeze swooping in through my window, which looked out at the hills and that magnificent sign that I hated and loved even more every day I saw it. The office was small and had no kitchen, but it was in an amazing location—right in the last piece of untouched Hollywood.

A stack of my old headshots that didn't even look like me anymore lay under a half-drunk bottle of Chianti. There were so many things I needed to take care, but I couldn't move.

A knock at the door startled me.

"I'm okay, Rob," I yelled with as much of yell as I could manage. "Don't worry about the rent."

The door pushed open, and when I saw her standing outlined in the black frame with the green hallway she'd painted in the background, I knew at least my heart was beating with its full force against by bruised chest. She was holding the top cup from a thermos.

"I brought you some ice," she said. "I thought you might be hurting more than you let on. Besides, I think I was a little too hard on you—it's not like you planned on getting beaten up. We are neighbors, after all, and neighbors at the very least should know each other's names."

"You look like that doorway was made for you to enter through," I said, noticing her looking at my Billy Bragg poster on the wall. "I'm Harold Hall and can't think of two things I'd rather see than you and a cup of ice."

"I'm Eliah," she said, walking in a few feet and putting the ice on the table next to the door. "Don't keep the ice on for more than a minute at a time. It's best to alternate between temperatures. I've got an appointment so, you know, I should get going. I'm right upstairs if there's nobody else around to help you."

A man's loud and demanding voice echoed down the hall, calling for her.

"I'm glad the first time I heard your name was through your lips and not his," I said, smiling, and then, I think, falling asleep. When I woke up, it didn't seem like that much time had passed, but she was gone and my head hurt even more. I was thankful I'd blacked out after I'd seen and processed Eliah.

Laying low with a mild concussion might have been a good idea, but I had an audition the next morning down on Vermont and Santa Monica, which meant if I went there early, I could grab myself a burrito at El Gran Burrito, which was right across from the spot holding the audition. Four bucks and I'd be full all day.

No time to go the gym for a full shower, so I went to the end of the hall to the community bathroom, did a monkey wash, pulled my bike from where it had been hanging from the ceiling since I first moved in, and rolled it down the stairs, knowing I wouldn't see Rob anywhere but the elevator. Back out onto Hollywood and into traffic that had no vision for bikes.

The sun above was always on, and I took off. The farther east you went down Hollywood Boulevard, the flatter and quieter it got. It's like they ran out of paint. The space for bikes was narrow, but I knew my way around every inch of that long boulevard. The flatness of the city rolled out in front of me. Past Bob's Frolic Room, the bar I knew Rob Larry was in, nursing one of his two at the start of the day. Past the old movie theaters playing double features for five bucks that you could escape into for a day if you were looking for such a thing.

There was the Pantages, which still had shows and was one of the few beacons of old construction that had been left alone to achieve landmark status. After that, there were only nondescript places that had lives of their own if you bothered knocking on the doors or knew the words to say to people to get them open. You could see, if you were on street level and not in a car, subtleties that got passed by. I grew up around here and had spent time on buses, on foot, and on bikes as part of the rhythm of the city. It always amazes me when people come here for a visit, drive around a few times, and go back home whining how the weather was nice but the place had no culture. We're bursting out here, but you don't want to get off those tour buses.

Just a little past Vine, there is the entrance to the 101 Freeway, right off of Hollywood Boulevard. I waited there, baking in the sun and trying to control my breathing so I could be as fresh as possible for the audition. That didn't matter, though—whatever casting directors would be sitting there knew what they wanted, and they just waited for that to come walking in through the doors.

Looking at the cars on the freeway locked up and fighting for every inch of space so they could move forward, I was glad at that moment to be on my bike. I likened it to having a horse and tried as much as I could to imagine myself riding through this undeveloped land of Hollywood East. The cars were all wagon train settlers pushing west toward something better, and I was on the overpass watching them go, walking a dirt road that hadn't been cleaned for a while, on my own mission toward a destination most had given up on looking for. My daydream was working until I got hit on the side of the face by a half-eaten apple thrown out of a low-ride Honda with tinted windows and a white-outlined cartoon of Calvin from Calvin and Hobbes pissing on the American flag. Welcome back to reality, Harold—the light is green.

I kept riding east, moving past thrift stores with random pieces of furniture grouped together to create a set that would sell. Buses took no account of me at their side, concerned only with staying on route time. A woman holding her baby in the bus window nodded knowingly.

The People Without Cars Society—Hollywood Division.

I took the mental snapshot of the living room and pictured Eliah and myself sitting next to the old record player looking at record jackets and deciding which one to play next in the middle of a lazy Saturday afternoon. She'd be wearing a slip that hung over her body so that when she lay on her stomach, her breasts would be revealed and I could look freely and then lie down next to her and roll her on her side, spooning her as the record ended, neither of us wanting to get up and move the needle.

A smile moved across my face and my muscles felt strange in that position, but it did me good to stay positive on the ride to the audition. I paused for a moment before I made a right on to Vermont, looking left toward the hills that had been following me in parallel during my journey. No wonder people here feel the constant need to climb.

Down Vermont, there is a strip of trees that allows you some shade relief, which I rode slowly under before continuing. Small hotels were still sprinkled on the streets next to the old buildings with odd fire escapes and cool old signs on the roofs advertising businesses that didn't exist anymore.

Finally on Santa Monica, I locked my bike to a parking meter and walked toward the building where the auditions were being held. It was a two-story post-noir job with a storefront that had a FOR RENT sign out front and a main showroom that looked like it had been vacated in a hurry. Glancing up, I saw that the rounded arches on the windows on the second floor looked welcoming, and that's where I needed to be. The warm feeling faded when the clock in the middle of the building read 1:00, which meant breakfast would have to wait until after my audition. I buzzed and was let in through the downstairs street entrance. I cast a hungry look across the street at El Gran Burrito, right in back of the Metro Stop that was finally beginning to show some age.

I took my black handkerchief from my pocket and wiped myself off as best I could while walking up the stairs that led to the second floor office. I opened the door, and there were fifteen people sitting there who looked like they could be my stunt double, though most of them were not sweating as much as I. The place was cool with AC, which only made me feel the heat I had just come from even more. A woman pushing her age down—and her breasts up—held a clipboard and looked me up and down.

"Do you need anything?" she said, observing my bruised face with some concern.

"I need this role," I said, laughing and looking around to see if anyone else found it funny. The other actors were silent except for the noise they made shifting around in their chairs, trying not to stare at my bruises.

"Just fill this out and take it in with you when your number is called," she said, realizing that I was, at the heart of it, just another guy looking for a job.

I filled out the sheet, trying my best not to let the sweat drip onto the paper. My stomach kept thinking about El Gran Burrito, so I told my mind that I should use the hunger in the audition. The part was for a man who worked at a newspaper stand—a good buddy to a cop on one of those crime shows that everyone wanted to see more of. Maybe it made watching the fake crime in real life bearable.

"Anyway, I could help you out, Chief. You know I'm here for you." That was the line. Fifteen people, on this round of auditions at least, in the middle of the day, sitting above a storefront, to read one line that's been said a million times in hopes of being number one million and one.

I kept reading the line over and over to myself, licking the sweat from the corners of my mouth for hydration. Who was this guy saying the line? What had he come from? How'd he end up at the newsstand? What did he think when he wasn't helping people? All of those questions you had to know—as if you actually lived it—if you want that line delivered with the right amount of truth. I asked myself those questions in a low whisper, and people were looking at me and nodding at each other, which I found strange, because most actors talked to themselves when going over lines—even when not going over lines.

I blocked them out and imagined Eliah next to me going over the line on our make-believe, pieced-together furniture set. The door to where the auditions were being held swung open, and a man looking like me, except with a more pronounced jawbone and a few inches taller, was backing out of the room, smiling ear to ear.

All you could hear was him saying, "Thank you! Thank you!" at whoever was inside. When he turned, his eyes were teary, but his posture—everything about his body—was shooting skyward. The women who was taking all of our names went into the room for a minute, but those of us who had been in this situation before didn't need to wait for her to come back out. Lucky bastard got the role. Well, that's how it goes. The trick is to take the punch to the gut that comes after a chance to move up gets denied and keep moving. Most of the actors stood slowly and headed for the door while a few of the newbies who had showered and made the mistake of buying something new for the audition sat there, waiting for someone to tell them they still had a chance.

At least I'd get a burrito, I thought—maybe even figure out how to keep the conversation with Eliah going once I got back to the office building. The weekend was coming up, so that meant my on-call waiter job at Rising Sushi might bring in enough cash for rent. All of these thoughts were coming in at once, but I could handle it.

Out the door and onto the street, which seemed to be even hotter than before, only to find a cut bike chain where my bike used to be. The other actors paid no attention as they exited into the sun, grabbing for their phones as one would go for a cigarette. At least with the audition, I'd never had a chance to mourn, but the feeling of getting your bike stolen is this odd mix of anger and sadness that attempts to draw down the shades on your worldview just a little bit more. What kind of animal takes a man's horse in the middle of the Hollywood sparseness? I grew up without swooshes on my sneakers. No crocodiles on my shirts. But I'd never lifted anything that wasn't mine from someone else.

The sun was roasting, and I needed to get out of it. Catching the subway at the Metro station across the way would at least would take me close to back home.

So instead of sitting at a table enjoying a burrito with the sweet middle time of not having to be anywhere, I made my five dollars work for me, got two tacos for two dollars to go, and went underground to the Metro station. There were no attendants, so you were on the honor system to pay. Thing is, if you got caught by any of the sheriffs whose job it was to check if you had a ticket, you'd wind up downtown paying hundreds of dollars in court fees for your attempt at avoiding the initial payment.

I held the tacos tight in my bag while on the immaculate train. There is no noise down here—no bustle like you see in the movies about New York. It's as solitary an experience riding the train as it is walking the streets of the city. A security guard off a long shift nodded off against the unscratched window.

I opened my bag and took out one of the tacos to eat, and just before I was about to put it to my mouth, a voice stopped me.

"Right now, you're still within the law," a man in a beige sheriff's uniform said. "But as soon as you take a bite, I'm going to write you a ticket. It's up to you."

I didn't even turn my head to see him—just wrapped up my soft taco and put it into the bag along with the little side of salsa I was about to open. I showed him my ticket, and he moved on to a group of teenagers who were eyeing him, knowing that perhaps they'd gambled wrong on whether or not to buy tickets. With the cutbacks in police and sheriff's departments around the city, you'd think they'd make the priority making the streets safe, but it generates more money to hand out tickets underground.

My stomach growled as I tilted my head skyward, thinking that stretching out would open up some space in my body to breathe.

"Tacos are better eaten when you're not moving anyway," a softer voice said.

I turned around and saw, under a hoodie, Eliah, with her face down in a book, still highlighting and taking notes.

"Thanks," I said, feeling a little less punched in the stomach by her sudden appearance. "Are you thinking of letting me sit next to you, or are you too into your highlighting?"

"That all depends. How open you are to sharing one of those?" she replied. "When we get out of here, that is."

I got up and walked toward her. The seats all still clean with multicolored fabric and the walls without so much as a tag or a Hello My Name Is sticker.

"Well, have a seat, before someone tells you not to stand there," she said, smiling but not looking up from her book. "I'm nearly done."

"Big test or something like that?"

"Not for me," she said, closing her book and taking the hood off her head.

"When you just did that, I felt like the sun was coming up and I was blinded of everything else around me," I told her.

"I like to keep it up. I don't want creeps bothering me on this train," she said, paying no attention to my compliment. "Hey, that swelling seems to be going down, at least a little bit. Looks like you listened to me about the ice."

"Not longer than a minute," I said, lying—I'd passed out as soon as she'd closed the door behind her—but convincing myself it was a small one to keep the conversation going.

We sat in uncomfortable silence for a minute. I looked down at the tops of her knees and then found myself only a foot or so from her dark eyes, which started to show a little texture that made up the blackness of her pupils.

"What do you do in that office of yours?" she asked. "There's no title on your door."

"I use it to create different personas," I said, trying to make what I do seem as normal as possible. "Hey, thanks for the ice last night. It sent me to sleep with a little less pain."

Before she could follow up on my description of what I did for a living, the train announced the Hollywood and Vine stop. We both got up and walked out together. I got a glimpse in the reflection of the window of what we looked like as a couple and caught her doing the same. The station had a huge escalator that ascended to the street and giant reams of film hanging from the ceiling.

As soon as a hint of light appeared from the street above, the people on the escalator all pulled out their phones and waited for a connection.

"What's so important out there that people need to check right away?" she said. "For me, I like to experience coming out of the subway and out onto Hollywood Boulevard. There's something special about it, don't you think? Why would you deny yourself that moment by looking at your phone?"

I moved my hand away from the phone I was about to check. "You wait until you get home to check yours?"

"I don't have one," she replied as we got off the escalator and put on our sunglasses to prepare for what was waiting. "The last thing I need when I'm alone and out in the city, trying to get something done or think deeply on something, is the distraction of a phone call or e-mail. We got along just fine for most of the modern age without any of it. That's actually what this latest paper I'm writing is about: the advancement of communication in the digital age."

"So you're a student?"

"Why are you so intent on figuring me out so quickly?"

"Why are you so intent on being so mysterious?"

She smiled and couldn't put it away once it was out, then pointed to a set of benches underneath an overhang made up of metal palm trees. We headed over and sat down to have our first meal together. *Take small bites,* I told myself. *It'll seem like more food that way.*

A man selling hot dogs wrapped in bacon wasn't too far off, and Eliah went over to buy two cans of soda, one grape, one orange, and then returned and let me choose the grape.

I handed her one of the tacos and then laid the napkin gently over her lap without touching her body.

We both took bites of the tacos, and we fell into the scene around us of old women pushing little carts, families waiting for the bus, and two skateboarders practicing kick flips off the railing not too far away from us.

"It's better than anything on TV," I said, motioning toward the scene.

"I wouldn't know," she said, taking another bite and holding the remaining piece up to me as if to show me how much she enjoyed it. "I haven't had a TV since I was a kid. But you're right. Most everything worth watching is in reality."

"What about movies?" I said. "Do you go to the movies?"

"In a way, I do. Not the movie theater, but I do go to the movies." She paused, looking ahead, then back to me. "How much of what you thought of me is matching what I'm actually saying?"

It was so direct and intimate. Amazing. "I didn't think of what you'd say," I told her, revealing a little bit more of myself than I had planned. "I only thought of you and wished that perhaps, somehow, I'd get to be doing something like this."

That was enough for both of us to finish the last bites in silence.

One of the skater kids who had been doing the same rail slide without success since we had sat down pointed me out to his friend, who nodded.

"Friends of yours?" she asked. "Never saw them in my life," I said. "Maybe we should get going, though. The mood just changed a little bit."

She finished chewing her taco, neatly folded the napkin I'd laid on her lap, and placed it in the back pocket of her jeans. We walked away together, back toward the building where I lived and she worked.

"Your face looks more healed in the sun," she said.

"Must have been the ice."

---

24 Hour Fitness in Los Angeles during the middle of the day is a full-throttle blast of energy drinks that give an extra push in the great race toward perfection. Makeup and surgery may be able to take care of you once you're famous,

but getting there—well, nobody has the money to properly cover anything up when you're struggling, so you best get it going at the gym.

Most people watch those futuristic movies where everyone is drinking and eating strange food out of shiny packages, but I'll tell you that if you're into dystopian thrillers, move on down to Hollywood and stay in the gym, because everything going on here suggests that we are being mutated from the inside out. The vending machines are filled with drinks like High Boltage, Double Pump, Flex Max, and of course, my favorite boost of choice, Ripped Fuel.

At the water fountain, gym rats popped handfuls of Pyruvate without any intention of concealing it. The code here is of absolute leanness. After a set of sit-ups, men and women turn to the mirror and lift up their shirts to check out their level of cutness.

Now, as I told you earlier, the 24 Hour Fitness I go to is smack in the middle of Sunset Boulevard right next to the Cinerama dome, so on your way in, you have to walk past a bunch of people waiting in line—couples on dates or night job workers spending their afternoons at the movies. When I see someone in Hollywood exercising when I'm not, I feel fat and guilty that I'm not at the gym. That's why people here touch their stomachs when coming in contact with someone leaner than them. Nobody judges anyone here for working out, and if they do, it's only because they've given up, and there's nothing sadder than someone who's given up but still lives on in Hollywood.

Normally I would have been in leer mode, looking at ass after ass of perfection and breasts that were made to be worshipped the way some people in the rest of the country worship a god. The bends and twists showcased features that eroded all rational thought and had you thinking of various sex fantasies all melting into one. However, just a day after getting closer with Eliah over those tacos, my desire for other women wasn't as strong. My heart was already going to her, and even though my life consisted of quests to be other people, I had this strange feeling now of just wanting to be with her as myself.

I hooked up my DashPLUS+ that would post my time to my Facebook and set off after my racing heartbeat and the internal swoon of my metabolism speeding up beyond what naturally should be happening.

The guy who had just gotten off the treadmill next to me had been going for an hour and a half at 6.3 speed and was dripping with sweat. His shirt read "Cardio Cuts." The treadmills were pushed up against the window so you could look out and up to the hills, and of course, run toward that sign.

I put the treadmill on a 3.4 incline, set the speed at 6.1, and started off on my run, playing the first Wu-Tang album at full blast in my headphones. On my left was a woman in tight spandex who might have taken her workouts a bit too far, as you could see veins popping out of her neck. To my right was a man who must have just started on his routines, as he was walking and already sweating—his gut sticking out and his head down, wondering how he was ever going to achieve the level of others around him. He got caught checking out the inner thighs and all that went with them of a girl in gray tights in back of us, so he kept looking right out the window at the hills through the rest of his treacherous climb on the treadmill.

When I was younger, I was a little heavy, so when I look in the mirror after a workout, it's memory that always drives me to turn up the incline and increase the speed just a bit. Most people looking at themselves in the mirror at the gym don't see the person they are—it's the person they're running away from.

In the middle of my second mile, my flow got interrupted by a buzz from Rob Larry. I let it go right to voicemail, but I knew he was calling about my rent being late again. As I looked at my phone, I saw a larger-than-usual number of messages in my inbox as well as text notifications, but I tried not to look at my external reminders when at the gym. It was one of the few places I forced myself to maintain focus.

Forty-five minutes of cardio. Off to the abs section. Checked myself out in the mirror with a quick shirt lift-up. A young couple who looked like they pushed each other to work out harder with shouts and butt slaps pointed at me and then looked at their phones. I must have still looked pretty messed up from the fight—though I thought the swelling under my eye was more or less a lighter purple and felt like it was on its way to healing.

In the abs section, the pain from my bruises shook me out of my love-tunnel-dream-cruise state, and shifted my thoughts back to rent. The numbers of what I would need added up in my head, and it could only be taken care of by seeing if one of the servers at Rising Sushi would be needing anyone this weekend.

I worked as an on-call waiter there, meaning that my number was available to anyone who didn't want their shift, but I wasn't part of the regular staff. It was a sweet arrangement and one that saved my ass from time to time. The only part that was a pain was Little Tom, one of the owners who, for some reason, just didn't like how I rolled. Perhaps it's just how I looked at him—because to me, any man with pectoral implants protruding from his chest is not a man. I guess my eyes didn't take him seriously, and he didn't like that.

What he did love was the amount of money I was able to get people to spend when they were sitting at my tables, and for most, love of cash money usually wins in the end. Personally I thought he was trying to store away enough to switch out the pectoral implants for a smaller pair that actually fit his frame.

I sent out a text blast to my servers' group at Rising Sushi asking if anyone needed me to work for them in the coming weeks. Rising Sushi would be jumping with all the graduations and celebrations that come with the start of summer in Hollywood.

Of course I would have rather been out with Eliah, but rent needed to be paid and I didn't want to be hurting that bad when I saw her. Sitting with her the other day eating tacos near the Metro station, I sensed that she saw the world as I saw it. I'd been at that same spot with other people, other women, and even some girls when I was younger. And even though it was the same spot, looking at it with Eliah—I realized how much she appreciated the scene around us. I saw that she loved the city the same way I loved it.

Time for abs. Other than what you do, it's the first thing people look at when they look at you in Hollywood. While doing three sets of everything from the twisting ab machine to the inverted sit-up, I planned out the perfect day with Eliah. How would I show her more of the Hollywood that I loved?

I was about to finish my ab set when I was blocked from completion by a woman on her phone, just sitting there on the machine I needed next, talking quickly and loudly. "I can't believe she de-friended me after I was just being honest," she was saying. "She's a ho anyway. You know she slept with Jason, right? She knew I liked him. Who cares? Yeah—I just added him and tagged him in this old picture of us. You know she'll be pissed. What a *lah-ooser*..."

I needed that last sit-up machine because it was super-important to my lower abs, and I was going to be damned if someone with no gym etiquette was going to keep me from achieving a solid six. But before I could interrupt her, something on the TV overhead caught my attention. *SportsCenter* was interrupted by a live shot of another protest taking place on Sunset Boulevard—right near Rising Sushi.

Now there had been rumblings in the restaurant about a possible unionization of the workers—that there would be planned protests right in the middle of Sunset Boulevard to allow all of the restaurant workers to unite. But what they failed to realize was that nobody working in a restaurant wanted to join a union because nobody wanted to work there for the rest of their life. The union leaders were trying to get a pulse on all the protests—trying to steer them toward a voice they could build on and get some of that leverage back that had been slowly chipped away at by enemies they thought were dead but were only being patient.

On the screen, everyone from Unbuttoned Ties and Unzipped Crossing Guard Vests were all chanting in unison, yelling, "No more (clap clap), ninety-nine." Over and over again.

Naibe Gonzalez, a reporter who covered the Hollywood beat, was there looking to get people to talk to her. When she asked one young girl wearing a bandanna over her mouth and nose what she was protesting, the girl took off her mask and looked right into the camera.

"We're not protesting anything—we're gathering. Talking about what we want. Communicating. Don't be so shocked—people do that. We blew this up in just a couple hours, using the same tools most of you out there use the same way you use your money—like morons. Wake up, fools, we're no longer in the shadows."

Many of the people she was engulfed in cheered and mobbed around her in front of Rising Sushi, along with Naibe, who was trying to give a closing summary but couldn't be heard. *Work should be a little extra fun this weekend,* I thought.

Not paying any attention to me or the news in front of her, the woman finished her status update by letting her friends know that she had just done two sets and was now heading for a shower.

As she headed to the shower, she did a double take of me, snapped my picture, and started texting. Maybe the combination of my bruises and my confidence with Eliah was starting to jump off me and make me seem tougher than I was. Perhaps now when I went on an audition, I'd walk in like I already had the part instead of wanting it. Fucking actors.

By the time I left the gym, it was already getting dark. Only a few blocks away—the walk wasn't so bad. So far, having my two forms of wheeled transportation taken away from me was working out all right.

I stopped at the newsstand before crossing the street to my building, observing how the real person working that job would have said my audition line. Though print sales were down and most people were reading on screens, this particular newsstand stayed afloat. They had a great adult section in back, and out front, newspapers from around the world, and the complete Holloway House selection of paperbacks.

Rob Larry came out carrying a magazine concealed in a paper bag.

"Just the man I wanted to see," he said, hiding the bag further under his arm. "That rent needs to be with me so I can give it to the people I deliver it to. You see? Don't break the chain of command, young man. The consequences could be dire."

"I'll have it for you by the end of the weekend," I said, bolting across the street. "I promise."

He may have thought about chasing after me, but there was no way his body was responding to that thought. I kept motoring until I turned the corner of the pizza spot and was at the front gate.

After an elevator ride up, feeling clean and lean, I arrived at my front door to find a note attached to it, written on the napkin I'd laid across Eliah's lap.

Paper done. Up for a movie? If so, pick me up tonight at ten.
—Eliah

Ever have an extra fourteen minutes before you had to be with a lady? I filled it by looking out my window and watching Hollywood happen. It was rare for me to be still and satisfied in my thoughts. I'd caught a few bad breaks lately, but I was still here, ready to take as many shots as the city wanted to swing with. You got to love it in some weird way. That pain. It's a harsh but sweet sting, because your hands would have to have gotten awfully close to the honey pot to have the sting hurt so badly, but not quite bad enough not to reach again.

Below me, I could hear the chains being dropped inside the steel gates that secured the storefronts. The rattle is like a whistle blowing over a factory yard. I sat, in my fourteen minutes of spare time, watching the night shift take over. Me, I had a glorious evening off, and I was taking full advantage of every minute I had.

Throughout the building, you could hear the sounds of a bass and drums from the kids who rented an office in the back on the second floor. The writer who lived next door to me yelled some curse every few hours while the singer/songwriter/actress/teacher/yoga instructor gave singing lessons to those who wanted exactly what she wanted.

I loved all the sounds and being able to stay awake without worrying about the consequences of having had no sleep. A day off meant my time was my time. What a shame that it's such a rare moment when we can actually stop and understand that.

Close enough to 10:00, I thought, so I took out the sample of Gucci cologne I had gotten during a street fair and dropped a bit of what was left in its tiny cap behind both ears and headed up. I'd never been up to the fourth floor in my two years here.

I turned the corner from the elevator on the floor and saw a guy with an envelope leaning casually in Eliah's doorway. He had a huge smile on his face.

"You really came through for me this time, thanks," he was saying, looking like he was trying to extend the conversation. "If you ever want to, you know, take our arrangement beyond business parameters, let me know."

Eliah was trying to push him out without actually pushing when she saw me.

"Well, you're right on time," she said. "That's impressive."

"Glad you think so," I said. "I'm going to try like hell to impress you each moment we're together."

"You'd impress me more if you didn't try," she said so that only I could hear. Then she backed away so we all returned to the conversation. "Harold, this is Derek, my client. He was just picking up something, and now he's on his way out."

"Really, if there's any way," he continued, paying no attention to me whatsoever, "I'd love to take you out. Where would I be without you?"

"Derek, don't make me think about things like that," she said. "You've been a great client who always pays top dollar. We've been working together long enough now that you should understand why that would be impossible."

He shrugged. "Thanks for this, anyway," he said, heading off to the elevator. "You saved my life again. This gives me what I need to graduate. Hope it was interesting stuff for you."

"Harold, have a seat here while I just return one phone call," she said to me, extending her hand so that I would walk in.

Hearing a woman you hope will touch you say your name, in any way, has more healing power than any of those painkillers pharmaceutical companies try to pass off as cures.

Her office was laid out exactly like mine, but Eliah had done a much better job of making it functional. The walls were all completely covered in corkboard and had articles, maps, highlighted pieces of paper, and math equations I wouldn't be able to figure out if you paid me. Surrounding me was a U-shaped mini-library that held books like cubbies used to hold our lunches in grade school. Her books were divided by subject. The whole room was laid out like a mini-independent bookstore.

My grandmother would always tell me: "Harold, you can tell everything about a person by the books they keep; just make sure the spines are bent so you know it's not just for show." All of the spines on Eliah's shelves looked intensely tested.

Just like in my space, the office was broken up by an archway that divided the two rooms. It gave me a view of Eliah sitting behind her massive oak desk. I tried to picture how she had gotten the thing into the building and through that narrow elevator gate. An image came into my head of all the merchants on the block coming together to help her while she directed them. Hard as they struggled, they were happy to help the beautiful girl who'd taken the time to learn their names.

I saw her like that.

"Hey, Will. So, it's a book report, right?" she said into the old green rotary phone on her desk. The receiver looked perfect in the space made when she had tucked her hair behind her ear. I loved the movements she made when she did that. She sat without regard as to who was watching, so I saw the hem of her sundress hike up a bit, revealing an amazing thigh I wished the palm of my hand would know at some point.

She wore her dress a little loose, and I imagined the slip I was dreaming about seeing her in was underneath.

"That's what you said over the phone—you needed, let me see, you needed a twenty-page paper on Ray Kurzweil's

The Singularity Is Near. That's pretty advanced stuff, if you ask me. What class is it for? Speak faster, Will, I'm heading out the door. Modern Technology and the Future of Advertising? That sounds very useful. You need it when? When? Impossible. Wednesday at the earliest. Four grand. It's Friday night and you waited, so now you pay. Me, I've got three other clients who need me at the same time, but you're my longtime one, right? We started when we were in high school—now look at you. *Two* grand? No way. Tell you what, I'll go thirty-five hundred, and that's at a discount. What? Don't be cheap with me or yourself. Thirty-two fifty—say yes or I'm hanging up and having a memorable evening. Good. Yeah, don't worry about it. I'll cancel my plans and read it this weekend. Right, see you Wednesday."

She hung up the phone, did the slightest of fist pumps, and then strode into the mini-library where I was standing. I was a little brokenhearted because she was about to cancel on me, but still a lot turned on by her negotiating skills.

"Don't worry about canceling," I said. "Sounds like you got a busy weekend ahead of you."

"Oh that." She smiled, looking over her modern technology section, searching for a book until she found it. *The Singularity Is Near.* "Read it when it came out. Sometimes you have to withhold a little information to get the deal you want. Getting a deal you don't want is never any fun. Now, you want to talk about writing papers for spoiled rich kids who have coke money to spend, or do you want to go see a movie?"

"Your business face is a little different than your real one."

"They're both real," she said with a sigh. "As little of the business one that I have use for in real life, the better for me."

"You look amazing," I said, backing up to take her in fully. "It should have been the first thing I said to you."

"That's how I'll remember it, then," she said, shutting off the lights and scooting me out the door.

CHAPTER 3

Reruns of Old Movies

"Hollywood Forever," she said, pointing at the name of the cemetery we were standing in front of on Santa Monica and Gower. "Rather appropriate for who's buried here, don't you think?"

"My grandmother's actually up in there," I said, trying not to think back to the last time I was there, but unable to help it. "We put her in some wall in one of the long mausoleums when I was thirteen. Seventeen years. I can still hear my mom and aunt arguing over what it would cost to actually put her in the ground. It's kind of exclusive, you know—the ground. Bugs Bunny is out there. Chaplin. It's an honor to go in the ground here."

"What about all the people in the mausoleums?" she asked, looking past me and into the cemetery itself. "Their accomplishments didn't warrant them prime real estate?"

"Pretty much the case," I said, looking in over the expansive green lawns. "She took me to reruns of not-so-old movies, you know, like *The Dark Crystal*—in one of those little theaters that weren't so little back then. To me they weren't, anyhow. I'd ride the bus with her and be embarrassed when she took her money in and out of her bra. She wanted to be buried here. Put it in her will. Ate up most of her inheritance. Oh, everyone was pissed. I do remember that day." I shook myself back to the present to spend my moments with Eliah, not looking back. "Sorry about that—I was drifting into a memory. Where's the movie at?"

"The movie's in here," she said, a little embarrassed. "Inside the cemetery. You didn't know that? Everyone here knows they show old horror movies on the walls in the back at night. What kind of citizen are you?"

"One who wants to be the entertainment, not watch it, I guess. You should know that, if you're going to be brave enough to fall for me." Trying to shift the mood, I said, "This is going to be amazing—hell, I'm here with you. What better way to visit my grandmother than before a movie? She'd think that's the perfect way to do it. Mind if we swing by her place and say hello?"

I took the chance at that moment to extend my hand to Eliah, and she accepted. We walked slowly up the slight incline that led us through the front gates with the gold infinity emblem that separated each time they opened. The first building on the right, the one with a hearse parked in front, was a tiny flower shop. Inside, the counter girl was putting on her lipstick and looking in her little antique mirror while counting out another round of daily receipts, her phone delivering updates on her soon-to-be evening.

Past the flower shop, there were two ways you could get to where they were showing the movie out back. The first was through the graveyard, which on movie nights is filled with young couples trying to remake romantic scenes from old flicks under the moonlight—the groans that came from the cemetery grounds where not haunting howls of lost souls but waves of pleasure from interlocking body parts.

Even though it had been so long since I'd visited my grandmother, I'd kept the memory fresh enough to remember exactly where she was. The entrance to the last long mausoleum was the only light on the end of the path, which was illuminated in a pink hue that resembled so many of the sunsets I'd seen over my time here.

Stepping inside, I saw that the walls looked to be painted the same pink color. The long aisles made the stacked-up, five-foot-high rows seem infinite, and the plaques didn't just read beloved mother or father of this or that or him or her but listed their movie accomplishments:

Silent flim star. Twelve films over her career...Assistant director of three documentaries and beloved husband...Writer of over thirty comedies during the '40s and '50s...

Over and over the credits rolled up on the plaques placed on the walls holding the departed.

"That's about the best you can expect, maybe," Eliah said. "Whatever you accomplish here on earth just ending up on a plaque on the wall that houses your remains." She shook her head. "It just proves that there's really nothing better to do with your life than to actually live it."

"Imagine being dead, though, without anything to show for it," I replied, glancing at a plaque for a silent movie actor I had never heard of then and have since forgotten. "Something about you should always stay behind after you go. For me, being on a screen, any screen, is the way to do that."

"When you're gone, you can't enjoy any of it," she said, moving in close to me. I could feel the thinness of her panties beneath her dress, stoking my imagination of what was beneath. I couldn't, and didn't want to, hide how turned on she made me. Like most men in that situation, arguments over life and death gave way to desire. She noticed and inched closer still. "You're too easy. I can't respect someone who can't put up a good fight."

"Been fighting all my life," I told her. An old woman holding a rolled-up *LA Weekly* approached us looking for the person she was supposed to mourn. Doing my best not to shake, I was overcome by feeling, for the first time, parts of Eliah's body other than those touched by everyone else. It wasn't just that I was close to her that made me aroused but that she wanted me there.

We held still until the old woman, who was now next to us, stretched her neck up while whispering to her husband, who she'd found in the wall. "I wish I had enough to bury you outside," she said, "but if you had just made the pictures that people watched instead of what you wanted them to watch, perhaps I could have buried you next to Chaplin in the main lot."

"Kind of harsh," Eliah whispered to me, pulling me down the hall past more of the same. "Who cares where you're buried? When you're gone, that's it anyway."

"Not in Hollywood," I whispered back.

I stopped when I came to the spot where I remember my grandmother being put into the wall. The space on the bottom and just to the right of me had more than enough flowers, so I took one tulip and put it in one of the little vases that were hanging on either side of her.

Her plaque was simple: just a name, the dates she lived, and those she left behind.

"I remember the fight over the plaque," I said. "My mother and aunt went on and on about what it should say and which of her two husbands should get the title credit."

It was amazing how nothing had changed—the light, the placement of things, even the movements of everyone shuffling around doing their visits with a whisper.

"Why do people whisper in cemeteries?" I whispered. "It's not like we're going to wake anyone up."

"It's so you can hear the spirits inside your head," she said a little louder. "They're talking to you all the time, you know."

"I'd rather listen to you than pay attention to anything that's going on in my head," I said, smiling.

"Funny. I'd rather know what you were thinking," she responded, matching my grin. "You think your grandmother would mind us acting like this in front of her?"

"That woman was always grooming me to be the perfect man for a woman," I told her. "Everything was always, 'Don't do that if you want to get a good woman.' Or 'You'll never get married if you lick your fingers after you eat.' She told me that at Norm's on a Sunday morning in front of a counter full of people after we'd just split one of those crazy ice cream brownie sundaes."

"We don't like it at all, Ms. Hall," she said to my grandmother up in the wall. "Thanks for straightening this one out." Then she turned back to me. "I'll wait outside while you have some time alone."

I watched Eliah walk on down the hall and turn the corner through the doorway and then I turned to my grandmother.

"We were sitting in the lobby of the Hotel Knickerbocker—remember when you lived there? You would do these plays with everyone in your building. We spent so much time together when I was younger. You took me everywhere. You brought me back little slot machines from Las Vegas when you'd go there on your senior citizen trip. You'd save me pizza from Shakey's—the all-you-can-eat pizza buffet—wrapped in napkins that you stuffed in your purse. I can still taste those little pieces of paper now when I think about it. What do you think about this girl, though?"

I didn't expect an answer, but I felt better after talking to her. Then a camera went off. I looked to my left, and from the hall we had just stepped into, I saw that a kid on a dirt bike with a fuzzy raccoon tail tied to his back bike buckle had just snapped a picture of me. *Probably taking a picture of someone famous in the walls*, I thought to myself as he peeled out of there.

Life was waiting outside. I could feel Eliah on the other side of the wall, leaning. I kissed my hand and then laid it on the cool space just under my grandmother's plaque and walked away from my visit.

As I stepped out of the mausoleum and into the back lot, the movie was getting ready to start. "It's *Carnival of Souls* tonight," Eliah said, excited and looking for a space for us to sit among the already ample crowd. "Drag-racing zombie picture. Hope that's okay with you."

I nodded yes and saw a few empty spots left toward the back, so we made our way through the crowd of Angelenos who were enjoying a rare occasion of sitting down with other people in one area and not driving or yelling or posing. A young man with pale skin and dark-circled eyes sat like a yogi with his guitar and unshaven face while being served a picnic by a younger girl excited to be with someone who already knew what age truly meant. Two men dressed as women, though only subtly, sat on lawn chairs perfectly positioned toward the screen. A crew of fitted flat-brimmed-hat teens were looking for possible matchups in the crowd.

Behind it all, you could see the gardeners working through the night.

We found the last small patch of space, and I quickly put the blanket down as if marking my claim and then set down the bag of groceries Eliah had bought at Trader Joe's.

"You can lean back on me," I said, moving down to the ground first and opening my arms toward her.

"I'll sit facing you while we eat," she said, slopping down cross-legged facing me. "Then we'll think about permanent positions." I took out the loaf of French bread and untwisted the jar of marinated artichokes. The carton of coconut water was still cold, so I poured us a cup in the thermos she'd packed.

"You don't mind that I'm not the one pouring a glass for you?" she said.

"I threw out conventional thinking a long time ago," I replied. "No matter how deep of a connection I feel with you, I'm not going to become another person. That's my only stipulation about this whole ride we're on."

"Why would anyone do that?" she said, taking a sip of the coconut water and reaching for the wine. "What's the use of being with someone who's not being real?" She unscrewed the cap, finished her coconut juice, and then filled the cup with wine and handed it to me. "Just drink half and hand it back."

The space between our lips was magnificently close and tense. Before either of us could decide how much closer we wanted to move, the movie popped on with those glorious trumpets that old films opened with, letting you know another world was about to unfold.

She spun and leaned back into me. I felt like a blanket I had been missing my entire life had finally fallen over me to keep me warm. On the screen, in black and white, two drag racers were about to start their dance at the Carnival of Souls. Couples lay on each other in various positions all around us, some jumping into each other's arms at the scary parts, some eating, and too many looking at their phones and letting the rest of the world know where they were and what they were doing. In the ground and in the walls all around us, people who had done whatever they could in their lives to live on films like the one we were watching didn't take a real breath, though I imagined they must have been gathered on the tombstones or lounging in the palm trees just outside the cemetery to get a good look at the movie—the one piece of immortality we haven't been able to dispel. And my grandmother was directing it all—handing out scripts in the lobby.

CHAPTER 4

Onion Rings

For me, there's no better place to be at 2:00 in the morning than at Astro Burger, eating a burger and onion rings and watching the show go down on Santa Monica Boulevard. The red-outlined neon sign rested just above the window that showed people eating, waiting, cooking, and deciding—all in one glorious painting come to life. The locals knew that this was the spot. People getting out of clubs had to fill their bodies with the late-night sublime menu. Moms drove in from the Valley and left their kids with their husbands so they could have a night out and wake up the next day to stumble to their spinning classes while tweeting Instagram photos of them getting low at a celebration for something.

And us—in that unique moment when your plans unravel and both of you are enjoying the mess. I was wild into a night I wished wouldn't end. There aren't many moments when your plans and expectations just fall away, and there you are.

Eliah's smell was still on my shirt from shifting back and forth against me in the graveyard during the movie.

"These are some mighty fine onion rings right here," she said, admiring the shape of one and looking at me through the center. "There are many things wrong with the world that could be solved over a perfect onion ring like this."

I grabbed for it, but she pulled it away and took a bite. Then she pushed the rest of the little red canoe across the patio table to me.

"Do you believe in things like people being made for each other?" I asked, not taking my eyes off her.

"Even if I were to believe in such things, I don't think the universe works according to human logic. Our means of communicating with each other are primitive."

"I don't mind being a primate."

"Why's that?" she said, almost taking a bite of her onion ring before I gently placed my hand on her forearm.

"That's means there's still room to evolve."

I leaned over to kiss her amid the madness around us, which all but faded away when I felt her lips return the pressure of mine. Then I heard the click, like the sound of a shutter snapping. I opened my eyes from the kiss and saw a young girl wearing a yellow T-shirt and two very skinny suspender straps clipped onto her Levi's standing in front of us, taking a picture with herself in the foreground between us and the camera.

"Yes!" she said, whipping around to us and holding up her phone. "Check it out! #DMVREVOLUTION at Astro Burger! You're straight up trending! I got you, dude—just uploaded the pic and put you on blast. Sorry if I interrupted your moment. That was one romantic scene. Wish I had something like that. One day."

She read aloud as she worked the words into her mobile: "'With @DMVRevolution, showin' sum style.' Damn I love this city! You two."

Eliah got up and started walking away from the scene, but I could feel other mobile lenses on me. I looked up to the crosswalk and saw the camera above the intersection recording everything that was happening on the heavily trafficked streets below, though I'm sure those shots had nothing to do with me.

The more cameras I realized were around, the more of them I could have sworn were on me. "Eliah," I yelled. "Where are you going? People are into our moment here. Maybe they'll make a bronze statue or something of us standing here, sharing an onion ring. Hey, what if other couples starting coming here and tried to do the same pose? We'd be famous."

"I don't want to be famous and certainly don't want to be on the other end of a photograph. Those things steal your soul, anyway. Let's get out of here, please."

I walked out with her and we kept going until we were halfway up Gardner, heading north toward Sunset. We didn't talk until I stopped her in front of one of those Los Angeles complexes that's covered in huge green leaves and bright lights to cast shadows on the walls of the building. I couldn't tell if the leaves were plastic—it might have been the lighting or it might have been the city or it might have been the fact that black-and-white movies make reality look a bit sweeter when you come back out into it.

It felt like were standing in a lush jungle while the rest of the world existed in concrete. I couldn't find another word to say, so I grabbed her and pulled her into me. The slight tease of lips that I had had before was now fully satisfied. I moved my hands up and down her body, from the tops of her thighs around to her backside, trying to bring her as close as possible right then. Nothing else was important at that moment. In the brief moments when we stopped kissing, I could feel her breath moving up and down my neck. She'd etched out tiny roads on my chest with her fingers, which let her fall further into me. I had to inhale all of her. The tall leaves covered us, but we weren't hiding from anyone.

Everything else spun, and I hoped that it wasn't a delayed concussion coming on. She put her head on my chest while I leaned against the wall and just held her for a few minutes. I gently rubbed her back and shoulders, taking stock of where we had just moved to in knowing each other.

"Why were those people taking pictures of you?" she asked. "What did they mean by 'trending'?"

"I've been with you all day," I said. "I could check my phone if you like and see what they're talking about. What did she say?"

"She said, 'DMV Revolution.' What the hell is that?"

"The DMV! I wonder how they would know."

"Know what?"

I pulled out my phone and checked Twitter to see what was going on, causing Eliah to step out from the leaves and back onto the sidewalk.

"Don't you want to see?" I asked. "It'll just take a second. Maybe I am trending."

"This is how you want to remember our first kiss—you want people to be watching it and talking about it? That just eats away at the moment."

"No, of course not," I said and then kind of trailed off when I saw what was waiting for me on my phone. I saw I had three hundred mentions. "Look, they have the video of the DMV. It's my speech! Hey, I sound pretty good. Want to see? I bet those people regret not standing up now."

"I don't look at any of that nonsense," she said. "Why would I spend my time listening to hundreds of people's insincere conversations? People are mistaking posting status updates for action. How can you equate liking something with pushing a button?"

I was caught up in watching myself on that grainy video and with how now it seemed as if the rest of the city was interested in me being myself, totally having a meltdown at the DMV. Perhaps that's what people were responding to these days—just brutal honesty. Maybe it was my time?

"Hey, dream boy," Eliah said, snapping her fingers in front of my face. "I've got some work to put in this weekend. Let's start heading back. I'm not so sure you're better, though—looks like you keep slipping into a daydream."

"What's wrong with that?"

"You're going to miss what's in front of you if you keep dreaming all the time."

"I'm not missing out on anything in this life," I told her. "I just might be planning on taking you with me through my fantasy."

We held hands and walked up Gardner until we hit Sunset Boulevard, which was starting to quiet down at 3:00 a.m. To the west, about five long Los Angeles blocks down, was the Strip, which I stayed away from as much as I could when I wasn't working.

It was now about the time I would have been getting off work at Rising Sushi, and I could pick out the waiters and waitresses from various spots up and down the strip heading back home.

Funny, but if I hadn't been knocked out by Superman, I might have been at Rising Sushi on that night, under the watch of Little Tom and his tits, under the stress of the threats of the busboys to unionize and strike, and under the worry of trying to make enough money to make rent. Sure, all of that still existed, but it existed later.

Those problems were to the west, and we were heading east, down toward La Brea—past the hotels that used to charge by the hour and were now filled with families who could take tour buses out to Disneyland and believe the postcard reality of Hollywood.

"Have you seen the statue?" I asked Eliah as we walked past a strip club being guarded by a large man with his arms crossed but his eyes looking deep into the night. "Right here, look."

"It's a bust of Hippocrates," she said, surprised and then delighted. "Here in the middle of Sunset Boulevard. Next to a strip club?"

"Where do you think he would go if he were visiting the city?" I asked. "Most people just drive on by this, and if they're walking, it's a quick walk to the strip club with a purpose, not a subtle stroll to notice statues in the middle of Hollywood."

LIFE IS SHORT, ART IS LONG was written right at the bottom.

"Where did this come from?" she asked. "It just seems so out of place here."

"I never thought about where it came from." I said softly, happy that I was the one to show her something she'd never seen before. "It's cool just knowing something like that can exist."

We walked by Rock 'N' Roll Ralphs, open twenty-four hours a day for those on odd shifts or out doing odd things at random hours of the night or early morning. Remember, this city breathes off the leftovers that don't make it up on screen. I smiled when looking at the bus stop and once again saw myself as a child sitting with my grandmother waiting for the bus, and holding those grocery bags and balancing in the aisle as the bus pulled out like a giant whale drifting down Sunset Boulevard.

We reached La Brea and Sunset and made a left, north toward Hollywood Boulevard. Looking up through the windows of the Hollywood Gym, we could see people working out, fueled by creatine or just the insanity of being alone in Hollywood late at night, working out in hopes of maybe getting tired enough to reach some form of contentment.

"You want to go in and do a few sets?" she asked, laughing. "I'll wait here for you—or even spot you if that's your idea of fun. I've got some serious guns too, see?" She jumped up onto the grass and flexed against the bright redness of the LA XXXPRESS sign.

"Those are some guns," I said, laughing.

"Go on and feel them—I can't stand here flexing forever."

I felt her smooth biceps and bit softly on the space between the neck and the shoulder blades. Traffic was sporadic but soothing in its odd rhythm. I wished it would never turn to morning, that this evening would just keep going on like one of those long pieces of concrete that pass themselves off for blocks in Los Angeles.

"You're looking at me very seriously," she said, pulling me with her as we got closer to Hollywood Boulevard. "Please enjoy the night for what it is, not what you think it might turn into."

"Why don't you fill in some blanks for me, then—you know, tell more about what *is*. Like, why is it you don't get credit for what you do?" I asked as we hit Hollywood Boulevard and made a right. "Others are getting degrees off of your work."

"That's just a piece of paper," she said. "I'm happy with what I'm learning all the time. How many people get paid, and paid well, I might add, to learn?"

Smiling at the moment we became that much more familiar to each other, we hit the start of Hollywood Boulevard with the wonder of first strolls through the night. At the all-night Internet café, people were playing World of Warcraft and searching on Facebook for someone else, somewhere, bleary-eyed in front of a screen as though it might provide the same feeling of relief that an open window provides.

I grabbed Eliah's hand and ran across the street toward the cement footprints and handprints that so many people had tried to fit their own into.

"This right here," I said, pointing down, "this is respect. Credit—being known and remembered for something you did. Leaving your mark out there so that it can never be erased. One day, when I'm long gone, I'd like people to talk about me being a great man."

"Well, today's not that day, is it?" boomed a voice that shattered the mood for the first time since Eliah had pressed ice to my face.

I turned and saw one of LAPD's finest sitting on his motorcycle, still wearing his helmet and reflective sunglasses, which showed me back my face, even though it was dark. He'd turned on his red and blue lights for effect.

"You just cut across the street when the law states you must go to the crosswalk. I have no choice but to write you up for that."

"Well, you do have a choice," I said, trying not to ruin the flow of the evening. "There's not a car for miles around. We just wanted to enjoy what everyone looks at every day here in the cement. We're residents! Can you please cut me a break tonight? I'm in the middle of something special."

He looked at Eliah and smiled and then back at me and at my black eye. "Just give me your driver's license, and we can get this over with quicker than if you are resisting. You're not resisting, are you?"

"I'm going to have to go downtown and take care of this. You realize what that's going to do to my time? Come on man, have a—"

"Just take the ticket," Eliah said out of the corner of her mouth. "It's already happening; there's no need to fight the fact that it is. Next time we'll cross at the light."

"That's not the point," I said.

"It's exactly the point," the officer said, handing me back my license, which thankfully he'd only copied down my number from and hadn't run through his computer. "Cross where you're supposed to cross, and we won't have these kinds of troubles."

He handed me the ticket, looked at Eliah, smiled, and roared his engine before making an illegal U-turn in front of us and running every red light back down Hollywood Boulevard until he disappeared from sight.

"See there, that's what you get for chasing immortality," she said, grabbing my hand, as well as the ticket, as we continued our stroll, disappearing into what was left of the neon evening.

The sky was starting to lighten by the time we arrived back at the office building. We'd stopped, laughed, kissed, hugged, and touched all the way through the night down Hollywood Boulevard.

"I need to crash out on my couch to get to work on this damn paper," Eliah said, standing up on both toes to kiss me. "I've got two other papers due besides that one, and you're going to be too much of a distraction, so don't be expecting to hear from me until Tuesday at the earliest. Until then, you go on back into your world, and I'll see you in ours in a few days."

The sound of the front gate opening was the sound of our first date ending. Shoes across the floor of the building. Elevator coming down to us and letting out the musicians, smelling of smoke and alcohol—sunglasses down and bodies twitching from trying to make music that reaches beyond the walls.

We closed ourselves off in that gated elevator, and made out a little more before she reached behind me and pushed my floor and then pushed me out when it stopped.

"Are you always so serious?" she said, smiling and then yawning.

The gate closed, and the elevator rose away before I could think of a comeback.

My office felt empty with just me in it. How sublime to finally be falling asleep to something beautiful happening during one of my days. On the streets below, I could hear the metal gates opening and business starting. My phone rang, but I shut it off, thinking that it was someone from the restaurant calling to offer up a shift. Tonight I'd go back to that; this morning, I wanted to sleep without attachment.

CHAPTER 5

Rising Sushi

I woke up with the sun flooding my office, ready to take on a world filled with people that had nothing to do with my love affair. Now, usually the first thing I did in the morning was check my phone to see if I'd gotten any e-mails or follows or likes or any other connections with the world out there to make me feel as if someone was paying attention to me. Today, though, I went to my minibar fridge and pulled out a cold bottle of water to take away the heat that was already surrounding me.

I looked at the mountain and the sign that had been taunting me for so many years, and there was a little less heaviness in my heart than normal. I took a full breath. When was the last time I'd actually taken in a breath? Eliah. Even saying her name had an exhale at the end.

My phone vibrated, and I left my water at the windowsill to check it. I couldn't believe my eyes when I saw the number of missed calls: twenty. The number of e-mails: forty-three. Forty-three e-mails—some of those had to be opportunity.

Mixed in with the notifications were texts from waitresses who wanted me to cover their shifts. I ignored those for a moment. I'd gone up two hundred followers overnight. I was getting tweets, and my Facebook page was just blowing up with requests.

The phone rang from an unknown number. "Who's there?"

"That's a very odd way to answer the phone, Mr. Hall," a female voice said while I struggled to hit the speaker button. "Then again, you're a very odd fellow, isn't that correct?"

"I hope that I'm odd," I said, going along with the fun. "What's the use of being normal? Who's going to call me if I'm normal?"

"You're right, Mr. Hall. We don't care for normal," she answered. "My name's Samantha Parsons, and I actually sought you out for a part. You certainly seem to have a flair for rousing speeches. Our production company is holding auditions for a role I feel you may just be perfect for. Would you be interested in coming in for a read?"

"Can you tell me a little more about what I'm reading, please?" I asked, getting serious as I realized this might be something real. "I like to be as prepared as possible when trying to fit into a role."

"We're not really looking for prepared. We're looking for something that's never been seen. As you might expect, the search is exhausting."

"I can try to make it there today, but seeing as how my transportation issue is a bit dicey, I'm not sure how long it's going to take."

"I figured that might be the case," she said, chuckling, "but I don't think you'll need to worry about transportation to us. I'll send a car for you; I don't want you walking to the Valley."

"Do you do that for everyone who's auditioning?"

"Only for those whom I'm pushing to get the part," she said and then asked for my address. "Look for a car within the half hour. I have a feeling this is going to be something special."

I didn't want to hang up for fear of the phone call not being real. I waited a few seconds to see if I was going to wake up, then, realizing I wasn't dreaming, smiled wide.

I still had time before the car arrived, and even though Eliah had told me she needed a few days to finish her work, I wanted to do something to start the day right for her. I got dressed and went down to the pizza shop to get her a little breakfast.

As I strolled in, two old men were exchanging sections of the *Los Angeles Times* on the table up against the window.

"My name's Harold," I said to the counter guy. "Figured that after all of these years, I might as well introduce myself."

"Mine's Louis," he said, extending his hand. "You look very different today. A bit—I don't know—lighter, somehow." He grinned. "Maybe that has something to do with Ms. Eliah. She lights up the place when she comes through those doors. I think maybe I'd save a fortune on electric bills if she'd just hang out in here all day. People need that, I think. Ms. Eliah drinks the tea, not the coffee. You were going to bring something to her, yes?"

"Yes. What about orange juice, though? I think I'll get her that and one of those blueberry muffins."

"I've never seen her get that before," he said.

"Perfect."

I gave him five of my last ten dollars and felt proud for being able to do that. I couldn't help but think that soon, if that call was real and the audition went well, I wouldn't have to keep track of each cent.

Knocking on her door a few times and trying to balance the coffee and OJ was tough, so when she didn't answer, I turned the knob and pushed. She had her Beats headphones on and was bopping her head to the music while cranking out words on her laptop. Somehow, she'd turned the desk around so that her back was now to the door and she was facing the window, though not looking out—only focusing on the work. At her feet were three Red Bull cans—not sugar-free, though. You should drink the sugar-free if you're taking in the Bull like that—better for your bottom rim and stomach.

I went on watching her work for a minute, lost in her movements and her way of interacting with her environment. For as long as I could, I stayed lost, and then I placed the muffin and OJ on the little table next to the door with a note that read, *Just wanted to be part of your day.*

I locked the door behind me because I didn't want anyone else coming in and walked down those green hallways like a man strolling through the middle of a park with the love of a good woman acting like the wind at his back. I was about to take a ride.

The black Lincoln Town Car was driven by a tall man who never said anything to me other than hello. During the drive, he was texting and jumping in and out of phone calls. I concentrated on the zooming world around me, happy to be in a car again going through Hollywood. We took Hollywood Boulevard down to Laurel Canyon and made a right, heading up the path that separated the Hollywood Hills from the Valley.

As we climbed, the skinny palm trees gave way to lush foliage that grew behind walls that got higher the higher up we drove. Masked men and women stood on ladders while they trimmed and watered the greenery.

We drove past the Mt. Olympus sign on our right, marking a private community that wasn't guarded but somehow managed to keep those they didn't want in, out. Perhaps it was the luxury of the houses and cleanness of the streets that made folks from the sunbaked lowlands feel like they didn't belong.

Houses started to appear on the side of mountains as we drove higher. Little turnoffs that led to tree-covered streets were everywhere, but in all my time in LA, I'd never had time to make my way down them, always sticking to the main road that we were on. Gated entrances to the houses higher up on the side of the hills were locked, and the higher we climbed, the fewer houses you could see from the road. It was as if the city planners had made a mistake and put all the oxygen up here for these few people instead of down below where the masses could have used it to take a decent breath in, escaping the smog.

On Gould Avenue, one of the little roads that turned up from Laurel, I saw a woman jogging with a group of dogs pass a man walking alone, seeming to talk to himself but really yelling into a Bluetooth. The dogs looked pretty happy.

The houses got more and more amazing; the sheer space and land they had was inspiring. I saw a couple sitting on their deck meditating and wondered how long it would be before Eliah and I had a place to look out on the world like that. The houses seemed to repeat themselves in their solitude and peacefulness as the road wound like a serpent, now starting its decline into Studio City, the entrance to the valley below.

We made a left onto Ventura Boulevard, and as if we had just emerged from a car wash, the world was suddenly immaculate. We pulled into a parking lot of a new office building that reflected the sun as if it were refusing its power.

"This is you," the driver said, still texting. "I'll wait here."

I felt the window to see how hot it was and dreaded the reality of the open car door.

After a deep breath, I stepped out into the blazing valley sun and walked to another audition I hoped would change my life.

This audition started out like most of the rest, though the nondisclosure they had me fill out was a little strange. It didn't bother me at all; I always thought it to be bad luck to talk about auditions until I knew one way or the other anyway. There was a room full of us, all the same body type, same look in our eyes, same hope-and-fear cocktail we all loved to pound. They kept calling people in—each audition lasting only a minute or two before the actor would come out looking pissed off and a little shocked.

A ripped guy with a Mohawk stormed out. "All they did was just ask me to take my shirt off and look into the camera and smile," he said. "Can you believe that?"

Then the door opened, and my name was called by a young woman with incredible posture, sporting a gray pencil skirt and a thin, white blouse that gave a little look between the buttons but nothing so obvious as a plunging neckline. "Nice to meet you in person, Mr. Hall," she said, handing me a sheet of paper with the words GOLDEN STATE BROADCASTING—OPENING SCENE written across the top. "I'm Samantha. We spoke on the phone."

She seemed to be looking at me from over the rim of her glasses, which were a little too big for her face. When she moved around the room, each stride moved the fabric of her skirt so that it seemed to rub gently against her legs.

"If you'll follow me, Mr. Hall—"

"Harold, please," I said. "Mr. Hall brings back bad memories of the principal's office in grade school."

She smiled slightly, but didn't seem to have the time to complete the motion as she reached for the doorknob and let me in. The room was lit with a few floor lamps that gave the huge ficus plant in the corner a significant shadow on the wall.

The man sitting in the chair behind the desk was dressed in jeans, a V-neck sweater with a white T-shirt underneath, and a blue blazer that hung open and showed about two-thirds of his watch, which looked perfectly rugged—like something a pilot might wear.

"Are you married?" he asked me.

"Does it matter either way in regard to the part?" I asked, looking down at the script and then back up at him. "You're not with the IRS, are you? I'm still gathering receipts. This isn't one of those sting operations, is it?"

"No, friend," the man said, smiling. "I was asking because you weren't distracted by Samantha's backside when she walked you in. Most of the others were. I was merely looking for a reason why."

"Well, and no offense to Ms. Parsons, but my mind is on another woman right now. Hey, what kind of audition is this?"

"One that's looking to do things a bit differently, friend," he said, leaning his head against the tips of his thumb and forefinger. "I just like to know things about people I might be working with. Information, after all, is the modern-day currency. At least that's what we're banking on. My name's Peter Wolfson, but everyone calls me Pete the Wolf."

"Harold Hall," I said. "You make one hell of a first impression, but I don't mind people saying exactly what they think. Kind of refreshing."

"Yes, we'll have to do something with that name," he said, looking at Samantha, who made a note. "He's trending—is that what you said, Samantha? You know, she's the one who begged that we have you come in and read. That was some show you put on at the DMV. However, I don't believe in giving away performances that are worth potential millions for free. Did you have a writer for that, or do you perform your own material?"

"We just couldn't stop talking about the speech," Samantha interrupted, though Pete gave her a look like she shouldn't have.

"A writer for what? My DMV meltdown? Hell no. I speak without filters, and writers put them on, no? It's how I've managed to stay sane. I didn't even know the cameras were rolling, to tell you the truth. Funny, I've been waiting my whole life to be recognized for being someone other than myself, and it wasn't until I thought the cameras were off that it finally happened."

"The universe enjoys a good joke," said Pete, pouring me a tall glass of water out of a crystal pitcher. "I was under the impression it was all part of your act. Some kind of show you're performing out there—to be seen and followed. Everyone's using social media these days to attack an audience."

"Self-promotion?" I said, backing up a little. "No sir, I don't put myself up on YouTube with little skits. It's not pro. I've always held out for something real."

"Oh, I see." Pete the Wolf chuckled. "You only do *pro* work. Only on TV and in movies. No Amateur Night at the Apollo for you, I see."

"You got that right, pal," I said, liking the way the word *pal* just came off my lips. "If you're here in Hollywood, you might as well strike it big. Go big or go home, that's what I'm about."

"Go big or go home," he repeated slowly.

"Go big or go home."

We both took long sips of water and looked at each other's eyes to see what was happening behind our shown selves.

He snapped his fingers at Samantha, who missed it at first and then jerked toward him and handed him her old, classic leather briefcase, complete with a latch that needed to be unlocked by a small key she wore around her neck.

"Samantha has quite a knack for finding exactly what I'm looking for," Pete the Wolf said to me.

"There was something so perfect about him when I saw the video, Pete," Samantha said, pushing up her glasses.

"Perhaps. However, Mr. Hall, we'll have to dispel your notions on what entertainment is and how it's delivered. You seemed to be under the assumption that the future is going to be as it has always been. We'd like to be part of an industry shake-up. What do you think about that?"

"I tell you, Mr. Wolf," I said, leaning back and trying to play it as cool as I could, even though I felt that odd sensation of being close to getting what I'd been waiting for all those years of wanting. "If you have a role you want played by someone ready to lose himself in it, you have the right person sitting across from you."

"Samantha, why don't you tell the rest of the people waiting to leave?" Pete said. "I'd like to talk to Mr. Hall, alone."

"Of course. Though perhaps I should be here?" she protested faintly, putting on her matching gray blazer to heighten her stature. "I'm going to be overseeing the writers and scouting out locations, so it would help with my understanding to know each part of Mr. Hall's personality—if we did decide to go with him, that is."

"There will be plenty of time for all of us to get to know one another," Pete the Wolf said. "For now, we'll just follow process and see where that takes us.

"She's an amazing woman," he said, taking a breath after watching her leave. "She came to *me*, you know. She was working in a law firm downtown making good money and on her way to being one of those power women who seem to have it all. Did she want any of that? No. She wants to write movies. You have to respect someone who does what they do because of passion and not reward."

"Maybe her passion is her reward," I said, starting to feel comfortable. "Some folks are just like that. Look at me—I guess it wasn't such bad thing after all to lose my mind at the DMV."

"Mr. Hall, I can see you're a friend who likes it straight," he said, finishing what was left in his glass and then pouring himself another. "You see, with the social climate being what it is—you wouldn't like a real drink, would you?"

I shook my head no, as I wanted complete sobriety for this moment of ascension.

"Good, good. Let's talk about Golden State Broadcasting. See, with all of the Occupy movements and attempts at government overthrow around the world, we think it's time to put something on television that captures that revolutionary spirit like never before. The people who are dissatisfied are no longer college students or the forever poor, Mr. Hall. No, if you look closely on the street at who's looking in the trash for thrown-out furniture or spare bottles to recycle, they're what the news calls 'everyday Americans'—though I'm not sure what that means. We're all Americans. Myself, I believe they are talking about the people who thought the dream of full refrigerators was a birthright. There are spaces now between the groceries, Mr. Hall. Are you still with me?"

I nodded and listened, as is best to do when you wish for someone to trust you enough to tell you valuable information.

"The premise for the show is this: A social networking site makes a play to buy out California's debt to gain control of how the state budget is spent. Facing massive layoffs of public servants, police, fire departments, and a disgruntled population, there is no choice but to privatize.

"Soon after, the social networking company moves the capital of California down to Hollywood. The present government stays up north and continues with their made-for-TV dances, because really, it's just a show anyhow. The power shifts to Hollywood, and a call is put out to all Americans who want to move to California. The promise to all who move here is that that they will be given their own channel on something called Golden State Broadcasting—GSB, for short.

"The state of the country being what it is, craftspeople, farmers, teachers, actors, office managers, writers, data entry technicians—anyone in America can come to work in California and broadcast government-subsidized TV shows on whatever their expertise is. We will promise them development folks who will help them create a brand for themselves. Their success comes in the form of followers. The more followers, the better you live. The underlying thought here is that most people would give up what's left of their normal lives for a shot at Hollywood. Golden State Broadcasting would be that shot. If you look at the current state of social media, everyone out there believes they can be famous. Why else would you devote so much time to maintaining a Facebook page, Twitter account, or blog, or post YouTube videos? The self-importance of Americans is at an all-time high, and we'd like to tap into that.

"Of course, the United States is not going to let this happen, so they order California to stop. But they won't stop and set in motion a plan to secede from the rest of the country. Among the millions now seeking refuge within California's borders, one man steps forward to lead the secession and claims that all who follow him will be part of the creation of a state run by entertainment. We won't be attracting viewers, Mr. Hall; we'll be attracting those who want to make something of themselves away from the offices and regulations they live their lives by. It's the Hollywood dream. That person to play the leader very well could be you.

"The content will be distributed on a massive social networking site, the Golden State Broadcasting network. In a nation full of content creators, there's no other place to be but Hollywood."

The door swung open, and Samantha entered again.

"I've sent everyone home, Pete," Samantha said, then gave a look at the script I was holding. "Maybe he should read a few lines. I wrote some thoughts down—nothing official, but it may help us. You know, Mr. Hall, that purity we saw at the DMV—what is coming from inside of you—that's what we want in our star. Ambition. Confidence. Purpose. Something to say."

"Yes, Samantha," Pete said. "If he has as much passion for the part as you, we'll have a hit on our hands."

As he was telling me the pitch, I was picturing myself playing that role and being known throughout the world as that character. It wasn't exactly a movie, but what the hell did I care? I was going to be famous, and the role would be written for me based on what I was doing in the real world. I'd been trying to get out of being me for my entire life, and here this man was offering me a role as, essentially, myself. I'd make it work, though.

I was near tears but held them in. After all, it was still business. I'd save the emotions for Eliah and what was to come with us. There wasn't a moment of my future that I didn't see her being a part of now. I'd look at houses, and I'd imagine us in them. I'd imagine walking through the pound to pick up a dog. Jumping on planes to other places or just sitting at home not caring what time of day it was. I was going to be one of those lucky ones who had it all.

"I think I'll be able to handle it," I said, doing all I could to restrain myself. "I'm sure it's not as easy as sealing it with a handshake, though I sure wish it was."

"Many times, friend, so do I," he said, resting his hand on my shoulder. "There are a few other people you need to meet first. Samantha will set up the meeting and contact you at the appropriate time. The one who controls our finances is always hard to reach. Money never sleeps, you know. Please keep all of this on the down-low. We're going to be letting out little pieces of the show as if it were real—you know, fake but real-looking commercials by Golden State Broadcasting telling people to move to California."

"That's not a problem," I said, standing up to shake his hand. "I play it that it's bad luck to talk about a part before you have it, and the last thing I need is a dark cloud hanging over this lucky streak I have going. I've been waiting for this chance for too long."

"Friend, I think it's we who have been waiting for you."

CHAPTER 6

Seeds

The ninety-nine-cent store on La Brea and Willoughby is a haven for the broke but not brokenhearted. I'll tell you, folks, that is one great thing about living in Los Angeles: you can have just pennies in your pocket and there's always something to keep you going—always enough gas to make it to the next station.

Now, normally I'd come here to buy some pasta or see what kind of little treats they had available. You didn't have to feel ashamed being here because everyone pushing a cart around was in the same position. There was a glorious freedom from the need to worry about checking prices, only expiration dates.

Walking up and down the aisles, I tried to find the perfect gift. I needed to eat, which meant three of my dollars were going to an orange drink and two Lunchables—so I had to make the choice more valuable than my remaining two dollars.

Finally, after examining an endless supply of socks and badly made coloring books, there it was. A rack full of flower seeds. It was perfect and enough to build an idea around.

While standing in line, I put the whole plan together. We'd go on a hike up the hills, and I could take the two Lunchables with me as little snacks in case we got hungry. We'd go to Runyon Canyon, where there would be infinite hiking trails and butterflies moving around as Eliah and I hiked up the trails, pausing now and then to look back and watch the city get smaller. The middle of the day would make the park ours alone. I'd find a patch under a tree with some moist soil, take out my packet of seeds, and then dig little spaces and plant them. This would be our plot of land, taken in secret, and each spring we'd come to watch the flowers bloom and kiss under the tree.

Up to the counter with my orange drink, two Lunchables, and packet of flower seeds. The woman at the register looked at the seeds strangely.

"Oh, I've never seen these before," she said. "There's no bar code—I don't think I can ring them up."

"But," I said, "everything's the same price here."

"That's true," she replied, holding on her U a for a bit so it sounded like "truuuuue" before looking at all sides of the package for the bar code, "but we need to ring it up as the item itself. That's how we put it in the system. I don't want to lose my job. Would you please go back and see if there's another one that has a bar code? I can't sell you this one."

Back through the aisles to the spot where I'd seen the seeds. I went through each pack, and they were all the same, unmarked by a bar code. I knew that returning with the same pack would net me the same response, so I looked around to see if anyone was watching and then slid them into my back pocket and headed toward the register.

"None of them has the bar code," I said, hoping she'd come to her senses and not turn me into a thief for trying to be rational. "Can I just pay you for this one and we'll be good?"

"There's nothing I can do about that," she said. "It happens sometimes. Just pick something else. Everything's a dollar, and none are worth more than the other."

I told her I understood, paid for my three items, and walked out of the store half-expecting some alarm to go off and to find myself in jail for stealing a ninety-nine-cent bag of seeds in preparation for a romantic walk in the park.

"What are you in for?" the man arrested for assault would ask.
"Stealing seeds. Flowers. You?"
"I shoved someone's head through a window for not paying me what they owed."
"I can see that."

No time for daydreaming and no alarms. I was done. Back up La Brea to go pick up Eliah and start the date before I had to go into work. Things were going well, I thought; plus, I'd beaten the system and had a pack of seeds in my pocket.

As I was coming into our office building, I saw a tall man wearing a V-neck T-shirt and a blue blazer coming out of the steel gate holding a manila envelope just like the one Derek had been holding. He wasn't smiling; he was wearing instead that kind of awkward look a man has when walking out of a strip club.

"What are you doing down there like a mope?" a voice said from what seemed high above. "It's Wednesday afternoon, and the city is ours. What do you think about that?"

Eliah was sitting on the top of the building with her feet dangling from above. Though the roof was only four stories up, she looked so far away from me. I could see the bottom of her white mesh Vans, which are always perfect for any entrance you make in Los Angeles, and the hint of the backs of her calves. As she leaned over, I noticed she was holding a giant red ball with a card attached to it. She let it go, but rather than falling, it rose. She repeated the same action a few times, and soon the sky was filled with red balloons disappearing into tiny red dots. I shaded my eyes and watched them go as far as I possibly could.

She walked down the fire escape and climbed into her window, and I didn't shy away from watching her move. Though she didn't wear clothes that were meant to accentuate her figure, a breeze was kind enough to kick in and push her T-shirt just above her stomach, which led to the tip of her cotton bra. Her shapely calves flexed as she walked down the cool iron, though she held her skirt to prevent me from looking up it—but the not-seeing was more erotic to me than a full view. Every now and then, she'd look up to watch the balloons on their ascent, but I'd lost any of that.

A few minutes later, after I watched the balloons disappear from sight, she appeared through the front gate and gave me her hand.

"If I never have to think about how humans and machines are going to be one again, it will be too soon. Ray Kurzweil blows my mind but also exhausts me. All of that's done and over. What magic do you have planned for me today, kind sir?"

"To the hills, my lady," I said, playing off of her and folding her arm into mine. "To the hills."

Moving past La Brea but still on Hollywood—that's where the Hollywood Boulevard that tour buses roll down ends and the strip where residents live starts up. The transition is subtle and starts with those old-style apartment buildings with decks and slightly open sliding doors. Up on one deck stood a woman in designer sweatpants talking in a loud Russian accent on her mobile phone through a mask of makeup, while below, a man jogged without his shirt singing to the Guns N' Roses song screaming to escape his headphones. Around them, gardens were being manicured and watered to keep from wilting by people who needed the same treatment. This was the start of the lowlands right before the Hollywood Hills truly started.

We made a right on Fuller and then walked up a few blocks to Runyon Canyon, where soap opera stars jogged and those who wanted to be soap opera stars walked dogs for execs who ran soap operas. I believed the Hollywood legend that the whole canyon used to be Errol Flynn's estate. I never wanted to lose belief in that story, which said that when he died, his will stated that it be turned it into a public park. Throughout the trails, there were tiny pieces of walls that I always imagined were ruins from his mansion—little pieces of stone serving as echoes from what might have been real so long ago. Hiking trails ran throughout the park, and I had been on each one of them alone many times, so I had no trouble planning out a route in my head and of course, checking my watch to make sure I had enough time to walk Eliah back, go to the gym and shower, and then race back to Rising Sushi to make money so I could keep it all going until I'd made it.

Now, you may be thinking that my mind was on the big part of the revolutionary, but I kept drifting to Eliah—daydreaming how her breasts would feel lying on my chest when we had an early morning with nowhere to go but back to bed. How amazing she'd look from behind getting up and walking to the kitchen.

"What's up with those balloons you were letting off the roof?" I asked as we climbed up through the main gates and headed up the path toward the rest of the park. "Are you sending secret messages to someone? I used to do that with bottles down at the end of the Venice piers. The fishermen looked at me like I was crazy, but fishing when there's already fish in the market is just as insane."

A midday yoga class was in session on the lawn to our left where mothers were practicing their inversions in front of their children, who were resting in baby carriages parked in front of them. The instructor stole glances of Eliah as we walked by and then went fully back to his class, moving his eyes over the trying-to-bend mothers.

"There's nothing secret about them," she said, bending down to pick up a pinecone and then tossing it away when she discovered it didn't have any smell. "The notes are for my parents. When it's clear out like this, I send them up words in hopes that there's nothing blocking them."

She looked at me right then, maybe wondering if it was okay to let me in a little more. I stayed with her eyes, which I'd never been able to do to anyone without acting before.

"They both died a while ago, together, in a car crash. My dad was driving home, and my mother was leaning on his shoulder, I think finding a soft place on that bumpy road to relax herself. We were coming back from dinner somewhere. My father used to just point the car and go until we found a spot that looked right, that looked like it had good food and a booth that could hold us. We never asked anyone or looked up reviews—we just went.

"I was asleep in the back—well, almost asleep. Kind of in that semi-lucid state when you're moving back and forth, in and out of consciousness. My mom was kissing him on the neck, telling him how much she loved him. She was talking about his smell. I remember that whenever she saw him, the first thing she did was sniff him, inhale his smell. Like this."

Eliah stood on her tiptoes and placed her nose on the base of my neck and inhaled slightly, eliminating my desire for anything else I was in need of.

"She could never get enough of him," she continued, though now looking off in the distance. "He turned to kiss her back and lost control of the car. The damn fool was lost in his wife's kisses—even after all those years. Our car ran head-on into an oncoming car, and they both went right through the windshield. Me, all I got was this scar under my cheek, and of course, the amazing memory of what happens after a kiss."

I stopped her and brought her face into my hand, rubbing my finger over the scar, thinking there might be a tear there that needed drying, but there were none. I smiled at her.

"You know that scar looks sexy as hell, right?"

"Please, don't show me any extra kindness," she said. "I've dealt with all of that. I'm only looking to move forward. To live my life as I see fit. You asked, so I told you. Most people don't even think to ask."

We continued on the path through a lush patch of trees. There were a few places like this along the dusty roads that rolled all through Runyon Canyon, most of which I knew. Even though she looked tough in her moment of reflection, I knew she had to be shaken, which I actually felt deep in that part of your chest that holds sorrow.

There was a huge tree that seemed to be waiting for us to take shelter from the sun beneath. We stood on the little patch of grass, leaned against the part of the tree that shielded us from sight, and kissed.

"I have something for you," I told her. "Now may not be the right moment, but I've always been about making the moment instead of waiting for it." I motioned toward the spot where the grass met a patch of soft soil, crouched down, and then took Eliah's hand and brought her down close to me. I felt the ground for the one moist patch and took her hands to get her to feel the soil. She reached back through the empty spaces in my fingers and gripped my hand as best she could, turning around to let me kiss her. I did, slightly, but her leaning in for me took me off my plan. I improvised and took the seeds from out my back pocket and showed her what I had brought.

"We're going to plant these together," I told her, ripping the packet open with my teeth and emptying the seeds gently into the lines in her palms. "Anyone can bring you flowers," I said. "I'm here to grow with you on this earth. We'll start here, in the soil, and then rise up together. This patch grows our memories now."

"That's quite a bit to offer a lady in the middle of the afternoon," she said, rubbing her hand on my stomach and then slowly lowering her lips to mine. "I want you to arouse me. I want you to lift me up to where the balloons are, away from the earth, not closer to it. Why do men always think that they have to save us? You've caught me already. I'm here, now. That's the only thing that matters."

Eliah started rubbing her hands on my chest and looking at my body as she took my shirt off. Her hands wouldn't move off of me. She couldn't decide which part to touch next. I tried to kiss her softly, but she moved her face away and let her lips trace the path that her hands had made. She unbuckled my belt and paused, giving her fingers a chance to trickle down just underneath the first button of my pants, where even the subtle muscles were ready for her to take her time.

Then her skirt was moving over my stomach, and though I could only catch glimpses of her panties, the wetness that was seeping through moistened the space between my chest and my abs. The occasional glimpses of white panties were enthralling, but I didn't want to rip her skirt off—I just watched it rising up and down like a curtain. Slowly, I slipped my hand up under her skirt and gently moved my thumb beneath her panties and between her outer lips, letting it move over above them and barely touching, waiting for them to open. She arched back, and I let my thumb move down, slowly, and I could feel her entire self starting to spill.

I moved to the inner lips, now drenched, keeping the motion but increasing the speed. There was nobody else but us. Then, gliding my thumb from inside her to her inner thigh, moving my hands quickly around her waist, I brought her up to my mouth, still with her panties on, and moved my nose right over the openness I had created, with only a thin layer of cotton separating my skin from her.

She reached down and pulled her panties to the side, and I entered her slowly with the tip of my tongue, creating room, which she filled quickly with bursts of explosions. I hydrated myself with her liquid, over and over again. She moved as she wished, and though I was aroused to the point of pain, I kept pleasuring her, feeling her body release and hoping her mind would follow the path toward an ongoing orgasm that melted away her past, if only for a moment.

The seeds had fallen to the ground, and I'm not sure if she had ever seen or valued them, but as I rose my head up, I could see them vanish into the soil and knew that one day they would sprout, and we'd come here to look at them.

After we gathered ourselves, we walked silently up the windy road to the rim of the canyon we had been climbing—past the old tennis court with the sagging net that nobody ever played on. The emptiness of the court—the lack of a game—always went perfectly with the mood up in the hills. We held hands and swung them back and forth like it was the first time either of us had done so. While the sun was still out, I had time to be with her. Still, the higher we climbed, the more I saw the city darkening and my time dwindling until I had to be at work. I'd been picking up so many shifts that, each time the sun went down, my mind was already ticking down to the time I had to clock in.

I wanted to tell her about the audition and the pending role, but my habits of superstition kept me from sharing completely. I'd learned never to say too much before it happened. Once that energy escapes, there's no way to reel it back in.

At the top of the incline, we reached the bench I had planned for us to sit on. This was supposed to be the big romantic gesture of the day—watching the sunset over the city—but now that I'd made her come already, an ordinary sunset seemed a little anticlimactic. The bench was in the perfect spot to look over Hollywood and Los Angeles beyond that.

"What does it look like to you?" she asked.

"Like a big Moroccan marketplace stretching for miles. I can almost hear bargaining merchants from up here. What's it look like to you?"

"Like Los Angeles at sunset."

A man sat down on a space of the bench not big enough for him, but he sat anyway, continuing to play with and take pictures of his red-nosed pit bull. (I know dogs okay because I did some work as a dog walker.) The man had an old Canon AE-1 camera that he loved to point at his dog. We made for an unromantic quartet, but sometimes that little element of randomness during a date gives a couple something light to talk about other than what's going on between them.

The man was one of those people who was really into his dog—totally content with his place in the world and the relationship he had with his pal.

"Cute pup," Eliah said to him, reaching down to give a good scratch behind the dog's ear. "You don't see too many of these without the ears and tail clipped. If you're interested in my opinion, I think she looks much better in her natural state. Most people look better in their natural state, wouldn't you say?" She motioned toward me, and the old man gave me a once-over before snapping a shot of us.

"I think so too," the old man said, turning the camera on the dog. "It'd be hard to see little Lucy looking any other way than how she is, but don't get too caught up on what's natural and what's not. This here is a made dog. Looks like the real thing, though, doesn't she? Why, just look at that face. How could you not just love it, regardless of where it came from or how it came to be in existence? I had one before that looked just like her, and then I found some people who could make me another when she passed. I just loooove her."

He bent down and started kissing the dog, which brought out a huge smile and a big tail wag.

"Even though they have the same genes, the personality is different. Life is not about replication," Eliah said. "Apologies for taking away any part of your moment."

"Oh, I couldn't care less about what you or anyone else thinks," the man said, tossing a tennis ball and snapping shots of Lucy shooting out after it. "I just care that, at night, I get to curl up with this girl and feel her heart beating. When I wake up, I see her smile. No need to go digging around out there for what's already inside."

All the while he managed a grand smile—all that existed, that mattered, was him and his dog. The rest of the world could do what it did. Eliah looked deeply at me and then out to the sky, forgetting about the man and his dog. They got up to walk away, but not before the man took a few pictures of us looking at the sunset before we noticed.

"Hope you don't mind," he said. "Usually I just get pics of Lucy here. I couldn't resist taking some of young lovers at sunset. It's one of my few indulgences."

"I don't like to have pictures taken of me," Eliah said, still not looking away from the sunset. "It's not right taking the moment and keeping it for yourself. What is this constant need we have to replicate and share everything? It's as unnatural as your dog."

The man continued taking pictures of us until she flipped him off. Each snap took away any amount of tenderness I had replenished her with. It wasn't going fully according to plan, though it was becoming a most memorable day, which is all I ever really cared about. I couldn't have gotten a funny woman feeding the birds as my random person wandering into my scene? The guy wouldn't stop snapping, despite Eliah calling him a list of names that suggested he might be doing unseemly maneuvers with his red-nosed pit. Finally, satisfied with his shots, not embarrassed by the names, he stopped.

"Well, then," the man said, lifting his fisherman's hat from his head for a moment. "I'll have to respect the young woman's thoughts. Good luck to you both."

He walked away, seemingly into the sunset, with his fake dog jumping around him and an old camera swinging from his wrinkly neck.

"You just let him keep going," she said. "Didn't you see how pissed off I was getting? Nobody has the right to just take pictures of you without asking."

"I've never minded it," I said. "That's what it would be like if I ever got famous, you know. How are you going to handle it when that happens?"

"*If* we're together and it happens," she said, a little taken aback by far into the future I was looking, "I guess I'll either have to learn to deal with it or stay inside a bunch. Don't look too far ahead, though. What we have is good. Just, you know, look out for the lady on your way to the top."

The sun was going down, and everyone else paused for a moment. That's the great thing about Los Angeles—no matter how messed up your day was, regardless of your expectations that weren't met, there's always a sunset somewhere to settle you down and tuck you into the evening.

"I need to work tonight," I said, trying to get her back into the space we had created before. "But if you can stay up, I'll bring you back some sushi, and we'll have a late-night rooftop dinner. How's that sound?"

"Sounds like a lot of heights in one day," she said, trying to catch the last bit of orange light before the sky turned monochrome. "You should crash after your shift. I'll be there in the morning. Don't you trust that?"

"Of course I trust it," I said, though I questioned whether I did or not. "It's just that, since I met you, I can't take a step without making sure it's toward you. Don't you feel the same?"

"Look," she said, grabbing my hand while watching the last bit of pink sun roll down beneath the smog, "I've been doing this life thing on my own for a long time. I enjoy you. I even enjoyed taking care of you and like that fact that you wanted to give me pleasure before yourself." She grabbed my face and brought me closer. "That was amazing, down there. Nobody has ever made me come that hard. But for now, let's not define things. Life always gets complicated when you try to define it. Let's just leave it that we give each other pleasure, and as long as that continues to happen, we should stay with each other."

"What if I want more than that? I want to create memories with you."

"I have no room for memories."

I think that's when you know if you love someone—or at least if you feel her in your heart. That moment when you see that you don't agree on what the world's all about, but you know sure as hell that there's no place you'd rather be in it than next to her.

CHAPTER 7

Little Tom, the Bastard

Like most waiters, my work uniform was all black, so I wore black baggy Dickies and a tight black T-shirt to give some definition to my form when working. You could usually tell who was going to work in Los Angeles by how they walked in the heat to their jobs, sweating and with that look on their faces of "How much more can I take?" Me, for the first time, I just drank it in and found that I could save the heat for those rare moments when it was cold.

I had showered, shaved, and gotten dressed at the gym. Though I'd used mouthwash, I could still taste Eliah. My mind was focused on dinner later that night and my meeting the next day. For now, this was going to possibly be my last night waiting tables, so I'd enjoy it. If it were just another day in the struggle, hell, I'd enjoy that as well.

If you've never been to Rising Sushi before, it is a three-level, faux Japanese Shogun-themed spot erected as a monument for good times and young girls from the Valley. A giant flag with a piece of California roll where the Rising Sun should have been waving gently in the soon-to-be late-night breeze.

When I got to the restaurant, I found milling around in front a gathering of men in different-colored windbreakers with yellow lettering spelling out which union they represented. Some mounted police were also stationed a few feet away, just kind of surveying the scene. Among the usual girls in short skirts and guys drowned in too much gel and cologne, these people seemed a bit out of place.

A man with a mustache and a proper bullhorn saw me and called for me. "This is the time to join us, you know," he said, first speaking into the bullhorn and then realizing he didn't need to. "Hey, you're that guy from the DMV video! Boy, I tell you that was something. We're all talking about it down there at the union office. You should really think about coming and joining us. We could use a speaker like you."

"What is it you're fighting for?" I asked him. "I don't see what's so bad right now. This is America—greatest country in the world. Plenty to eat if you're willing to work for it. You'd be surprised what I do to survive—and I get to live my dream. What other country can you do that in? Besides, of all the places to protest in, why Hollywood? Everyone here is an actor or writer or something like that."

"Only actors and writers think they're the only people in Hollywood," he said, but in a matter-of-fact way, nodding to the busboys walking into work and then to the homeless guys down the street, who were looking over but didn't dare cross that imaginary line that was drawn for them. "This is the time to join us. Pretty soon there won't even be a choice, you can believe that. Those things you shake your head at when you see it in other countries will be happening just outside of your front door."

The sushi chefs sat on the wall checking out the protesters. They looked hardcore in front of that small wooden gate—sitting there with their knives hanging off their sides. They were an odd mix of characters, most whose names I didn't know, except for Sigh Gonzalez, who sported the same bandana with Hello Kitty on the front every night. He was always down to trade me fine slices of toro for Sapporos. Through the third-floor window you could see the servers, who were getting their stations ready for the night, eyeballing the gathering people in the street.

The unrest outside was palpable, which was strange in Los Angeles. Just before I was about to go inside, I spotted Naibe Gonzalez, the reporter I'd seen on TV earlier, trying to direct her cameramen to get the right set-up shot. Then she noticed me, and her expression moved from one of concern and anger to one of happiness and interest—something you'll need to master if you're thinking about rolling out to Hollywood.

"You're the man from the DMV video," she said, brushing her hair back over her ears and showing me a smile that was formed to look like it was only for me. "My producers have been trying to get in touch with you for days. How about an on-the-spot interview? Are you here to lead the protests today?"

"I'm here to go to work," I said, gesturing to the club behind me. "To tell you the truth, I don't even know what these people are protesting about. If you can tell me that, I might be interested in doing an interview."

She looked good—wearing black slacks that hugged her hips but flared out just enough at the bottom, and a sleeveless tuxedo shirt with ruffles she kept playing with to attract my eyes to the outline of her ample breasts.

"I don't think there is a general message of what they want," she said. "I think they're just angry. You seemed pretty angry at the DMV the other day—care to talk to me about why? Maybe you all are angry over the same things. That's a very real possibility, you know. There might be some connection. It would make a great story if *we* could find some connection.

"You know, between you and me, I'm here because this is taking place on Sunset Boulevard. My producers want me to see if I can get a story about how the protests are going to affect the partiers or something like that. You know—'Here on Sunset Boulevard, those looking to blow off steam for the night don't seem to be affected by the unrest that's happening throughout the city…' That kind of thing.

"I was supposed to get shots of happy clubbers coming out and showing what a good time they were having despite the unrest—you know, kind of to get people to keep coming down and partying—a 'Don't worry, LA, it's still on' kind of thing. But I'm working on my own little piece about what's behind all the protests. That's what I'm after. Maybe you can help me get it."

She stood close, letting her breasts touch slightly up against me before pulling them away but not making any motions that suggested she'd done anything wrong.

"I need to get to work," I said, more than satisfied with the taste of Eliah that I still had on my tongue. "I'm sure you'll get your story from the folks out here. Everyone with a sign out here has something to say. That's why they put it on a sign."

"You'd think so, huh?" she said, lowering her microphone as well as her smile. "People aren't as smart as we are, you know. Maybe I'll stop in for some sushi after I get my story."

She walked away, and Sigh and the rest of the sushi chefs watched her go.

"Dude, next time bring that over to us," he said, jumping off the wall and tightening his bandana. "I'd have given her a story to tell. I know exactly what everyone's protesting about. Hell, I might just jump right in. Sooner or later, everyone's going to have to pick a side."

"That's what the union guy said to me," I told him. "Is tonight that night, or are we going to get paid?"

"Paid."

We both hung our heads at the reality a bit and went into work. Sigh and the rest of the sushi chefs went in the through the back stairs that led to the sushi bars on the second and third levels. The second-level bar was a little mellower than the top. It was my level, with huge couches available for big parties—that was the section I always worked—and a long sushi bar running parallel to a row of two-top tables looking out over Sunset Boulevard.

The top level was the wild show, with a main bar that girls would be dancing on top of and little islands of sushi chefs that people would sit around and as the night descended, and would be dancing around as the restaurant gave way to the club experience—the main dining room just erupting into a dance floor available for all.

By midnight, with still two hours to go before closing, most of the servers, who were in their younger twenties, would be so housed themselves that they'd forget about their tables and just start partying in the darkness with the clubbers. By that time, Little Tom would be locked in his office with whomever he'd found out there on the dance floor that night.

It was my time to scoop up the cash, so I stayed away from the alcohol and drugs and just pounded sugar-free Red Bulls and ran around taking drink and sushi orders, giving customers their fill, and asking them to pay in cash so I didn't have to report the order and could keep the profits for myself and my busboys, whom I paid to stick close to me.

I had an exchange system going between the bars and the sushi chefs, where I would bring the bartenders sushi of their choice and bring the chefs liquor of their choice, which they kept beneath the sushi bar and shared with the customers, and everyone drank shots and yelled *kanpai*! I would slip my chefs my orders, and after they'd make it, I'd take it and run out to the floor, dropping a bit off at the bar and the rest at the table, where I'd just give discounted prices, stick the cash in my pocket, and tip out the busboys and of course, the hosts.

The hosts, usually the youngest and newest to the city, are the people you need to take care of most. They may be naive and wide-eyed, with good skin and clean clothes, but they're broke. Before each shift, while the others were chatting about auditions or getting their stations ready, I went and talked with the hosts downstairs as they gathered around their little stand, which was carved out to look like it should hold a sacred scroll but only had the night's reservations written down on large parchment paper to complete the effect.

There were three hosts, but my man was Andre. Andre was from Brooklyn, and I'm not sure why he even came out to Los Angeles. Perhaps, like most, he wanted a taste of the West Coast and the freedom he thought it would bring.

Now, most of the servers through the night would just come down and complain about the people who were getting seated in their sections. Nobody wanted two girls sitting a table that could hold six college guys—who do you think is going to spend the loot? So—and I'd see it every night—servers came down and bitched about who's getting seated where, only to tip out a lousy 3 percent to the hosts at the end of the night, which is what the rules state you should tip. Now, do you think that these people getting handed three to five dollars peeled off a stack of three hundred are going to seat you well? I made sure to give them a fifty each night I worked in exchange for making sure the good parties—big guys without girls—were seated in my section. You could always get the girls to come over with the promise of a free round of kamikazes, and then the guys would buy the next round. Then, well, people get drunk and nobody cares about money until the check gets dropped down—with an automatic 18 percent gratuity added on for parties of six or more. Little Tom is happy because I sold more than anyone else, and in that time between 12:00 and 2:00, I was pocketing my own cash. Restaurant systems are easy to game if you do what makes sense and pay everyone off.

So on this night, just like most of the other nights I had worked, I stood with Andre for a bit and checked the reservations to see where the large parties were. Things had kicked off a bit early because it was graduation season and all the folks from USC and UCLA were looking for places to party after dinner with their parents.

"No girls, okay?" I pleaded. "They're all out tonight looking to be taken care of. We want the people who are taking care of them, right?"

"I got you," Andre said. "You know why I always hook you up, Harold?"

"Because I pay you better than anyone?"

"Well, there's no doubt about that," he said. "But it's more than that. It's about respect. You don't paint it pretty man, but you paint it. Know what I'm saying? You're different than everyone else here. That's a good thing."

"Yeah," I said, heading toward the downstairs kitchen. "Everyone keeps on telling me that."

The first floor had a door that led to the back stairs that led all the way through the three floors of the club. There was already a huge line of girls who had started early waiting to use the bathroom, anchored by a girl with a kind of horse face holding a glass of what had the unmistakable smell of Patrón.

"This stuff makes me piss like a racehorse," she said, knocking back her head and finishing the rest of what was in the glass. "Whoo-*hoo*! I had my finals this week and now those are *oh-ver*, so I'm out with my bitches and we're celebrating! Right, bitches?"

They all cheered and then turned again to the bathroom door.

"You're celebrating your finals," I asked, "or that fact that you're finished with them?"

"Everything! We're all celebrating everything," she continued, trying to find her center of gravity as well as the ability to hold on to any semblance of enunciation. "And those fuckers outside are out there protesting—protesting what? You think I'm going to let those losers take away my good time? I'm celebrating—why don't they come in here and celebrate with me?"

"I could bring them to your table if you like," I said.

"That's not the point," she said, turning around to her nearby table of girls who matched her state of intoxication but not her need to relieve herself. "We don't have space for anyone else that's not celebrating at our table, right, bitches?"

They all cheered.

She reached to balance herself on my shoulder as she turned, but I had moved away by then and saw her fall on the floor, to which her table cheered even louder. Not wanting to intrude on her celebrations, I moved on through the swinging doors that led to the inner workings of the restaurant. If I was going to have to eventually choose a side, I sure as hell wouldn't be choosing theirs.

On the other side of the walls, the busboys raced around feverishly with heavy bins of dishes, half-eaten crab rolls, and empty edamame-pod skins. They were sweating heavily and moving quickly. The waitresses were standing around taking sips of the apple martinis they'd stored in the side cupboards and were talking about how little they were going to make tonight and how lazy the busboys were.

I started taking a tray of dishes up the back stairs with me toward the kitchen on the third floor.

"Why are you taking that?" one of the waitresses called after me. "That's not your job."

"It helps out," I said. "Besides, the fewer dishes the busboys have to carry, the more time they can spend on my tables. It all works out."

"Maybe you should be a busboy," the blonde one said, checking her ass out in the mirror. "Man, I need to do my flexes. Do you think I'm starting to sag?"

I went up the back stairs with one of the older busboys, Martin. Now, Martin was kind of an institution there. He ran the show behind the scenes, and everyone knew it. Back in Mexico, he had been a big rodeo star. Once, when we were counting out the cash for the night, he showed me the scar where he had been cut by the horns of a bull.

"Reality, eh?" I remember him saying.

I imagined him now in an all-black bullfighting outfit with thousands of people cheering for him while the bull kicked at the dirt, waiting. The restaurant smell and noise wouldn't subside, so I placed it into my vision, the dishwashers working in the steam to the ranchero music coming from their tiny radio suddenly becoming Martin's cheering crowd in their white dishwashing outfits, waving their drying rags as he walked through the arena. As Martin and I dropped off the round of dishes and headed through the third-floor kitchen, the background ranchero music faded a little bit, giving way to the sounds of heavy electro house, and as we moved through the swinging doors to the dance floor, the stadium faded away, and we were back in the third-floor reality of the club in full swing.

Sushi chefs cut up their meals on tiny islands while young girls and boys danced away their youth around them. The busboys moved quickly, and I used Martin as a blocking back until I sprung out on my own, only to run into a giant brick wall disguised as a celebrating college kid wearing too much hair mousse and a ton of Drakkar.

He spilled his drink all over me and instead of apologizing, turned around and went ballistic. Derek looked a little different all dressed up and ready to party, but I recognized him as Eliah's client right away. I smiled at him, thinking that he would find the chance encounter funny, but all he saw was his drink on the ground and his buddies laughing at him.

"Dude, that was my graduation drink!" he said, getting right in my face, not showing the least sign of recognition. "You need to get me another. Right now, bro!"

"Derek," I said. "You don't remember me?"

"Dude, this is my *graduation* party—I'm done. Freakin' USC, man. I'm holding that degree now, and you're trying to take it from me by spilling my drink just because you're a waiter here. Are you upset because I'm making it?"

The girls from downstairs had appeared on the scene and were cheering Derek.

"I'm making it, too, you big bitch," the Patrón girl said, ready to roll after relieving herself. "You're celebrating with us, right? We're not protesting, are we, bitch?"

"No protest here," he said, grabbing her and pulling her close. "We're in this together, and this *guy* right here, this *guy*, is going to buy us a round of drinks."

When he said *this guy*, he poked me in the chest pretty hard.

"I'll buy you drinks, pal," I said, "only if you're not careful, I might be buying you a new finger. You better watch who you're pushing."

"Duuuude," he said, now holding on to the Patrón girl like they were on the cover of some twisted Harlequin romance novel. "*You* are here to serve *me*. That's why I'm here, so I can have people like *you* serve people like *me*."

He poked me again, this time even harder, and then stuck his tongue down the Patrón girl's throat, at which point both of their crews cheered.

"Just go over to the bar and get yourself a drink," I said. "Tell him that Harold sent you, and you'll be taken care of. I need to get back to work."

He pulled his tongue out of the Patrón girl and squinted at me. "No, dude, I think I want you to get it for all of us," he slurred, this time using the hand of the Patrón girl to poke me. "We'll be waiting for you to serve us. Better get used to serving us. While you're at it, why don't you get a round for those damn protestors outside? You can charge it to freakin' USC!"

They all cheered.

Slowly, I walked over the bar, which was now being danced on by girls pushing the limits of what was acceptable clothing to be worn in public. How much pubic hair needed to be shaven to wear pants that low? Even amped up by the Derek business, I had to appreciate the care that everyone put into being part of the show. I love watching women dancing by themselves. There is this incredible freedom they have while doing it, moving their bodies every way possible, like they're giving themselves such pleasure by feeling every note of the music. It's so erotic and voyeuristic, but a woman dancing on the bar by herself isn't worried about who's watching. She couldn't care less about anything other than controlling her movements. I'd heard while working during the holidays in the Prada stockroom in Beverly Hills that those expensive shoes that women pay so much for actually arouse them when they walk and shift their weight. It's like constant foreplay that can be controlled by how one steps.

Perhaps it was the freedom of the movement of the girls on the bar, or seeing all of the students up there drunk and telling me what to do. No doubt there was also much in it of the fact that Derek hadn't earned any of it himself but had still made his way through the system and was now ready to take his place, like so many others, on the other side of the bulletproof glass.

"Bottle," I said to Corinne, who was one of those bartending women who was trying like hell to land a part in the city before her stretch pants could no longer hold in what was back there. "Doesn't matter what, just let me have it. I'll pay out whatever it costs to empty it."

"I can't give it to you, honey," she yelled over the music, "but when I walk away, you do whatever you want to do without me seeing. Don't go getting yourself in trouble; I'll miss you if you disappear. Who else is going to read to us?"

She was talking about how, when the shift was done, I would read a bit of my Richard Brautigan books to some folks while they were counting out their cash. I left one of the books in my locker and would take it out sometimes after a tough night.

Corinne walked away to serve the crowd gathered at the bar, and I reached over to grab the bottle and a stack of glasses. Making my way back out to the dance floor, I found the two graduation parties now merged into one caravan of celebration.

"Got your drinks right here," I said. "Come on down to the second floor, and I'll take care of you. I've got a big section and some couches where you all can party without all these people bumping into you. How's that sound?"

"Sounds like the server is finally doing his job!"

"Follow me," I said with a smile. "I'll take care of you."

I led them toward the front staircase, making sure each of them was walking ahead of me.

"I'm right here, team," I said, pointing to where they should turn. "I'm going to take good care of you."

Martin stopped me.

"Look, eh," he said, looking into my eyes. "I don't know what you're thinking about doing, but realize what it could all lead to. Things are good for you right now. Good for us, too. Don't push it."

"I'm not the one who pushed, Martin," I said. "Besides, like the man outside said, I'm going to have to make a choice sooner or later. I've been talked down to by guys like this for my whole life. I know him too—the man doesn't even recognize me."

Little Tom came up behind us both, eyes wide and nostrils red. "What are you two doing standing around during prime time? What the hell are you doing with that bottle in your hand, Hall? Did they pay for it?"

"They did, Tom," I said, "and they're about to get served. Don't you worry about a thing. I think I saw Lisa waiting for you by the office door. She said she needed to talk. She's looking pretty good these days, huh?"

"I've got my eye on you," he said, twitching a bit and then checking to see if his fly was open. "One day I'm going to figure out how your sales are always so high, and when I do…"

"Yes?"

"Well, something's gonna happen, that's all."

Martin laughed, Tom went to find Lisa, and I went down after my graduation party, who were all waiting for me on the first giant couch, which sat ten comfortably and eighteen stacked on each other, which, when drunk, was what most people wanted.

Derek had the Patrón girl on his lap and couldn't stop his hands from moving all over her, though I'm not sure she was feeling anything. Such is the case when you're celebrating.

I lined up the glasses in front of each of them and held the bottle at my side like a cowboy might have in this same spot two hundred years ago.

"Well, what are you waiting for, *waiter*!"

"I'm waiting for you to say please."

"How about you do what you're told?" he roared, confident with the attention of a grinding woman. "I am the king right here! Recognize!"

I grabbed tight the neck of the bottle and crashed it across his face, sending him flying backward and the Patrón girl screaming from his lap and back onto floor, just like I'd seen her when we first met.

There was this moment of stillness and fading music. I could hear Martin breathing over my shoulder. Sigh was standing in shock at the sushi bar, his knife in hand. The footsteps of Little Tom coming back down the steps. The looks on the faces of Derek's boys. Everything was frozen, but only for a moment.

Two of Derek's boys jumped on me right away, and from there, fists and kicks were coming in every direction. Martin jumped in out of rodeo instinct, and I could see that some of the fists that were flying were his in addition to some vicious towel whips to the faces of the graduation party. Next I heard Sigh and the rest of the sushi chefs jump over the bar. Derek's group was joined by another who looked similar, and the brawl was on. Glasses, fists, and sushi knifes were flailing.

"Take this shit outside, please!" Little Tom was screaming. "This is not the place. People should be partying in here. You are fired for sure, Hall. That's it for you!"

As if on cue, the brawl rolled down the stairs. Derek's friends charged me down the stairs, quickly followed by Sigh, his chefs, and then the busboys. We tumbled past the host stand, where Andre was talking up a girl only to get swept up in the brawl. It was like one of those giant cartoon rolling balls that took up everyone in its path. Once you were inside, it was tough to really know whom you were punching.

Out the doors and into the streets, where the protesters saw what was happening and joined in. I caught a glimpse of Little Tom standing at the steps watching the whole thing, keeping the waitresses inside.

The union leaders were moving into the fray, trying to stop the unplanned riot from happening. Naibe jumped in front of the whole thing with her cameraman and started reporting on the spot. Had I not had fists and feet coming at me in every direction, I might have been able to catch what she was saying, though I did see her smiling at the chance to finally be in front of some real news. Glad I could provide her with her amazing moment.

The mounted police, who had up until that point just been keeping watch, galloped directly toward us and started pepper spraying and clubbing the busboys and the protestors, though I never saw anything hit the college boys. Martin was in there kicking ass, losing himself in the moment and perhaps finally letting out the frustration of all those years of hauling dishes.

Someone dropped a smoke bomb and fired a couple of shots in the air, which caused those of us still engaged in silly antics like fistfights to scatter on the real. I could barely hear Naibe's voice giving the report from Sunset.

The protesters, after hours of inaction, had stormed the club, pulling out gradation parties in hopes of disrupting what would have been an evening filled with celebration for hard work.

We all ran in different directions, away from Sunset Boulevard, away from Rising Sushi, and for sure, away from my on-call job as a waiter. That career was over.

In my head, I had two thoughts: Get to Eliah, and make sure you get that part.

CHAPTER 8

Being

Funny, but after the big fight with Little Tom and the USC boys, I didn't have a scratch on me. Now, of course there was no doubt that Naibe's story would get on the evening news and put my face even more out there than before, but that was okay by me. The way I figured it, the more I was out there in the public space, the more sway I might have with the producers of the show when they determined just whose mug was going to carry out their vision.

I took the elevator up to the top floor of my office building and made my way out to the roof, knowing I was a little early for my scheduled time with Eliah. Another job lost—I could add that to the endless list of employment opportunities that were never quite enough for me. I think that line in *Casablanca* when Louie asks Rick what he was doing back in New York and Rick answers, "Looking for a job," says so much about Los Angeles. I imagine the screenplay writer who put those words down walked the streets of Hollywood looking for something or was starving for something or worried about losing something.

Myself, I might have found that hope, though there was a feeling of regret for smashing that bottle across that kid's face. He had his whole life ahead of him, and he was going to have to explain to his parents why the side of his face was going to need some money to be fixed just until he could get into the right position in his new company. Of course, he'd have to take a bit of time off before he actually sat down in that chair.

On the roof, looking out over the city and watching it all move, I kept jumping in and out of lives that were playing out all around me. Inside car windows where hands turned up the volume to make the streets blow up with bass. Kids sitting at bus stops wondering if they'd be able to stay high enough for the night. Men pushing shopping carts full of oranges home. Graffiti writers wondering how they could get to the top of the sign on the freeway. My eyes moved to the blurs of the sped-up traffic.

In front of my vision, a red balloon floated. Then another—and I looked over the edge of the roof and saw Eliah's hand letting them out of her window. I lay on my back with my head as close to the edge as possible so that as the balloons passed by, I might be able to hear the sounds of their ascension moving past my ears. Her hand had just let go of that string, so I wanted to follow the flight that she guided.

My phone was alternating between text messages from the restaurant and from Rob Larry—both of whom would want money. Right then, I didn't care about any of that. Everything I wanted was in that window below, letting up balloons.

It was incredible watching them float off into the night but never disappear because the sky was never completely dark here.

I heard the door to the roof slam shut and heard footsteps walking to me. "What are you doing up here so early?" Eliah asked. "You weren't supposed to be here until much later. Did they move up last call time or something?"

"Things didn't exactly go as planned tonight," I said. "That's fine. I don't need them anyway. Hey, I thought you didn't let balloons out unless it was a blue sky?"

"I said when it's clear. What happened at work?"

"You didn't see the news?"

"You know I don't have a TV or Internet," she said. "You blew your job?"

I laughed a bit at what she said, but she didn't see it as that funny.

"Don't get so serious about this," I said, a little confused at where the passion from the hills had gone. "I wasn't going to talk about it, but I have a big callback tomorrow. I think there are people out there who want me. It's about to happen—and I can't wait to share that moment with you."

"Sounds like since we've met, you've lost two jobs and have nothing but a callback to show for it. Why would you need anyone other than yourself to want you? Nobody is more important than you."

"You're taking this all wrong," I said, grabbing her hand and trying to guide her down with me. "Those jobs were just temporary. They have nothing to do with what I really want."

"What do you really want?" she asked and then stopped me before I could answer. "And think about it for a second—who do you want to be?"

"Someone who's remembered," I said. "What else is there?"

"You might never be happy then. Waiting for the world to know who you are—do you even know yourself well enough yet? Nobody just gets to do whatever they want without paying for it."

"You do," I replied, with the fear-backed feeling of wanting to be right in an argument.

"That's different," she said. "I didn't have a choice. My parents died when I was super young and I didn't have enough to go to the school I wanted, so I decided to learn everything that took place inside of those schools. Life handed me some shit, and I made something out of it. I didn't act on my emotions. Neither should you."

"As long as we're together, things are going to be fine."

"What about when we're not together?" She scooted away from me. "I can't support you until you make it."

"That's not what I'm asking for."

"I'm going away on assignment for a few months," she said, without emotion. "How are you going to handle that?"

The silence between what she had just said and my reaction was immeasurable.

"What are you talking about?" I asked. "Like a long-term gig, you mean?"

"It's for a very affluent woman who wants me to tutor her son or something. We have to meet on the details still. They need him to cram a few years' worth of information into eight months of intensive study. I usually don't take these long-term assignments, but she pretty much handed me a blank check and told me to name my price. My thoughts were I could do this gig, then, I don't know—take a year off after that and just let my brain work for me instead of for other people. I could use the rest. It might have been you who opened me to up realize that."

"Well at least I did something right," I said, sulking a bit.

"You did everything right," she said, holding her hand on my cheek. "I thought we were close enough to say what we felt to each other. No filters, right? You shouldn't be hurt by my trying to help you."

"How will I know you're safe? Besides you, what about me? I can barely spend a minute without you, and we just got with each other. We have a true love story going on right here—now you're going to tell me you're breaking away?"

"You need to trust that I'll be back, and when I do return, things will be just fine. We'll have life to talk about—our own lives, different eyes on the world. We'll get to see life through each others' eyes."

"What about others?" I asked. "Are you going to be with anyone else?"

"That's just like a man," she said, recoiling even further. "I'm telling you I'm going somewhere for my career—to get paid—and your mind goes directly to sex. I'm talking about life, Harold. Why do men always go to the cock? It's unbelievable. Why don't you just leave now? Things would be easier. Take a long walk into the Hollywood night or whatever you do when you get into your head. I'll be gone by morning. We'll see if we connect when I get back."

"Calm down," I said and then realized it was the wrong thing to say when someone is pissed at you. "When do you leave for your new job? We can talk about this more tomorrow night. After my meeting. I've had a long night, anyway. Maybe I'm not acting right."

"You just showed me who you really are," she said, laying down on the roof and looking up into the stars. "I'm just going to do my thing—like I always have. If you're here waiting for me, that's fine. It will do you some good to do some self-discovery. If not, I can take going at it alone—I've done it before."

"If you tell me where you're going, what you're going to do, it won't be a problem. I can't just let you go without knowing."

"That's called trust, though," she said. "Without that, love is just a greeting card. You and your gestures can't stand up to trust."

"I know myself," I said. "Waiting for you like that is going to kill me. Eight months is a long time—can't we visit?"

"Why don't you take that time and make something of yourself?" she said. "You keep saying that you're close to it—try it. Be it. I'll be back at some point, and if it's meant to be, then it is."

I grabbed her and tried to pick up from that feeling we had together in the park earlier that day—to start touching and feeling her where I had before, to try the same moves and give her the same pleasure—but though the motions were replication, the feeling wasn't the same.

I tried to force the moment—but she pushed me off her like I was a stranger trying to take liberties that were never mine to take.

"What are you doing?" she said. "This is not the time for it—not the place for this!"

"What about in the hills? That was different?"

"It was," she said, holding back tears. "It was a moment. Something passionate and real. Something that made my body shake. Something totally unselfish and unlike anything I've ever experienced. I gave you everything I possibly could right there. My trust. My body. I flowed with you. You didn't feel that?"

I did feel it. I should have told her I was sorry for trying to take more right then. That I'd never felt anything as deeply as I did up there in the hills. That she was the calmness to my pounding heart—the being that finally allowed me to sleep at night.

I got up like a filthy man overflowing with ego and told her an untruth.

"I already know who I am," I said. "I know I don't like to be teased. Maybe this was just another random Los Angeles encounter by two people who were too lonely not to have someone next to them. I'll think of you when I'm sad and smile—maybe you'll do the same."

I walked off the roof and couldn't believe what I was doing—what I'd said. Perhaps I was repeating a combination of lines that I'd heard in a movie somewhere and thought they were my own. Down the stairs I walked, ignoring my heart, which was screaming for me to turn back and beg her forgiveness. My mind pushed me forward, back down in the elevator, through my office door, and as I was just about to crash on the office couch, Rob Larry held the door open and prevented me from closing it.

"You've been ignoring my text messages, Harold," he said, still in his outfit and sad, saggy face. "Hey, you look like you had a long one. You don't have my money, do you?"

"I don't, Rob, I really don't. Believe me, though, and this is the truth, I did everything I could do to get it to you tonight. You have my word, if you'll take it, and I promise you'll have it by the end of the week. If you want to put me out, I understand, but at least let me stay until morning. I'm pretty sure I haven't slept for a long while."

Rob Larry looked at me deep in the eyes, and there, for the first time, I recognized him. His face was old and no longer had any hint of youth. No doubt he'd made the same mistakes I had. Maybe he'd said the wrong things and didn't have the smarts to turn around and correct them, either. Here we both were, though, in this old building, trying to stay at least a little bit ourselves.

He smiled, looking at me the same way I had looked at him, seeing him sweeping up those halls day after day and knocking on doors to pay the rent.

"Doing the paperwork would be too much for me," he said. "I trust you to get it to me when you can—just make sure it's all of it. You get some sleep. I think you can use it."

He closed the door behind me, and he might as well have tucked me in and read me a bedtime story. Amazing where and whom the tender moments come from.

CHAPTER 9

The Snow Queen

The big meeting was at one of the main producers' houses up in the Hollywood Hills. Pete had told me only that she was known as the Snow Queen, partly because she always dressed in white and partly because of what she was known for serving at the parties that made her famous. I pressed a bit for her real name but couldn't get it. Hollywood was the place where you came to reinvent yourself—away from the life you were running from. Those ex-lovers or memories of a family member getting too close were going to be squashed down with fame and success, and then the world was going to know you for the new you, and you'd hope—pray—that the old you would slowly fade away.

I'd seen it a bunch of times when talking to or going home with some of the waitresses I'd met on a job. Or junior executives I'd met while filing papers. Or young girls handing out flyers for Jamba Juice when they first got to the city. They were all from somewhere else—trying to be something else. Me? I was born here. I knew that people spent so much of their time in Los Angeles trying to meet the right people. That's half the job, just being invited to the right party so you can casually meet the right person who likes you enough to be friends with you and then finds out something about you that can help them, so they decide to help you.

Sitting in the living room of the Snow Queen's house, I was trying to forget everything that had happened with Eliah the previous night, but it was impossible. My heart was beating so hard the bottom of my tongue was vibrating. I wished I could have texted her or gotten to her before I hit the gym in the morning, but she was already gone.

The Snow Queen was late, but I think it was just because she knew she was the most important person to come into that room. If you want to know who has the power in a room, just watch who's the last one to come in. Eagerness is oftentimes taken as weakness.

Pete the Wolf was sitting just to my left, pouring a little bit of cream into his coffee and adding a half spoon of sugar, which he stirred in slowly while never once hitting the inside of his mug.

Samantha had on a tight long-sleeved shirt with a modest neckline that hugged her body and high-waisted pants that stopped an inch above her ankles. I didn't know how anyone could walk in those kind of heels. She fiddled with her glasses, which she never could seem to get right. Noticing me notice them, she leaned in and whispered, "Peter likes me to wear them during meetings. Says people take me a little more seriously with these things on. Can you believe it? Hollywood is full of silly rules, but so is every other business."

She smiled, and I felt her honesty. She still had that purity of being herself, of doing everything because she wanted to, because it was inside of her to do it.

Pete was wearing an oatmeal turtleneck that looked good against his skin color. The line at the top met the bottom of his neck just right. Turtlenecks are hard to pull off because if you have the possibility of extra fat hanging from the bottom of your chin, it's sure to rest over the brim, and that's just not going to look right.

"If the Snow Queen likes you, it's a go," Pete the Wolf said calmly, finally taking a sip of his coffee. "Just be you, that's all she wants to see. Whatever else is on your mind, forget about it. We'll talk about what happened on the news later."

"You saw that," I said, having not turned on or noticed a TV since I talked with Eliah. "I haven't seen a thing. Been in a fog today. My lady left me—or I left her—I can't really remember."

Samantha put a consoling hand on my shoulder, but Pete the Wolf took a different approach.

"Look, friend," he said, "I've been searching for someone like you for too long. Everything is set up and ready to roll. Just be yourself, and everything else will fall into place."

Funny, but right then when he said it, I started really thinking about what I wanted. When's the last time you truly thought of that? We all have that initial drive to go out and get what we want. Then we spend most of our lives focused on the pursuit itself and forget what the actual thing was. Maybe it was Eliah. Love. That moment of happiness that I had walked away from. What was I doing without her other than fighting and starting riots? Those questions all fell out of my head when the Snow Queen made her entrance. It was too late to do anything about it anyhow.

There was a white, spiraling staircase that she glided down—wearing a white Adidas jumpsuit with matching shell-top shoes. It was no doubt the most comfortable thing you could wear in the middle of the day, and she was rocking it to perfection. When she reached the bottom of the stairs, she took off the shoes she was wearing and put on another pair just like them, only these had the backs removed so they looked like house slippers.

As she approached us, each step was measured so that there wasn't so much as a squeak on the white marble floor. We all rose up to say hello, Pete the Wolf moving first with a big smile on his face and genuine affection in his eyes for this woman who was moving toward us. Samantha was timid in her presence and moved her body closer to me—looking up to smile, as though asking me if it was okay to do so. She seemed to shiver just a bit, which made me notice how cold it was in there.

The AC was turned on full blast, which may be why all the servants had on coats and jackets—some even had on earmuffs. Everything was all white and marble, hard angles and nothing soft, not even the couch we were sitting on, which was more like a park bench than an actual couch.

From far away, the Snow Queen had appeared to have an incredible body and features that were made to be fawned over. The jumpsuit fell on her just right. As she moved closer, though, her age became more apparent, and the youth of her physical being washed away—but not the grace with which she moved.

"My apologies for the deep coldness in here," she said, grabbing a piece of Nicorette gum from a crystal bowl in front of her. "The cold air keeps one young. That's something all these girls in tanning booths just don't understand. Longevity, my dear."

"Well, I'm from LA, myself," I said, reaching out to shake her hand before she bent it for me to kiss her. "Anything below sixty-five is winter to me. If you invite me back, maybe I'll wear a matching jumpsuit and we can start a fire or something."

"What did I tell you about our friend?" Pete the Wolf said, leaning back. "This is the guy right here. Have you ever seen someone so comfortable in a potentially life-changing situation? That's going to come through so real on the camera, don't you think? The audience will eat it up. He's going to be so huge people are going to be wearing T-shirts with him on them instead of Che in a few years. You can't deny how much passion he exudes."

"Take it easy with the hard sell, Mr. Wolfson," the Snow Queen said. "Tell me, Mr. Hall, what do you think is wrong with this country? What of yourself are you going to put into this role? You're already becoming famous for your acts against authority—but what the Queen wants to know, my dear, is what's inside of you. What do you think?"

Thoughts raced into my mind and overlapped like one of those old slot-car sets where you snapped the tracks together and controlled the car with little guns attached by wires to the metal grooves inside the tracks. I thought about the DMV and how they took away my license, and how I wouldn't need one to drive around on those little tracks. About every role I'd ever been turned down for. About the cop who gave me a ticket for crossing the street because it was against the law, then broke the law himself. About Eliah and her balloons—would I ever watch them vanish with her again? About all those windows in all the buildings all around the country where people were locked in and typing away on a keyboard or looking for a connection in their life but couldn't find one, so they just turned to porn or chocolate or sports or something else to distract them from themselves.

My head was about to crack open, and though the thoughts were stacking up on top of each other like the bodies in the Hollywood Forever cemetery walls, only a few seconds had gone by.

"You know," I said, honestly and directly, "I don't even know what I think. I'm not sure the thoughts that are in my head are even mine. I mean, how much are we even alone anymore? How many minutes do you spend without checking your Facebook or Twitter feed or to see who e-mailed you? When's the last time you took an elevator where everyone was just standing there thinking, instead of hunched over some device? My thoughts are snippets from tweets or postings of others, all attached to some icon that I've chosen to represent myself with.

"I started off—a long time ago, I started off thinking that I would be able to make something of myself, to really lose myself in a singular character. But all of this mess out there has gotten me lost in other people's personas. The whole world is becoming Hollywood, so a show that makes Hollywood the center of the universe, there's no better fucking person to do that than me."

Samantha had taken off her glasses and couldn't stop looking at me. It's how I looked at Eliah.

Pete nodded, took out a contract, and handed it to the Snow Queen. "I'll let you look it all over, and if there are terms you're not comfortable with, we can have the lawyers work them out. We might have gotten even more than we hoped for with him, wouldn't you say?"

"Is he willing to do whatever it takes to keep the role?" she asked. "Because I have a feeling that, while this young man has the passion, he might not realize all that is going to be required of him. He might not know the sacrifice that is going to be required. People think they want to be remembered and sought after, but nobody realizes the total price. Have you explained everything to him?"

"I wanted to make sure you were comfortable with Mr. Hall in the role," Pete the Wolf said. "We'll take care of everything else if you're good."

She leaned over to me, put her hand on my leg, and an inhaled with such force that I felt all of the oxygen around me evaporate.

"Shame," she said. "I'm rather fond of how his face looks now. In another life, perhaps we could have used it as it is. I'm fine with him. We can move on to the rest of the casting. Make sure they're all meshing with his look and ways. Everything must look real, understand?"

"Of course," Pete the Wolf said. "It's the only way any of this is going to work. Samantha will make arrangements with the trainers and then start in with the publicists—schedules and all of that will be taken care of in the next few days. I'm beyond excited."

The Snow Queen stood up and moved toward the front door, where a parka-clad assistant handed her the leash for her dog. As the door opened, she seemed taken aback at first by the blast of sunlight that flooded the room.

"I knew she'd love you," Samantha said, but not completely out of earshot of the Snow Queen, who turned and eyed her. "You did just perfectly. We had some others make it this far, but nobody with your voice. You realize that it was *you* that she wanted? Nobody else could have—"

"Samantha," Pete the Wolf said, stopping her after seeing the Snow Queen's reaction. "I'm sure there's scheduling that needs to be done—plenty to do before we kick into celebration mode." He turned to the Snow Queen.

"She's a bit new to the business and can't seem to hide her emotions."

"She seems very enthusiastic," the Snow Queen said, looking directly at me when saying the word *enthusiastic*. "That kind of passion needs to be rewarded."

The Snow Queen was escorted out by her assistant under a cream-colored umbrella, and Samantha, following the dog, left as slowly as possible, as if hoping to catch a last snippet of the conversation that followed.

With nobody in the room but Pete the Wolf and me, the coldness was palpable. This might be what it feels like to get exactly what you want—exactly what you asked for. You think that, perhaps, you'll be able to hold it—to touch what your dream actually feels like—but it doesn't work like that.

"You no doubt have questions for me," Pete the Wolf said. "You might as well ask them now."

"Not sure what she was talking about with my face. Am I going to need to wear makeup during production? These bumps and bruises are going away anyhow—don't worry about that. I'm not planning on getting into any brawls from now on. I won't even leave my office unless it's to get out to the set. You have my word. The only revolution I'll be leading is the one in the scripts."

"Oh, I have no doubt about that," he said, leaning back. "But I'm afraid we're going to need a bit more than your word to go on with production. You see, your body type is perfect. Sure, we'll have to have some trainers do a bit of adjusting to put some weight on you, but that will come soon enough. You've become a bit too famous now, with your two videos. We think that, if done right, we can use that to your advantage, though. That brawl last night involved many of the protestors out there on Sunset Boulevard. The cops came in and broke it up. People are furious, but there were no deaths. No real deaths, anyhow."

"Yeah, things got out of hand, that's for sure," I told him, reflecting back on the madness. "Glad that nobody got too hurt."

"Well, what if we were to tell you that you vanished afterward? That there was no record of you after that night? Maybe you took a bus out of town, crazed at what Hollywood has become. What if you just stayed in your apartment for months and didn't let anyone know where you were? What if you just vanished into the sea that is Los Angeles, which swallows up people greater than yourself every day? What if your life, the life of Harold Hall, became a mystery?

"Theories would jump up and rumors would spread that the state of California wanted you put down because you were becoming too big of a social media star—that you were provoking the already simmering protests erupting throughout the city."

"You want me to vanish?" I asked, confused. "I thought you were offering me a role."

"Not you, Harold. I'm offering Pace Skillman the role of a lifetime. Of course, this is only if Harold Hall accepts it. We'll create a new character, based on you—the you who's disappeared," he said, taking one of the folders that Samantha had left on the table and pulling out a bunch of pictures that at first glance appeared to be old headshots. "This new character, this Pace Skillman, would have all of your passion, even your exact build, only the face would be a little more...I don't know how to say it."

"More Hollywood?"

"That's half right," he said, spreading the pictures across the table. "Not so much more Hollywood but more a representation of these men. The spirit would still be yours underneath. Nothing would change underneath your skin."

On the table, the pictures that were spread out were of Malcolm, of Che, of Michael Collins, of Castro, of Lenin, of Bobby Seale. The pantheon of recognizable revolutionaries.

"It's the role of a lifetime, and it's yours if you want it. You, the person you are, what's underneath you, is perfect. The face, though—nobody is going to believe it. Nobody is going to believe you are capable of leading a revolution."

"My...face?" I was having trouble tracking. "And me, vanishing?"

"Don't you see?" Pete the Wolf said. "The press releases and PR around this stuff is all going to be focused on how the character you are playing is inspired by you. A young revolutionary who was too early for his own time. It's so sublime. The public will eat it up, believe that. You'll get everything you always wanted.

"The face we create for you is going to be a mixture of all of these. Teenage girls are going to have your picture on their walls. Women will wish their men were more like you. Everyone will want to *be* you. They'll believe you're someone to follow. There will be campaign posters put up all over the city to make it look like there is a true revolutionary among them. It's going to be a show like nobody has ever seen before, and it will all be you. Of course, this is Hollywood—and we've got the best plastic surgeons in the world."

"My face?" I said, making sure I'd heard it right.

"I'm asking you if you want the role of lifetime," he said. "This show will revolutionize the way things are done in this town. Who better to be part of that than you, a product of this city? You were born for this."

I got up and looked around at the cool whiteness surrounding me. It was unsettling, but it did allow me to focus on my thoughts. The role of a lifetime. The chance to be part of something huge and no longer run after those small scraps left on the floor after the giants had finished feasting.

"My mom," I said, realizing that she would never go for it. "How could I put her through that? It's not right—how will she live with that?"

"She'll live very well," he said, taking out a picture of an amazing beach house in Malibu. "Your mother will live out the rest of her days in comfort. She'll have it all—never worry about money again in her life. Think about that for a moment. What's going to happen if you don't take this? She's got to be getting older, right? You have to start thinking about these things."

He had tapped into one of my deepest fears: How would I be able to take care of my mother when she was unable to take care of herself? She had worked since the moment I could remember—always coming home late and when the sun was down but always managing to tell me that she loved me. How could I go the rest of my life without hearing that? But at the same time, how could I go the rest of my life without paying her back for that?

I drifted to a vision of my mom sitting in her house in Malibu sipping on Bloody Marys, living free of burden.

His voice low, Pete the Wolf said, "When my mom got to be too old and couldn't work anymore, that fell on me quick. Real quick. I had to put so much money together it stopped my life. She felt crazy about it—I could see it in her eyes. Nobody wants to be like that for their children.

"This would be doing your mom an enormous favor. You can't think of it in your reality; you need to think of how it is. Of the results. Friend, you people from California have rather thin skin. Man up and think of your mom. Think of yourself, if you like, it's the role of a lifetime. Everyone is getting exactly what they want. There aren't many times in life when that's possible. Think of what you could do for her."

"But it won't be me," I told him. "It'll be someone else's face. Plastic surgery is not a mask—it's real. It's forever."

"This here is Hollywood, friend. Do you want this or not?"

"I need a night to think about it," I told him. "It's not the kind of thing one just says yes to. You're asking for my life."

"My gut tells me that you've already made your choice," Pete the Wolf said, "but your mind is trying to convince you of something your real self already knows. That's fine. Take your night. I'm going to proceed like everything is happening because I see that you're not a fool. Just let Samantha know when you're ready. She's at your disposal from here on out. Don't make the mistake of thinking that this opportunity is going to come around again. Life doesn't work like that, even if you want it to."

"I'll give you a call in the morning," I said. "We can talk then."

"No, friend," Pete told me, putting his hands on my shoulders. "I need to know before you leave here. I can't let you walk into the world and tell anyone about this. You either want it or you don't. There are plenty of rooms to sleep in here if you so desire."

He could read me from deep inside. I'd wanted it from the moment he told me. I didn't care so much about the surgery. Hell, who did I know, anyway, but some casual acquaintances I'd see once in a while? I'd lost Eliah and now, at least, had a chance to take care of my mother. I'd have to hide her from it for a bit, though—send her on a trip around the world for a year or so—put her up in hotels and give her the high life that she always saw but never touched. The money Pete was offering would take care of that.

For me, I wouldn't be doing it for the money; it would be for the recognition I'd always been after. I could build myself into someone women would never say no to and somehow build upon the pain I was in from leaving Eliah so that it became a memory rather than a feeling. In some strange way, I would become the person that she wanted me to be, only she'd never see it.

For the friends I had, I could keep my old Facebook account up and going. That's how we all exist, anyways, these days. There's no real-life communication. No real world. Hell with it, I pushed all my chips in and gave it all to Hollywood.

Why not?

CHAPTER 10

Choices

"You're going to be just fine, friend," Pete the Wolf said to me. "Just remember, you wanted this. Nobody ends up in these situations if they didn't want it from deep within."

"Where is she?" I said, half out my mind from whatever they had running through the tubes in my arms. "She should be here before I go away. I need her to know how I feel. It's not too late for us."

"Now listen, young man," said Dr. Addison, the surgeon looking at every inch of me from the space between his mask and the cap on his head. "There's no one better at this than I. Do not fool yourself into thinking you're the first in this town to have a few adjustments made. Believe me, I'm responsible for much of what you see up on that screen and fantasize about."

In and out of consciousness, I felt pieces of myself slipping away, like they were falling off the side of a rollercoaster that I was screaming at to slow down, but it wouldn't. Then everything went black. I didn't pass out. I didn't sleep. I remember just being away and moving through the darkness—through this black space that never ended.

I was letting go of everything. Every worry. Every thought. I just was, without any judgment at all. It was so clear. Into the blackness. How long I was under, I couldn't tell you. Red balloons were the only moments of color in my darkness.

The first thing I remember is Samantha typing away furiously on her laptop, only to stop when she realized I was awake. She was about to press a button or call someone but stopped herself and looked me over. I could barely make out that it was her. I grasped for memory, finding it in the bits and pieces that were floating through the sedation.

"You're okay," she said softly. "They have you on some heavy medications, but you're okay."

I tried to move but couldn't. Each attempt sent some kind of shock through my body, which ended in a burst of acute pain. Everything was hazy, my vision was blurred, but I still felt the sensation of bandages on my face and tubes running every which way through me.

"You're fine," Samantha said, pushing the button for the doctor. "It's okay."

The door swung open, and Dr. Addison came in with Pete. A good part of me was happy that I recognized everyone in the room and hadn't been in some horrible accident where I had lost my memory. That would have been one bad movie to be stuck in for the rest of my life. The pain was intense, and the doctor must have noticed me rolling from it, as he touched my hand and let me know that if it felt too horrible, I could push this button, although he warned that too much pushing of the button might be addictive. Nothing wrong with being addicted to feeling good, so I kept pushing until I couldn't feel anything.

From what I could see, I was in some kind of surgery room—small but extremely modern, though the only similar places I had to hold it up against were the free clinics and county medical centers I'd visited during my adult life.

"Don't try to talk," the man who I knew to be the doctor said. "I'm Dr. Addison, you remember me? You've been in and out for a few days. We're going to ask you to be patient with us, and with yourself. You're going to need to learn some new tricks for speaking and some other functions you may have taken for granted. Also, I'm quite sure you've already noticed the bandages on your face. I'm going to insist that you not touch those. Just let everything settle for a bit. Pain is something we're quite tolerant of given the proper time to adapt. You're strong and in good shape. That helps us. Can you hear me? Move your finger if you can hear me—oh, and please, don't blink your eyes any more than absolutely necessary. Here." He leaned in close and put a couple of drops in each of my aching eyes. "Push the call button whenever you need more tears. The eyelids are always the most challenging part to get right, and they take the longest to heal. Why is it that everyone wants to speak with their eyes?"

Out I went.

Every time I came to, it was pretty much the same thing—Samantha in the room with me letting Pete know that I was awake. The doctor would come in and tell me to move my finger if I needed any more pain medication, which I did most every time. He administered. If there was one thing that there was plenty of in Hollywood, it was pain medication. Eliah—I looked around for her, hoping perhaps that she would be somewhere in the room. I saw pieces of her: Spread legs. Tilted-back head. Breasts moving across my tongue so that I could just taste her nipples in my memories, but when I tried to swallow the memory into my stomach, there was nothing there.

Out again.

They had moved me—perspective changed. My bed was propped up against a window that looked out over a pool, where I saw the Snow Queen sitting in a white wicker chair and sporting a huge, wide-brimmed hat that shadowed her face. Pete was next to her getting her signature on a bunch of different papers as men and women paraded past them in a steady line. It seemed as if both of them were picking people out for something, though I couldn't be sure what it was. The palm trees that surrounded everything barely moved.

I reached up to touch my face, but Samantha moved her hands in the way so I couldn't get to it. "I don't like to listen to doctors, either," she said, "but this time, I think we better. You'll be fine. Do you feel better? You're actually moving like yourself again."

I reached for the button that was controlling whatever drug they pumped into me to make me feel better, but again, there was Samantha's hand, stopping my movement.

"Why not just try it for a few minutes without it?" she said. "I believe you might be able to take it."

She may have been right, but it didn't stop me from clicking the morphine drip as many times as I could before I passed out. I had a dream about floating away on a giant balloon with Eliah—somewhere in the skies over Los Angeles, while somewhere below, in the graveyards, there were couples falling in love over horror movies before falling into their graves. Still, there were giggles because they had at least died together.

Fading out. Fading out. My Eliah—how could I let you slip away? You step on all of my moments from here on out. You're the weight that keeps my heart from rising out of my body—impossible to give freely to anyone else.

At least in front of a camera, I might be able to survive.

It was hard to believe how very gentle Dr. Addison was. How do doctors get their hands like that? The touch of a doctor's fingers is so light. I wonder if it's because of the level of respect they have for the human body—or perhaps they just know how it all really works from the inside. He peeled the bandages off slowly, and instead of seeing myself revealed, I used the reactions from Pete the Wolf and Samantha as my mirror.

As soon as the last bandage was unwrapped, I was finally able to feel air on my face without the separation of material. They seemed like proud parents looking down at their baby boy—which is what I guess I was. Dr. Addison checked each area of my new face and applied various creams and lotions that were all neatly placed in an old medical satchel. Though his touch was light, even the lightest touches are still harsh on sensitive bones.

"That there, friends, is our leader," Pete said, crossing his arms so hard I thought his armpits were going to snap off his fingers. "I hope you got the writers rolling, Samantha. I want the first script done by the end of the month. Once the swelling goes down, we are all systems go."

"I've worked in a few edits to their initial drafts," she said. "As soon as I'm done with those, I'll let you see them."

"I never asked you to edit them," he snapped.

"Why not just do what needs to be done instead of waiting around for someone to ask you for help? Besides, I know I can do it better than anyone else. You should know that by now as well."

Pete smiled at how right she was and at how much more right he was for being smart enough to hire her.

I laughed until it hurt just a bit and then got up and walked unsteadily to the mirror hanging over the white marble dresser. I was amazed at what I saw. Even through the puffiness and discoloration, I could see that they had done it: created a face that was made up of a composite of recognizable parts of iconic historical revolutionary figures. It was a face I had never seen before but immediately knew and would follow. So trustworthy. Some feelings of regret and anger at the choice I had made lifted just a bit, and I just stood there, allowing myself to love me. My new self. With this face, there was no way anyone could resist what I had to say.

"You're not looking so conflicted," Pete the Wolf said with a grin, as if he were reading my mind. "Are you ready to do something amazing, friend? Are you ready to lead a damn revolution?"

"I am," I said, feeling that first taste of power. "I'll do whatever it takes."

His cell phone rang, and the attention switched from me to whomever was on the other end of that call. Pete was addressing everyone as Captain this and Colonel that. I didn't care—that world out there was for me to grab. No way would I ever let go again.

CHAPTER 11

Sunrises over Sunset Boulevard

The first time out of the recovery room was out on the front lawn, which extended like a giant mossy moat that seemed to be on the verge of overflowing down the steep incline of the Hollywood Hills. I stuck my face out to feel the air's full weight and enjoyed the unexpected lightness that was waiting for me. It was time to call my mom and tell her the *good* news.

"Sorry I didn't tell you about it before, Ma," I said. "They just called me in when they saw my DMV video."

"What video? Never mind: I don't watch those stupid things on the Internet, Harold," she said, annoyed. "But I'm happy for you, though. It's a good part?"

"It's an amazing part, Ma."

"Isn't that wonderful," she said. "Well, when you have time, we'll have lunch at Canter's and have a decent sit-down like we used to. Didn't I tell you to just be yourself and the world will love you like I do?"

Strange how you think as you get older and become an adult that you somehow know more about life than your parents, then one of them drops a piece of knowledge on you so sublime you feel like you have to start life over just to fully understand it. "You did tell me that, Ma."

I looked over and saw Pete and Samantha sitting in lounge chairs, each talking to different people on their cell phones. Samantha looked up and smiled, giving me an okay sign with her hand and lifting her eyebrows as if asking if things were going well.

"Look, Ma, they've advanced me pretty well—well enough that I'm going to give you your dream. Remember when I asked you to tell me what your life would look like without any restrictions?"

"I do, Harold. My old dream of traveling the world—just moving. Yes, I visualize it some days when it gets rough. I usually end up thinking of you, though."

"I listened all of those times you said you wanted to visit those old streets and stand on cliffs that lead out to fantasy worlds. You're flying first class and staying first class. I've got a bank account ready for you, and a car's going to pick you up in about an hour to go get your passport and go shopping for the trip. Just buy a suitcase, fill it up, and you're off. You don't even need to pack—you can shop wherever you go. Just call me and post your pics so I can keep track of your dream."

After a stunned silence, she said, "Lord, whatever I didn't do right, I know I did something good enough to deserve this boy right here. I love you."

"When you get back, we'll meet and celebrate. I'm going to be shooting for the remainder of the year."

"I'm going to call the school board and tell them they can go fuck themselves with their offers of a substitute teaching job. Oh, I am so excited."

She was crying with happiness, both for her new freedom and her son's success. Perhaps that is the reward all parents are looking for.

"I love you, Ma," I said. "I'll see you when you get back and keep track of you on Facebook. I'll always make time to chat with you."

I hung up and looked out over the wide expanse of the Snow Queen's lawn, putting on my sunglasses so that my tears couldn't show.

Pete was lying on a lounge chair talking on his phone, while Samantha had kicked off her shoes but still looked corporate, continuing to create schedules on a giant dry-erase board. I walked over, admiring her mural of organization.

"If I tried for a month, I couldn't do any of what you're doing," I said. "It goes to a new level of analog infographics."

"If I don't put it down," she said, finishing up her last column of times and tasks, "I'd stay up at night thinking about it, worried that I'd forget, and then my thoughts would all go to waste. Missing chances is never an option."

"Hey," I said, stepping back so that I could get a view of the whole board. "Thanks for taking care of all those plans for my mom while I was under. They're all of her favorite spots. Not sure how you knew that."

She capped her dry-erase Sharpie and turned to me. As she did, I couldn't help but notice how well she filled out her gray flannel slacks.

"You don't remember because you kept on squeezing that morphine drip, but you took me through all of the places your mom ever wanted to visit," Samantha said, moving beside me and folding her arms to observe her finished schedule. "She must have talked a bunch about it, though, because you knew each spot and each detail. To tell you the truth, it was kind of fun to do. I imagined myself doing such things one day."

The board was a schedule with the name Pace Skillman on the top. I took me a minute to remember the name they'd given me.

"Your schedule doesn't leave much room for free will, does it?" I said, half joking.

"That what the sleeping hours are for," she said. "Those are yours completely."

I was feeling more like myself. I no longer looked like I'd had a major operation but more like I'd been in a huge fight. Hell, I couldn't remember the last time I didn't look like I'd been in a big fight. The only imperfection on my face was a big scar running from the right corner of my jaw over my cheekbone, but even that they had put there to make me look tougher—which I thought they could have done with some makeup instead of a permanent blemish, but who was I to mess with what they created? They were the experts, after all.

The Snow Queen's grounds were huge. Samantha and I wandered them for hours, talking so I could get used to speaking with my new face, but my thoughts of Eliah were tough to remove. I kept going out to the edge of the lawn that reached over the cliff and looked out for signs of red balloons with notes for me.

On the day the Snow Queen really broke it down for me, instead of a balloon I saw a small man wearing an equally small bellhop's uniform made out of an Adidas jumpsuit pushing a cart of ice across the lawn to fill the Snow Queen's glass. She got to her feet, slid her arm through mine, and walked me slowly over the perfectly manicured grass that stretched out for what seemed to be miles along the cliff behind her house. I took a look back at the exterior of the place I had spent so much time inside of and was struck by the enormity of the structure and amount of land it took up. From the entrance on the opposite side, you couldn't really see the depth of the architecture, but here, behind the locked gates, the spectacle of a mansion done up in white marble looked to be the immaculate escape I so desperately needed. It was a little different from the cramped quarters I'd lived in my whole life, and I actually teetered a little, dizzied.

"You're confused," the Snow Queen said, steadying me. "That's natural. It happened to me as well. I'm not from any of this. I came from Atlanta back in the eighties, and when I first got here, I worked ten hours a day in a phone room somewhere in Culver City, cold-calling companies to see if they wanted pens with their name and address on them. I realized, though, that running around the city looking for someone to make it happen for you wasn't how it all worked. You needed to create your own. So I created the Snow Queen.

"I started having parties every Thursday—inviting everyone I knew from the phone room, knowing that if the party was good enough, they'd invite their friends. It went on like that for a few months until my parties became the place to be on Thursday night.

"Now, of course the thing to do in the eighties was cocaine. Everyone thought they could inch a bit closer to the top if they were high—makes sense when you're high, I guess. Son, I had so much of it at the house that people started asking so much that I quit my day job. Pretty soon, I had enough money to move out of my apartment and get a place closer to the hills. The closer I moved to the hills, the more elite the selection of people who started coming to me.

"My parties became my job as well as my identity. New people started showing up. Hollywood people who were tired of their lives being their jobs—tired of people wanting to be friends in hopes that it will lead to somewhere. The closer you get to the top, the more you need a mellow place hang out and be human. Have fun. Not talk business. You'll see that soon. Anyhow, I got to know all of these folks, and when those parties got to be too big, I moved up here.

"I found the kind of people hanging out because of the cocaine to be a bit, let's say, less interesting after a while. I'm into interesting people. Interesting things. That's when I met the good doctor. He was a big man in Hollywood plastic surgery circles back then, but FDA guidelines and other rules and regulations were keeping him from doing the kind of work he wanted to do. It wasn't even the rules, really—I need you to understand that. He just didn't want anyone overseeing what he was doing, especially his side projects. Most doctors have these little side projects that the general public doesn't care too much for. I made him a deal: I told him I'd allow him to do his side projects up here and run a secret plastic surgery center, away from the public eye. My new connections through my parties starting calling on me because, well, whatever movie script was hot in Hollywood at the time, I just happened to always have a new, fresh-faced star who fit the open role perfectly. You just listen to people talking about themselves, trying to impress at parties in Hollywood. Don't make a fool of yourself trying to talk—just listen. They'll tell you everything. A few months later, I'd introduce them to one of my new 'talent finds' and—*whammo*—it's the perfect fit. The Snow Queen always finds her perfect fit because the good doctor makes it perfect."

There was something almost hypnotic about the Snow Queen that made her voice move around both inside and outside of my head.

"Together, over the years, the good doctor and I have created some of the best-known faces in Hollywood. Of course, if you become known like that, you don't want anyone to know where it happened. No records of such things. It's a dangerous time we live in, with records and information so readily available. Pete could have just taken any one of the wannabes out there and offered him the chance to change his face to fill the role of a lifetime. You know better than most that there are millions down there who would do just about anything for this chance.

"How wonderful for you that you were smart enough to seize your moment. The changing of your face can't just be superficial. To play it real, this must become the real you. Who knows, this might be the person you've wanted to be your whole life but were afraid to let out. That's what keeps everyone else out there with their heads down; they're afraid to be who they are destined to be.

"None of us are who we say we are. We are our own projections. These clothes, hairstyles, the way we dress—all of it together is what we project as our truth, our way of being in this world. You've changed how you look, but I think—and this is why we chose you—that you've always been this person. That we've brought it out in you. We found you, and we want to give you everything you ever wanted. It'll work out, and it'll work out for your mother as well. She'll be better taken care of now than she would have ever been.

"This show is going to be legendary, and when that happens, you get your immortality. For that to happen, you need to find the balance of leaving behind everything you've known but holding on to that sense of loss. That's the vulnerability of a leader. That's where you'll get viewers on the same page as you. They'll wish you existed in real life. Now, are you ready to enjoy it all?"

Her voice's exit from in and around my head left a disorienting vacuum for few seconds, but I was finally able to tell her, "Been ready." We had ended up right back where we started, at the end of the bluff that looked out over the rest of the city, a similar but grander view than the one Eliah and I saw together, when the city looked like a Moroccan marketplace under the smog. There was no doubt that this was the Snow Queen's show, which was just fine for me.

Samantha was sitting in between the two writers across the big table from us with a pad in her hand and a pen behind each ear. Her hair was tied up in a ponytail, and she was still rocking those glasses Pete the Wolf had her wear. Seeing her relaxed me.

"What are you doing with the writers, Samantha?" Pete said. "We've got to set up meetings with the military branches and get those contracts signed."

"I thought it would be a good idea, Peter," the Snow Queen said. "We've got to have a female voice on this show to give it some balls, isn't that correct, Samantha?"

"You're damned right."

"That's what I like to hear."

"Well, I guess we can make some arrangement," Pete said.

The guy on Samantha's left was big in both his stature and his slow, giant-like movements. He must have been six foot three and had thick arms, but not muscle thick. His eyes looked like he'd been on the other end of a twelve-pack the night before. He said his name was simply Tare, and though it was interesting to have just one name, I think he did it only so he didn't have to say two words to people when he introduced himself.

Randy, the other writer, shook his foot and stared directly at me as I read the script through to myself. There was nothing casual about him. He kept getting up and walking behind Pete and me to see where we were in the script, wincing when something made us raise an eyebrow or scratch our heads or asking *"What? What?"* when I read something that had made me smile.

Samantha was in the middle of them, watching everything, writing down whatever she saw.

Pete marked his place on the page and leaned over to me. "You know," he said, almost in a whisper, "I have to admit Samantha and the Snow Queen might be onto something. I'm seeing that Samantha rewrote a lot of your dialogue. If you ask me, without her, your character wouldn't be anywhere near as believable. Her name won't be on this, but her passion is there. Incredible."

"This stuff is amazing," I said back softly. "Why not give her the credit? She deserves it."

"Friend, nobody deserves anything," Pete the Wolf said. "You get what you get. What you make of it is up to you. When she wants to be recognized, she'll ask for it. Better not to hand anyone anything."

"What about me?" I said.

"You've been asking for it your whole life," he replied. "The day you came in to the audition you were asking for it."

We both turned the last page at the same time. I had trouble putting the script down. You know the feeling when you read something for the first time and it just jumps inside of you? When the understanding of what's been created takes over 100 percent of your insides? I got it when I first read *The Outsiders* by S. E. Hinton—turning that last page, knowing there was nothing left to read, was a devastating feeling. I felt the same about the script I'd just read, only I knew it would continue and that I would be the one carrying it out.

"It's amazing," I said. "The concept itself is incredible! You'd told me before, but to see it all fleshed out in this way—these three are amazing."

"The concept is mine," Pete said, smiling as he put his copy down, "but I realize it couldn't have been executed by anyone but our team."

"Do you know how it all ends?" I asked. "It's killing me not to know."

"That's precisely what television is supposed to do," Tare said, cracking open another beer and finishing half of it before letting his arm drop. "Just make sure you get the words out right."

"He will," Samantha said, standing up and stretching high to grab some oxygen, showing her bare belly as she did. It lay flat, allowing the space between her black panties and pants to canyon for an instant. "It was written for him." She'd been so buttoned up till now that seeing her flesh peek out from under her clothes peeled away another layer.

"Not all of it," added Randy. "You see, the *story* has to be the star. Remember that. You are just the mover of the *story*. He has to remember that. Will there be someone there to make sure he remembers?"

"Relax," Pete the Wolf said. "Your nerves are making me nervous. We're all on message here. Nothing is going to stray from what's been put down. You'll find both of your bank accounts have been taken care of. Samantha, you, of course—well, you know our arrangement."

I saw her discomfort and made the mistake of thinking it was about money. Then the look slowly washed away from her face when the Snow Queen nodded in approval of what she'd read. With that knowing look, I could swear I saw Samantha's legs open just slightly.

The first episode was set in Los Angeles in the present day. The Occupy protests had started to gather a real following, but the members weren't organized and were in need of a leader. People were ready for it. There was too much information out there for them to ignore. The stories on the news were no longer events you shook your head and said "Too bad" about, but were now happening to you.

The economy was imploding in the middle of the country, so California started a Real Jobs for Real Americans program, offering people a chance to come out to Hollywood and have their own show on a new network.

Golden State Broadcasting.

My character, Pace Skillman, was the pitchman who'd make it all seem real. Pete was talking about a five-year run—and then, when I was no longer under contract, I'd be free to do what I chose.

It all just unfolded for me up there. Pete and the Snow Queen were going back and forth on numbers, while the two writers had left after they'd heard there was something waiting for them in their accounts. The Snow Queen kept looking at Samantha and smiling at her actions and passion.

She had taken quite an interest in the girl, which made me look at her more closely as well.

Samantha and I watched the sky get darker, but it wasn't black yet. I had to tell myself there was no Rising Sushi shift to report to. Nobody to serve down there.

"You see it, don't you?" Samantha said, looking out at the blank space with me. "You see how amazing it can be."

"I've always seen it," I said. "It's just that the people I saw it happening with are not here to share it with me. It doesn't feel whole."

"Why do you need people in your past to share in your present?" she said and then wrote it down as a note to put that line in her script. "If they're not here with you, there must be a reason why."

She placed her hand on mine, and I was struck by the warmth I felt from her touch. It was a tender moment that kept me from floating too high over the skyline of Hollywood.

CHAPTER 12

Fresh Faced

My bruises were gone, and for the first time in longer than I could remember, my face was clean. I say "my face" because, well, that's how I was dealing with Pace Skillman.

Though I was comfortable staying at the Snow Queen's house during the final stages of my recovery, I was getting restless. I'd always been restless in my former life—always needed to be moving—so here, confined to one place, there was that need inside me to move. Perhaps that's what being from Los Angeles does to your insides—that wide space, that flat skyline that stretches out over the horizon, always gives you the sense that you can take off and keep going, but still be within the limits of the city.

During the day, Samantha and I would go up to the Hollywood Reservoir and run laps in the sunshine to firm up and tan up. She wore those American Apparel shorts that were short just past her backside, the thin fabric falling around her curves. Her San Francisco State T-shirt bounced as she ran, making trying to keep up with her enjoyable.

"You look freer out of the power suits," I told her as we went for another lap. "No makeup suits you."

"I'm comfortable in anything," she said. "Still, it's nice to be noticed honestly by a man. Nothing I hate more than those who take a peek and then turn away when I try to look them in their eyes. What happened to men who don't act like little boys?"

"We've always acted like little boys," I said, trying to pull ahead to no avail. "It's just that women weren't allowed in the places where we played. Those days are over, so your illusion may be a little shattered."

To say I was into her wouldn't be a lie, but it wasn't that all-encompassing feeling of lust I felt when I was with or even thought about Eliah. It was funny, but the fact that Samantha was so gorgeous and yet I wasn't drooling over her like a fool gave me a sense of power that I actually enjoyed. It allowed me to stay in control and ease into the small crush I thought Samantha had on me.

My runs were quicker and smoother than they ever had been because I was able to block out the worries that crept in: money, rent, success, Mom—all of that had been taken care of. I still had all my Facebook and Twitter accounts. Sometimes while I was jogging, I'd get a notification that my mom had posted something on my wall—a picture of her in Florence eating tortellini in the center of a square or relaxing by a pool in Costa Rica holding a drink I could tell wasn't the first of the day. She had a smile on her face, and I could see, for the first time in my life, that her face was relaxed and unstressed.

Samantha and I would do four laps around the Hollywood Reservoir and then drive back to the Snow Queen's house, where I had my speech therapy lessons to learn how to enunciate. I had to be of an educated background to lead this movement. Our target audience wasn't crying for religious freedom or civil rights; they wanted solutions and not rhetoric. Underneath everything, I think Americans were wondering how they were going to keep their grip on their lives of privilege (in comparison to how the rest of the world was living, not how the rest of America was living). How could they afford their cable, Internet, cell phones, and all of the other devices that had become necessary but not so long ago didn't exist? I'm not sure a decent meal and a place to live was enough for anyone, myself included.

Back at the Snow Queen's house, Pete was constantly on the phone, breathing away from it only to ask Samantha to help him with setting up meetings or reworking schedules. She was getting paid to be his associate producer, not a writer for the show, so she needed to be at the ready for him and work on scripts on her own time.

The thing about Samantha and Pete was that, if you looked at their relationship objectively, they needed each other equally—but Pete's ability to make Samantha feel that, without him, she would be nothing, never allowed her to demand what she was really worth.

Pete was trying to find working tanks and jets to line up on California's borders. These clips were going to be in the trailers—just quick shots of California's new military bracing for any backlash from the rest of the country. Now, there is a long tradition of cooperation between the military and Hollywood. Movies and TV are always good places to show off some brand-new toys picked up with taxpayer cash—and man, do Americans love to cheer the hardware. It's always a big win for the US military to showcase all of the weapons and vehicles at their disposal—gives the public a sense they're being protected. The partnership had been going on since the days of those glorious World War II movies where John Wayne teamed with the military machine to make those propaganda posters really come to life. Hell, it was free advertising for them—and nobody turns that down. War movies are a great way to advertise war toys.

When Samantha and I came back to the Snow Queen's house after one of our runs, Pete was wrapping up a meeting with four men in military uniforms. They looked straight out of Central Casting for what a hard-nosed, kick-ass military type was supposed to look like, except for the fact that they were all smiles and seemed quite relaxed. I guess an afternoon in the Hollywood Hills with visionaries like Pete the Wolf and the Snow Queen is going to do that to you.

A tall man with multiple medals and a perfectly fitted hat was nodding at Pete as we approached. "As I said, Mr. Wolfson, I can't imagine we'll have any trouble loaning you whatever your production needs." He lifted one meaty finger into air between them. "We will, of course, have to ensure safety by providing experts, and that will entail some compensation. We don't want anyone firing that artillery without knowing what they're doing, do we? Marines are protective of their goods. Your budget accounts for such things, I presume."

"And you can be sure that the air force will be willing and at your service with our planes and pilots," said the man in the powder-blue uniform. "As long as we can get a few shots of them in the show. Does the men some good, you know. This country used to be more supportive of its men in service."

"Now you'd have to include the women as well, isn't that right?" said Samantha, wishing to cover herself but not having the material to make that wish possible.

"Not bad for recruiting either, huh?" Pete said with a smile, trying to shift the awkwardness back to business. "I think it's a fair exchange—you giving us the contracts to do your commercials and your recruitment ads that everyone, of course, must watch before the show starts. Young people aren't watching as much TV—but we know where they are."

"Wouldn't have it any other way," the light-blue man said, not taking his eyes off Samantha. "Nobody makes us look as appealing to the young folks as your talented people behind the cameras."

We listened politely, Samantha inching closer to me, as the navy man said his piece about the ships that would be used for filming down off the coast. "I can't wait to see my fleet shot against the sunset of the great Pacific," the navy man said, looking out over the water as if he could picture it.

"That's going to be a money shot," Pete said, sidling up next to him and settling in to enjoy his vision with him. "I think we'll have a camera on the ship so we can see your view—you know, protecting the coastline. Of course, we'll have to have a waiver from you saying it's okay to paint our Golden State Broadcasting logo on the side. After all, in the show, it won't be the United States protecting us, it'll be GBS."

"They'll still know who it really is, though," the marine said. "They'll God-damn well know."

They all gazed out together then, each lost in imagining how those cameras would showcase his respective military outfit. They loved their men and loved their country even more.

"Hope you gentlemen don't mind being on the other side of the revolution," I said, doing my best to break the ice.

"Though, after seeing the pictures Pete showed me earlier about what you have in your back pocket, I'm not sure how any revolution would ever stand a chance against you."

"Always in character, this one," Pete said, bringing me to the forefront, trying to shift the attention from Samantha. When Pete sent her off with a stack of paperwork to process, there was no doubt in my mind that the men wished it were me being dispatched. "This here is our star," Pete said. "The leader of our 'revolution.' Don't worry, though, boys—inside he's a true-blue patriot, you can believe that."

"There's no other way to be," the marine representative said, slapping me on the shoulder without taking his eyes off of the departing Samantha. "And you're beyond right, there, son," he went on, absently. "There's no chance of a revolution here. We're trained to spot those before they happen, don't you worry." Finally he sighed and snapped out of it, turning to me. "Still, it's fun to play in Hollywood with you all. Don't worry, I'm not going to put you on my list."

They all burst out laughing, and I laughed too, figuring it was just the thing to do.

"Well, then," I said, raising my eyes in a good-bye to Samantha when she turned to look back before vanishing into the house. "I'm glad it's just a TV show. Now, gentlemen, while it's been an honor and pleasure to meet all of you, I've got more lessons to attend to. I just hope that nobody attacks when we've got all of your gear. What state would the country be in then?"

"Well, son, I'll tell you," the army man said calmly. "The likelihood of you knowing anything we don't want you to know is pretty much zero. You just keep on watching the news."

Noting not to make jokes to military men, I excused myself and headed inside for my speech lessons. Waiting for me was Lionel Wise, elocutionist to the stars. Whatever accent you needed to have for a role, he could teach you. I enjoyed my time with him. He hated what he called "the Twitter" and was in a state of constant anger because people were losing the ability to speak with each other. He was old and a step slow, but when he spoke, each word he delivered shot right through you.

"You young guys have access to the most amazing women in the country walking around every day, and what do you do? You use your spare moments looking at a phone." That was the start of his hello but not the end of it. "All you want to do is send text messages and check to see if someone else was talking about you. If I were your age, I'd be in a different woman's bed each night, because most of you guys don't even look anymore. It's a shame, is what it is. Nobody's asking me, though, are they? Indeed they are not. They have hired me to teach you how to pronounce the words you'll say to a screen but not to a person."

He used old records to go over speeches with me and always carried a powder-blue portable record player with him, complete with built-in speakers. When he undid the silver locks, he opened it as if he were undoing the single strap on a woman's nightgown. The actual turntable was wrapped in a silk scarf that his wife had worn before she passed a few years earlier. When he took it off the turntable, I could swear he was imagining undressing her before they went to sleep. I caught him smelling it a few times.

On this day, he brought over speeches from Malcolm X: "The Ballot or the Bullet," "By Any Means Necessary," and "Message to the Grass Roots."

"Lionel, do you think I could get some of these speeches on my iPod?" I asked, sitting down next to the record player as he always asked me to do. "When I'm running, I'd love to be able to listen and get down his patterns. What do you think?"

"I think you had better sit your backside down and really, actively, listen to these records," he said. "You have to strain to listen to everything on a record. Those warps and pops and crackles are the background noise essential to your ear's ability to peel away distractions and concentrate on how a speaker delivers. Listening is an active event. That's how real-life speaking—*good* real-life speaking—distinguishes itself from someone standing on a street corner yelling out slogans.

"Here, train your ear to listen to how, despite the poor audio quality, you can still hear what Mr. X is saying—not only the *what* and the *how*, but the *feeling*. All of that is articulated despite the surrounding static. A great speaker must do the same. If you want to play one, you'll have to become one who speaks through distraction."

After he had put the scarf perfectly on the armchair, Lionel started playing the first record. Malcolm X's voice exploded through the house, rattled off of that clean white marble and just kept on going, bouncing off the walls and into every inch of my understanding of language.

"Listen to how different he is from all the others we've listened to. He's not yelling. He's not preaching. He's speaking and demanding that you listen to the words. There is that delicate, very rare balance of power and enunciation in each syllable. That's breath. The key to it all is confidence that what you're saying is one hundred percent true. Now that's going to be the challenge for you, because these words are not your thoughts. You must convince yourself that they are."

"I believe I can do that by forgetting my past," I said without hesitation. "I won't let what's happened before determine who I'll be."

Pete burst into the room as he usually did, as if he had a marching band behind him and a red carpet being rolled out ahead of him.

"That's true," he said. "The past is going to hold you back. If you drift into a memory while playing this role, you're going to shatter the illusion. How's he doing, Lionel?"

"Not quite as bad as some of them and not quite as well as some of the others. I need to relieve myself. Keep listening—we'll start practicing with actual speeches when I get back." He eyed Pete. "That is, if the scripts are ready. I do not like having my students practicing with materials that are not relevant."

He left the room, and Pete ripped open a pack of gummy bears he had in his lapel pocket.

"We've got all the equipment ready for the coast scenes," he said. "I've got Samantha working on getting us permits to shoot those tanks on Sunset as well. We'll shoot the trailer over the next few weeks, and things should start rolling from there. We'll leak it out in the form of actual commercials for Golden State Broadcasting and make sure all the connectors out there spread the word. Those gentlemen from our armed forces have agreed to share marketing resources and vendors to make sure we get plenty of play in the press. Soon I'll be able to get all of those with one phone call as well."

"Those military guys seem awfully eager to loan you their equipment."

"Indeed, friend," Pete said, smacking down on a red gummy. "They're like the cigarette companies—they need a constant stream of people to support the use of their product.

"Let's keep the focus on you, though. I know Lionel, and he doesn't seem too happy with your progress. Speaking is more than just words, you know. You have to understand what's behind them. That's how you get folks to follow you. To want to *be* you. Don't worry about it, though, I have more experts lined up to help out. I had a feeling we'd have to dig deeper into the understanding of who you are."

"Does every actor go through this much training for a major role?"

"Only those who become their parts."

"The surgery took care of that, wouldn't you say?"

"Exterior, friend," he said, finishing the last gummy, then checking the bag to make sure he had. "That's just for the posters. If you want them to follow you, you need to make them believe."

Lionel came back into the room and started in without checking to see if Pete and I were done. He played the record again and glanced over at the scarf while I practiced keeping time with Malcolm X, lifting up the needle and putting it back in its grooves, until I no longer heard the words, only the inflection in his tone.

"Repetition makes it real," Lionel said. "Repetition makes it real."

With Eliah gone and my mom on her dream travels around the world, the only woman who knew me was Samantha. My time with her became my most natural, as I didn't need to hide anything. Pete wanted her close to me so she could keep tabs, and she told him that spending time with me allowed her to write for my character. She was all about making sure the Revolutionary had some kind of vulnerability behind the inspiring words. I think, deep down—or perhaps not so deep down—we were both thankful for the enjoyment we seemed to give each other.

Samantha and I would take long walks through the Hollywood Hills and go over lines—which never seemed like work to me. The cool air helped to continue the healing of my face, which, though the visible bruises had gone away, was still sore and getting used to being in the outside world. That part of me was still a child.

Dr. Addison had been weaning me off the Vicodin for fear of addiction, but I had it under control and would share them with Samantha, who liked to take one with a glass of wine during our strolls through the hills.

Together we discovered the multitude of hidden little spots along Mulholland Drive and other areas of what we started to call the West Beautiful Mountain Range. There we made a game out of finding and naming out-of-the-way benches that look over the city—and believe me, there are hundreds scattered throughout the hills. We started a map showing where each of them was and indulged in fantastic plans to bury it and send others on a magnificent treasure hunt when all of this was over.

It was becoming our city. Any bitterness or sense of things being unfair had gone away; for both of us, our years of struggle had paid off. I hadn't run away screaming from the madness like so many had done in the past. I'd stood my ground and believed in myself, and now, finally, I was about to arrive. Well, I had arrived years ago at UCLA

Medical Center, but there was no announcement or fanfare. Nobody wrote about the event. There's no doubt they will now.

We stopped and sat on an old, graffiti-covered stone bench looking out through the gap cut by a long power line. Far in the distance, downtown Los Angeles lay like a spaceship turned upside down waiting to get its belly rubbed. Most folks miss these spots because they're zooming around in search of something instead of walking around just to be walking. Samantha and I read lines back and forth, and I used my new, learned voice. The scene dealt with the last part of the first episode, where the man who was chosen to be the face of the California rebellion finally realizes what he is responsible for.

"I can't see the page," I said, squinting through my new eyelids, which felt heavier than the ones I had before. "What's it say?"

Samantha leaned over and turned on her BlackBerry to give light. I could feel her thigh push up against mine. She held it to make sure I was into her movements. She trembled just a bit, and my natural inclination was to put my hand on her shaking thigh to quiet it down. As soon as I touched it, I felt her muscles relax and our body temperatures shift.

"Is that better?" she asked, looking me in the eyes and moving her lips close to mine while still leaving enough space for the soft breaths to travel. "The light, it makes it better, right? I wrote this last part, so I want you to really feel the words. I've pretty much written all of your lines. I tried to get away from making you some giant penis standing up there letting everyone know how powerful you are. There needs to be something to blend with the toughness—something viewers want to pull out of you while you do everything to keep it hidden below the surface."

"That's beautiful," I told her, moving my hand slowly up her thigh, pressing down to apply a little weight. "Do you think all this is going to work? We're all taking so many chances here."

She clicked off her phone so that the only illumination came from the distant city. "There are always shots at the mainstream, and we're definitely an outlier here. Outliers, though, if timed right, can become the new center—like a magnet. Don't you feel as if the center is changing?"

I looked into her eyes, and everything was right for me to kiss her—for me to finally be with someone who not only understood me but understood who I wanted to be. Perhaps she was my destiny after all—Eliah was still in my heart, yes, but Samantha was right here. Maybe that was enough, I was telling myself, making myself believe that it would be impossible to move on alone.

We leaned in slowly, the moments of near touches and subtle hints about to pay off here in the almost-darkness above Los Angeles.

"There you are!" a voice bellowed from the road. Pete, bumping his head out of his Escalade with that idiot grin of total self-satisfaction, had broken the mood. "I've been looking for you two for hours. Your final coach is ready, the one who's going to take it over the edge. I can tell from how you've been speaking that you never really did much reading on these people, so I found you someone to bring it all home. It's going to be fantastic. A few more weeks and we can get you started, but for now, we'll get you all the knowledge you need. Oh man, I am pumped! Samantha, you're not getting our boy here into any trouble, are you?"

"We're just running lines is all, Pete," she said, folding up the little map we had made and getting into the backseat of the ride.

"How do you always know where I am?" I said. "That's not going to work for the long run. I may be employed by you, but you don't own me."

I got into the front seat, and he turned up the Bob Dylan he was playing, smiling at the moment he thought he was creating and oblivious to the one he had just ruined.

"I'm not trying to own you, friend. I'm trying to make you. Let it go. I just brought you the teacher you've been missing."

"I thought I was doing a decent job," I heard Samantha say from the backseat.

"What was that, honey?" Pete said, looking quickly in the rearview mirror before returning his eyes on the road.

"It was nothing."

We zoomed through the Hollywood Hills with Pete's system shattering the stillness of our night. His phone was buzzing every few seconds, but he never checked it.

"Eyes on the road, my man," he said. "Anywhere else, you're bound to crash. We're too close for something like that happen, don't you think?" I felt sad in my chest, knowing that this maniac was in control and what I really wanted was right there in the backseat, or maybe it was somewhere in the city below, unable to be found because she never wanted anyone to find her.

We got back to our place. "Our place"—funny to be calling it that. Truth was, it belonged to the Snow Queen, and the rest of us were just playing around in her sandbox so she could keep an eye on her investment. Samantha jumped from the backseat of the Escalade to the front seat of her car, a used Volkswagen Rabbit, and raced away into the night that we had just been losing ourselves in.

"I'm not sure she should be behind the wheel," I said, watching as she sped off.

"Don't mistake her admiration for you for weakness," Pete said. "Besides, you need to meet your last coach. It's the final piece before you move into your new place."

"New place? I'm moving?"

"You didn't think you were going to stay in recovery, did you? I don't need to be away from my wife and family to babysit you twenty-four hours a day, do I? We got you a sweet place up in Hollywood, just by Runyon Canyon. Nothing too fancy, but it's newly constructed, there's a pool, and there's people there who are all trying to be what you have become."

Wife and family? I hadn't thought about the life Pete the Wolf lived outside of his involvement with me.

We walked in through the giant white doors. The Snow Queen was watching TV, and I could see the back of the head of another person with her, not paying attention to the show the Snow Queen was watching.

"Ah, good," Pete said, clapping his hands and doing a little skip. "You're here. Thanks for coming. I didn't see your car in front. You could have pulled up."

She turned around on the couch, and my stomach nearly fell to the floor.

"No worries," she said. "I don't drive." She extended her hand to me. "A pleasure to meet you. My name's Eliah."

I was silent on the outside. I might have imploded like a black hole, sucking all of my energy and attention away from myself and directing it toward her. Without a doubt, even in that instant when she first appeared, even in my shock, she was my sun. I wanted to grab her, hold her, do and say everything, but I caught a glance of myself in the mirror and stopped.

"This is Pace Skillman," Pete said, the first time I had ever been introduced by my new name. "Pace, meet Eliah Harper. She's a wiz at, well, what the hell aren't you a wiz at? The two of you are going to be spending some time together for the next few months, which, by the way you're both looking at each other, doesn't seem like it's going to be the worst thing in the world for either of you."

"Pleased to meet you," she said, reaching out her hand again. "We've got tons to do, but I've got most of it in my head. The trick will be getting it into yours. I'm confident I can do that."

I stood there silent, nothing coming out. My heart was just quieting down from the almost-kiss with Samantha, and now, here in front of me, was the love I thought I'd lost, and somewhere inside of her, there was a memory of me. I wanted to shout and scream that it was me—to grab her and spin her around and around—to tell her that I never stopped loving her and wished I hadn't been such an ass that night, but none of that came out. Nothing came out. I stood there like a mope.

"Not very talkative, is he?" she said, looking over at Pete. "Is he supposed to be the strong, silent type? If so, he has both of those things down."

I noticed her eyes looking over my body. You can always tell by holding someone's stare if they are checking you out. Those bouncy eyes are key giveaways.

"Now," Pete said, putting his arm around both of us, "Eliah runs the kind of business that doesn't need any kind of publicity, so you two will just have to be seen together in public as, well, let's say a young couple. We have a few photographers hired out to take some pics of Pace out and about, so for the time being, let's just go with it. It's good to have young actors be seen with mystery ladies. Don't worry, dear, I'm not going to mention your name."

"No pictures," she said. "You just make sure whoever you hire keeps me out of frame."

"You have my word," he said, clasping his hands together and bending the combination of the two toward her.

Eliah didn't look too happy—I remembered how much she hated having her picture taken—but she took Pete at his word and carried on. This must have been the gig she was talking about when we had our big fight—the one that was going to take care of any financial troubles for months to come. I mentally slapped myself. My guts were pounding against my skin to be let out and spill truth all over the place, but my mind, now firmly in command of the entire situation, knew that any kind of truth would in no way be helpful. In fact, right there, I thought of this encounter as a second chance. I could get her to fall in love with me again and not make the same mistakes as last time. How wrong could that be? I was still myself under this mask. We all do unreasonable things when we think it might be the only way to save a love.

"So, we'll get started tomorrow, right?" she said to Pete. "I'm on the clock as of now, so it's up to you how you want to spend your money."

Pete seemed to be enjoying what was happening in front of him, and because I knew him so well, I was wondering if he was thinking how he could get more out of his investment than was originally promised. The Snow Queen was looking at Eliah from her chair as if examining her.

Pete shook himself out of his thoughts and smiled confidently.

"Tomorrow's moving day for our boy here. Let's start fresh on Monday. There's something about the start of a week that gets everyone excited about what's ahead of them. Now, young lady, can I offer you a ride home?"

"I don't ride in cars," she said, "thanks for asking. Besides, it's not that cold out. I'll walk. The exercise is always nice."

With that, she shook my hand like she must have done a million times with other clients but never with me. The only times we'd ever touched, she'd either been healing or loving me. Perhaps I should have let her know then what was happening, but I couldn't. I had the possibility to do something that only exists in romance novels: The chance to retrieve a love that was thought to be lost.

CHAPTER 13

Chances Are

Pete was a crazy megalomaniac who only cared about success and greatness regardless of the cost—and that's what made him such an amazing director. He had a drive within him that attracted those who wanted the same thing but didn't want to put their desires out there for the rest of the world to see. He never minded the world looking at him. I'm not sure he slept—just stayed up all night working out how to make the show even better. How to make *me* even better.

Because of the feel of the show—that the main character was supposed to exist outside of the system—Pete was determined to make it outside of the network system.

Samantha was busy scouting locations and texting me places she saw while I was moving into my new place. There were little messages underneath with things like, "I think it's the perfect place for a bench." I didn't know what to do about that, because though I thought she was amazing and fit perfectly into my heart, it was Eliah who made it explode and caused me to go mad, and love—I thought, at least—was supposed to drive you crazy.

Pete set me up in a place two and a half a blocks down from Runyon Canyon—one of those multi-unit complexes filled with hustlers and pimps dressed up like independent producers and actresses. Everyone walking around that place looked like they could be stepping out of a magazine—but their eyes were never focused on the steps in front of them. When you walked by, they always checked to see if you were somebody.

There was a pool in the middle of the courtyard, which was surrounded by a seven-story building with an underground garage and a secured front door to a lobby that led to a tiny gym with treadmills right by the windows. It was like a sign for all those who were thinking about entering—like a rollercoaster sign saying how tall you needed to be to ride, except this one said you needed to be "At least this fit to enter."

The place was immaculate and new—it stank of newness—but that didn't bother me. I stank of newness as well.

My favorite thing in my apartment was the closed-circuit television security station—you could have a four-screen split of the front door and all three elevators. Real people were always a bit more enjoyable to watch than anything on television, but that's because I hadn't been on television yet.

I made sure the only entertainment I had in my place was watching the people coming in and out of the building and the script that I took with me into every room of the apartment. I was going over my lines a few days after I'd moved in when the phone rang its special ring to let me know someone was buzzing at the door for me. I looked at the camera and saw Eliah out there, trying to figure out if she'd pushed the right buttons. Amazing—she hadn't changed one bit—not in her discomfort with digital devices, anyway.

She had been coming over for about two weeks steady now. My apartment was getting more and more lived-in—a few new pieces of furniture, unwashed dishes, and some of the downgrade from perfection that comes from just taking the wrapper off. In my head, we were starting our courting period again—that's how I saw it, anyway. She, of course, was looking at it like just another job. I told myself to control my emotions and play it smart so that she'd fall in love with me slow. After all, I knew her secrets, her desires, and what she wanted from a man. I did love her, and she me—at least I thought she did. All she'd been asking for was for me to trust her, and now I did.

For this session, she brought over a 1975 *Playboy* magazine and tossed it down on my brand-new glass table. I'd polished the table before she got there, but it hadn't dried fully, so the back cover stuck to the glass.

"What kind of lesson is this going to be?" I asked her, slightly stimulated, because every boy—well, I shouldn't say every boy, but most boys—had their first sexual encounters with a *Playboy*, so anytime you see one later in your life, you can't help but get those feelings, imagining the women waiting for you inside those glossy pages.

"Calm down there, Pace," she said. "I have these in my files because most major publications back then, the ones we consider to be at the forefront of news, wouldn't publish interviews with the likes of Castro. I wanted you to get a sense of the times as well; that'll let you know more about him. You want to know about a man, you need to know about the times."

"I'm not sure about Castro and his politics," I said, trying to make a romantic situation out of any chance I could, and all this talk about Fidel and death and communism was killing my mack-down mood.

"We're not here talking about his politics," she said, without much emotion other than a little frustration. "I'm talking about his ability to get people to follow his lead. It's his impact that we're after, not his ideology. The writers fill in the ideology."

Whatever words came out of her mouth during our lessons, I'd imagine that she was talking to me about us—about how she missed me and couldn't believe that we had found each other again. How she wanted the role to be such a success that she'd spend any amount of time trying to get me ready for it. In my fantasy, I had convinced myself as best I could that Pete wasn't paying her to be there—that she came each day out of love for me.

Of course, that's not what she was saying at all. She was showing me what it took to be a leader—what I had to have inside of me if I was to be believable on-screen. I kept looking at the tops of her knees and remembered what existed up beyond that point and then gave her a look that said I'd been there before—like I owned it—hoping that she'd feel it.

"What each of these people had," she said, "was something worth dying for. They had something greater than themselves. You're going to need to find that inside of you—somewhere. Now, for them, it was their country or their people. What do you have that's going to motivate you? Obviously, you're not married—no girl either?"

"There's no time for women right now," I told her. "I've put everything I have into this role. It's the chance of lifetime, and I'm not going to throw it away to get between someone's legs."

When I said the word legs, I looked down at her thighs and imagined myself between then.

"I can respect that," she said, letting go a smile, perhaps feeling my attempts to shift the energy. "You have to put yourself and your dreams first. If someone's in your way, you need to push them aside. And if you're in someone's way, you need to step aside, even if it devastates you to do so."

She seemed to have triggered a memory and got up and looked out the sliding door. The AC was on full blast, but she asked if she could open it anyhow. She did, and we both walked out on to the deck. Below, there were people lounging by the pool. Everyone looked so small from up here. I was a bit tired of being high up and needed to get down on ground level.

"Let's get out of here," I said. "I need to move. Being cooped up all day is not anywhere close to my style."

"Where to? I don't want to lose my job because you can't sit still."

"Relax," I said. "Learning takes place everywhere. Let's roll out for a bit and see where that brings us. You look like you're fiending for some fresh air. When's the last time you were at the beach?"

"And how do you propose we get there?" she said. "I'm not big on cars, and we're a ways off from salt water."

"There are these magnificent things called buses. Most people use them to get around, though in Hollywood, you wouldn't think so. Come on. Pack your things; we're taking a field trip. I'm not even asking you, I'm telling you."

"Telling me, huh?" she said. "That's a new approach, for sure. Fine, that's what a leader's supposed to do anyhow. I'll play along—but realize, if you were a regular guy telling me what to do, I'd tell you to go screw yourself."

"Good thing I'm not a regular guy."

On the thirty-three down Fairfax Boulevard—past Hollywood High School, where kids were spilling out and heading down Melrose for a few minutes of freedom—Eliah and I were stuck in the stop-and-start motion of the Los Angeles public transportation system. When I was sixteen and seventeen, when everyone else was getting their licenses, I was still riding these buses with my grandmother, going food shopping or to the movies. I don't regret any of it because I know plenty of people—well, not plenty, but I know people—who had crazy cash to do what they wanted and never had as much fun as I had with my grandmother on the bus.

Nobody liked riding the bus in Los Angeles; buses were always hot and flooded with sunlight. The bus drivers were on edge all the time, and for me, they can be as insane as they like. Navigating through Los Angeles traffic in a giant whale requires even the harshest of critics to silence their know-it-all attitude.

Ever try to be a teenager and take a girl on the bus for a date in Los Angeles? Show up at her door and start walking on the sidewalk. She's looking around for your car—"Where'd you park?" And then you lay it down that you're walking to the bus stop, where you'll be able to catch one to Westwood in about twenty minutes. The look on her face makes you realize that at school on Monday she'll be telling all her friends about "waiting at the bus stop with him forever!"

That was fine for me. I knew that when I grew up, there'd be plenty of time for cars and quick rides through life. Being on the bus when I was young and learning about Los Angeles from that perspective—from the slow-moving, improbable pausing perspective, from the perspective of having to be somewhere and then waiting for an extra twenty minutes while someone with a wheelchair is loaded on and made room for in the back and seeing the bus driver coming back and sweating from being outside in the hot Southern California sun—it gave me a different feeling about the people that make up this great city. I felt like I was part of the millions here, and now, because of that patience, because of rubbing up against all those people on their ways through the veins of Los Angeles, I was calm and comfortable—and of course, with one of the only women in Los Angeles who would rather take a bus than ride in a car.

Eliah was looking out the scratched windows as Fairfax Boulevard moved by, populated by young couples who looked old in their orthodox clothes, teenagers from the high school who didn't have a group to hang with, shop owners stepping out from what held them to get some air, and sporadic sun-wanderers looking for shade.

We moved past Canter's Deli, which never closed, with waitresses and waiters inside that never retired—where I used to sit with my mother and listen to her crunch the bagel chips as she watched everyone moving and clanking dishes. She always looked so happy during the moments we shared in those booths. If I could bend time and stick two pieces together that didn't fit, I would have gotten off at the stop right there with Eliah and had my mother join us. "Ma, this is the girl I'm going to marry," I'd say.

"Oh, Harold, she's just beautiful," she'd say. "I always knew if you waited you'd find someone special."

Back to the moment.

Fairfax was one of the few streets that remained basically untouched by the attempts at the modernization of Los Angeles. It's funny, because when it was originally constructed, Los Angeles was supposed to be the most modern of all cities. New York and Chicago and Miami existed in so much tradition that Los Angeles had the feeling of being cookie-cutter and unoriginal, but as time moved and the rest of the big cities continued to build upon themselves, Los Angeles aged well and became locked in a form of noir reality that started to sit well with its age. The more people came out here for fame, the more they realized they could make some kind of home and foundation for themselves outside of it.

To the west you could see the Beverly Center, which opened thirty years earlier and was space-age then, but now felt retro. On the side was an escalator covered in a round tube that I imagined was a giant waterslide people could shoot down. I thought this when I was a kid, and now, here as an adult, I believed the same thing, only now I had to use my imagination, while as a child I actually believed it.

To the east, if you looked fast enough, Third Street stretched forever to downtown.

Eliah flipped through her notebooks and highlighted passages she wanted me to look at in the old *Playboy* as the bus continued its slow crawl, now moving past Third Street, where the buildings flattened out and the sun took over once again. A few school buddies who might have just moved past looking up what they thought to be dirty words in the dictionary were looking over at the *Playboy*.

"Maybe we should let those two have the *Playboy*," I said, looking at them and nodding. "That way we could use this time to get to know each other a little better. How's that sound?"

The two kids nodded back.

"You know that most great leaders have been assassinated," she said, disregarding my attempts at a shift. "Maybe you need to feel that kind of fear inside to give your character the depth Pete keeps asking for. Maybe that's the element that's missing. How would you go about working with that hanging over you? Knowing that you could be taken out at any moment."

I grabbed the *Playboy* from her hands and gave it to the little boys, who acted like they'd just received the Holy Grail. Who knows, they just might have. The bus stopped just then, and they jumped off and sat down against the wall of the Farmer's Daughter Motel and started turning pages, slowly, from the beginning.

"Los Angeles through the windows of a bus is such a different kind of city," I said. "It's been a while since I've seen it like this. Amazing if you have the right person to look at it with, wouldn't you say?"

"Who the hell do you think you are taking my materials from me like that?" she said. "That was a very important interview in there. Now it's gone—those kids are probably going to take turns learning how to masturbate with it."

"Good for them," I said. "Makes me proud that I was the one to give them their first *Playboy*. That's an honor, you know. Besides, I can find that article online if I need to. Right here on my phone, if you're really stressing about it."

"That's not the point," she said. "It was the experience and history of the magazine, the context. There is a certain weight that comes with things of age that the Internet can never duplicate. Now what are we going to do?"

"Maybe I wanted you to experience the bus ride through the city with me," I said. "Ever think about that?"

"I've been on a bus before."

"Not sharing the ride with me. This is all a memory now—all of it being created with each crazy stop. Each freak or horny kid or madman who comes onto the bus and takes a ride—we'll have them in our minds, together. That's irreplaceable.

"Don't worry about prepping me for the part; I've studied everything you've brought me. Believe me, I have nothing but time for that. I've been holed up in my house or Pete's house or some trainer's gym or some speech therapist's spot for months now. I need to be out in the world experiencing it as my character. I'm in character now. The least you can do is play along with me and jump into my world for a bit. Might help you relax—you look like you could use a break. You must have been going nonstop for a while now."

"What makes you say that?"

"I can smell the Red Bull on your breath when you come over," I said, putting my hand on her knee. "Maybe you need to come down just a bit."

She moved my hand off her knee, which made me feel a bit awkward, but then she smiled at my observation. She exhaled and leaned back on the chair of the bus.

"You know," she said, sighing. "I spend most of my time researching and looking things up for other people, finding out facts that would back up arguments and then fitting it all into a neat, twenty-page paper or a stack of notes or checking off a list of things that I have to get somebody to retain. I'm not sure I have any of myself left. You know what I mean?"

"I do."

An older woman in front of us wearing a pink handkerchief on her head, her bus pass hanging from a leather wallet fixed to a string around her neck, had turned around in the middle of our talk. "I just know you from somewhere, don't I?" she said to me. "You've been on TV or something?"

"Not yet," I said, smiling. "You might see me around sometime soon, though."

"You look so familiar, I can't believe it. Even your voice—I'm sure I've heard that before. You can tell me, I won't make a scene."

The bus driver announced the Beverly and Fairfax stop.

"Oh, this is my stop," she said. "I *know* you're somebody."

"Everybody is somebody," I told her.

She smiled, gathered her bags tight to herself, got up, and left out the front door of the bus. I looked out the window and saw the old Farmers Market sitting still next to the Grove, a giant outside mall with fake streets for people to walk down in case they wanted that cobblestone feel. I used to sit in the middle of the day at the old Farmers Market with my grandmother, and after she passed, I'd go back to our usual table and eat, hoping that I'd feel her there, but it was empty and cold—and the people who seemed like warm characters before just turned into people waiting for the sun to go down so they could go on to their next scheduled thing to do in their day.

That memory loop slipped back into some other portion of my brain as the bus continued farther south down Fairfax. The traffic was thick for a few blocks, and the lack of AC in the bus, coupled with the sun shining in, caused a drop of sweat to start running down Eliah's cheek, so I grabbed a napkin from the pocket of my blazer and wiped it clean for her without her asking.

She looked at me but didn't say thank you. "That's never happened to me before," she said. "Nobody's ever wiped my face clean. Feels nice, I have to admit."

"You know," I said, "it's okay to let people do things for you. Life isn't all about taking in information and selling it back."

The bus crossed Olympic and headed through a strange block of houses and manicured lawns until we came to Venice Boulevard and pulled to a stop like it was a wagon finally giving its horses time to rest. The back doors opened and I jumped out first, then took Eliah's hands and walked her down the steps. Some of the women inside saw the gesture and smiled out their windows, while others looked off into the distance and may have wondered when their hand was coming to help them down during their tired journey.

We were the only ones at the stop. I looked at the faces in the cars that were paused at the light and at how they were looking at us—humans stranded in the middle of the concrete intersections. In one of the backseats, I could see two kids playing on their phones, taking pictures instead of watching the world.

In the distance, I could see a bus coming down Venice Boulevard toward us. How long had we been in transit? For me, it was golden time—time spent with nothing to do but to get to know one another. I had made a conscious decision not to check my phone one time when I was with her; I knew how much she hated it. To tell you the truth, my mind was so calm without looking at it. I'd kept the same number, in case my mom called or anyone from my past life needed to find me, and created new mailboxes and separate Twitter and Facebook accounts for my new personality. That was the best thing about this new age—changing your identity wasn't all that difficult because you could exist without ever really being in front of someone.

On this day, I enjoyed not looking to see what was happening beyond the present moment. Who cared what anyone else was saying or thinking right then? Normally, if there was any moment of silence, I would have checked to see if there was somebody calling or if someone had posted or commented on anything I had done, and if they had, my mind would race off to thoughts of them and what they were up to and how it affected my life. Now, though, in the hour or however long it took to get down to Venice Boulevard, I was free from all of that. Free from the pings and vibrations and red numbers.

"Can I ask something of you?" I said.

"Well, I'm working for you, so I can't see any reason why not."

"When we get down to Venice, why don't you let me show you a few things? There's plenty of time for you to teach me what I should know. Those facts aren't going anywhere. The day, though—this day—is only once. Can you allow me to show you the now? I promise to walk with the fear that at any moment, someone is going to shoot me."

"That sounds very relaxing for you," she said as the bus pulled up. "But fine. Seeing as how you gave away my materials for the day, I'll watch to see if you stay in character and correct you if you step out of line."

She walked onto the bus, handed the driver her transfer, and waited for me to be right behind her before she continued down the aisle. We paused before we did, looking at the sun-faded pictures of the driver's family he had pasted on the dashboard.

The doors of the bus closed, and we continued down the long, straight stretch of Venice Boulevard, the slowness of our progress allowing both of us time to think.

Once in Venice, we got off at Windward Circle in front of the old post office. I smiled every time I saw a post office because I thought of Bukowski and his long adventures there before he finally made it doing something he always wanted to do. He had that great fearlessness to live a life worth writing about. Most of us have to create the lives we want others to write about.

Before you reach Venice Beach, you walk that last block past all the old tattoo parlors, juice bars, and used clothing stores and pass under the sign that stretches across the street that reads: VENICE. In the distance, you can see the nothingness that exists over the ocean. Walking that last block is like turning off the rest of Los Angeles and having a curtain close behind you.

The first thing we saw when we hit the boardwalk was a man in a tight, leopard-print leotard moving a cannonball around his body like there were grooves in each of his muscles that wouldn't allow the ball to fall out. We could smell the great Pacific in front of us.

Eliah was struggling a bit with her backpack, so I took it from her without asking and put it on my shoulders. We started our walk down the boardwalk, leaving the man with the cannonball for a man crushing up glass and gathering people around him before his show started with him jumping on the pile, bare feet first. Kids on skateboards flashed past us while husbands walking with wives who'd been landlocked for years tried not to look at the roller-skating girls in their jean shorts and bikini tops, but neither of them could help but look.

Eliah stretched out her arms and smiled but squinted against the sun shining down on us. "Come on," I said, "my treat. Don't you know the best part about Venice is the four-ninety-nine sunglasses? You can't go wrong. Go on and choose."

She looked at the stretch of hundreds of sunglasses—the mirrored pilot glasses, the old '80s glasses with the little shades adorning the temples, the old-school Flavor Flav bat glasses. She tried on countless pairs in the mirror and then turned to me, gauging my reaction.

"How about these?" she said, turning from side to side with her new, extra-large, round-framed glasses. "They're kind of fun."

"It's like they were waiting for you to grab them from their slot," I told her, handing the man five bucks.

"You make a pretty good mirror," she said to me.

We continued down the boardwalk. Here, kids were still breakdancing on cardboard, and artists were selling their still-dripping-wet paintings. A group of cholas walked by in a perfect line, hair stacked three feet tall, sporting black eyeliner and matching black nail polish, and wearing T-shirts and pressed khaki Dickies.

Those who didn't have a license to sell from tents and little stands on the right-hand, developed side of the boardwalk set up on the ground just in front of the grassy knoll. I bought two slices of pizza from the man in the window who'd been selling them to thousands of other tourists and handed Eliah her slice before walking up toward the beach. A small skate park covered in graffiti where all the young riders were learning new tricks was the perfect entertainment venue for our meal. Back and forth they skated: trying, moving, failing, and doing it all again until they had made every attempt to achieve perfection.

The sounds of the tails of skateboards hitting the cement bounced off the waves in the background. We sat on the graffiti-covered wall and looked out at the ocean. I'd grown up here, watching the waves move while the rest of the world moved at my back. You could see people walking in deep reflection up and down the coastline. Couples were trying to find privacy under blankets just above the ever-changing tide.

"People are themselves in front of the ocean," I said. "It's why I've always done whatever I could to get down here."

"Why don't you get a car?" she asked, chewing on the edge of her pizza crust, then tearing a piece of it off and flipping it to a seagull. "It'd be easier that way."

"Easy is not fulfilling," I said. "It's best if you leave some things in the distance so you can race toward them."

"What are you racing toward?" she asked, laughing a bit when a seagull finally caught one of the pieces of the crust she had been tossing into the air.

I leaned in and kissed her, going light at first, allowing her to think about if she wanted to respond, then just taking over and pressing her lips in, taking deep inhales of her, now that I had her close to me. She pulled back for a moment and then shook her head.

"Tell me," I said.

"It's just—something still in my brain. Never mind."

She gave in and went with it. I'd like to think that in that moment, she felt me and remembered me—that even though she was kissing a person she'd never been with, there was something so familiar about it that she didn't mind the speed at which everything was happening. For me it had been an eternity without kissing her, and from the moment I saw her again for the first time, I had been restraining myself from acting. This moment, the opportunity, was there, and I had to take it.

She leaned her head on my shoulder, and we sat watching the ocean. It was all I could do to keep from shaking.

"What about studying what it takes to be a great revolutionary?" she said. "Everyone is going to be able to tell if you're faking it. I have a job to do—last time I got distracted from that—"

I kissed her again before I spoke and then pulled her close to me, allowing her to rest her head on my chest and just watch the world move a bit without doing anything about it.

"In all of those articles you had me read—in all of those books and all of those pictures—I discovered what was missing. What they never talked about. There was never any mention of a woman. Nothing. At first I thought that they had just sacrificed their love life for the cause—that they gave all their desires up for what they believed in. But then I realized I was wrong. The absence of mention—that blank spot—was a hiding spot. They were protecting their love. Everything else, whatever they believed, they spoke of freely and passionately because if they were to ever be gunned down, they would be a martyr for their beliefs.

"That's why there was no talk of love—because as tough as any of them were, they could never have been the ones that caused their loves to fall. So they hid them by not acknowledging them.

"For me—for my character, at least—if I had a woman like you, I'd stash her away so she could never be found. I would fight for freedom so she had a world to exist in that she could be safe living in. But I would hide her. I wouldn't let anyone know of my love for her. That's the way it would have to be—agonizing and fantastic. The absence of attention makes each touch all the more sensual. What an amazing way to love. Think of the yearning, of the wanting, of what it would be like when he could finally enter her without fear. My revolution, though for the people, would secretly be for her. That's how I am going to play it. You are going to be my unseen love. Nobody will know what I'm fighting for but you."

Her body dropped right there. I finally had her, only it wasn't me.

CHAPTER 14

Ready, Set

I was nervous and excited for the first day of actual shooting, so I went on an eight-mile run up and down Sunset Boulevard at 5:00 a.m. and watched Hollywood wake up. On my run, I remembered walking by movie shoots when I was doing some other gig to earn cash, whatever it was that week, and seeing those big spreads of food. I'd snatch a bagel or grab some fresh-squeezed orange juice when the crew wasn't looking. They always looked like they belonged to something—despite their late nights or dark circles under their eyes, there was a sharing taking place I envied and could never find.

I ran through all of my past lives and looked toward the hills to imagine what the future had for me. A text came in from Samantha notifying me of my 8:00 a.m. call time. She also asked if I wanted to meet before for a good-luck breakfast at the spot where Denny's used to be. Her texts had become less frequent as my involvement with Eliah grew. There was always that inside of me, that pain that comes from knowing someone else is hurting because of you, but this was my second chance with Eliah and that's where all my focus was—aside from my role.

Sunset Boulevard before everyone else woke up was magnificent. All the streetlights and neon were still on, but there were hardly any cars out; the air was light, and a slight breeze blew down the wideness of it all. Whatever kind of mania had been happening during the night had vanished, and all that existed was a day of hope for all of those trying to be something in Hollywood. Newspaper trucks, the ones that still had a product to push, filled the boxes with the *Los Angeles Times.* Made me think of my mom and those Sunday mornings when she'd give me the funnies and the sports section while she pored over the rest of the world. When I got through with my sections, I'd go through the TV schedule that came with the paper and read through all of the times and imagine each of the shows—all the characters and families that smiled together around a dinner table—looking forward to the moments when I could join them. I never went in for anything with a gun or violence in it. When I think back, they were all family shows, situation comedies that were funny and a little painful.

To remember who I was and where I'd come from before the shoot, I went to the 24 Hour Fitness on Sunset and showed my ID like I always did, forgetting for a minute that it had my old name and picture on it, but the person in charge was texting back and forth on his phone and paid me no mind—just let me in without making sure I was who I said I was while he chewed his gum.

I went to my old locker and looked through the various changes of clothes that I had in there, thinking of all the jobs I'd worked and people I'd answered to, all of the mindless tasks I'd done just to keep my dreams going.

I showered slowly and enjoyed being a new person in a place where I used to be someone else dreaming of being someone else. When I was done, I changed into my new clothes and walked back out to Sunset Boulevard, ready to start a new role.

Because of her dedication to finding the perfect location to make the scripts come to life, Samantha had found an amazing two-story brick building just above Sunset on Gardner Street. It began after an alley and had two storefronts on each side of a big archway that was the entrance to the second-floor row of eight apartments.

In those days, the old brick building was still used as a backdrop for headshots by the actors who took classes across the street and smoked cigarettes on its steps while reading lines and trying to not let their empty stomachs break the scene. I remember when Samantha had found it and came to tell me how excited she was to see me inside of it, how she'd imagined how I'd look wrapped in those old bricks.

"No studio lot for us, friends," Pete said as we all took it in together. "We'll build from here and make our own legends. This space will become known because of us. We're not a part of anything anymore."

The two storefronts to the left had FOR RENT signs in front, and Samantha was looking in the window at those near-empty spaces. The two storefronts on the right were an old antique shop and a modern furniture studio that didn't sell furniture but rather decorative pieces for people to showcase in their homes or on movie sets. Pete was looking at those before he called us both over to the steps that led to the second floor.

"I wanted to let you both know how amazing I think this moment is now," he said, smiling at me and then at Samantha, who smiled back at him but looked away when it was my turn. "It's been a long time—many falls but many brushes-off and stand-ups—that got me to this point in life. I know for a fact that without both of you by my side, there's no way I'm standing here."

He asked Samantha for the keys to the front door, which was made mostly of glass save the dark blue frame that looked as if it hadn't been painted for years.

"It's character," Samantha said, seeing us wince at the condition of the paint.

"Certainly is," Pete said, opening the doors and leading us up the flight of about ten steep stairs. The first thing I saw when we got to the top were windows of equal proportions that ran up against another building's side, so light struggled to get in, but still managed its way through the long hallway.

The apartment we were using to shoot in, in what would become my character's apartment, had been recently vacated by someone who couldn't afford the rent and decided to just roll out without notice—something not uncommon if you talk to a few landlords in Hollywood.

Apartment number eight was devoid of furniture save an old dentist's chair, which, the manager of the building told us, was ours to do with what we liked if we could move it. Pete had told the man to leave it exactly as it was because of how authentic it looked. There were hand-drawn maps of the Hollywood Hills all over the walls, with coordination points at each spot, but the math was nonsensical and didn't add up to anything. The room was clumsily painted a deep aqua blue with red-wine trim that had spilled onto the floor. The floor itself was furiously scratched up. Cue cards covered with writing were tacked to all the walls.

"Just like I told this young lady when she was poking around earlier this week," he said, drifting from watching me to holding his eyes on Samantha. "The guy who lived here before fancied himself to be one of those science fiction writers. If you look in the closet there, you'll see stacks of notebooks filled with pages of stories about these little people who live inside of the hills. The book was called *Hollywood Underground*—bunch of little creatures living inside an active volcano or something like that. I think he wanted to blow up the Hollywood sign at the end. Why does everything have to end up with an explosion these days? What happened to those kisses against the sunsets? Bah! Nobody can write a movie about this town if you ask me—if you try, you're bound to go insane like this fella did. What's your story about?"

Samantha thanked the super, handed him an envelope of cash, and walked him out in a way that said, *Don't bother us again. This money should take care of everything.*

"There's not too many folks still in these apartments," he said on his way out the door. "The ones who are won't bother you none—they're all in the process of being, let's say, asked to move."

"The Snow Queen has made a great deal with our military friends to secure financing throughout," Pete said, closing the door and looking around the place. "We can just concentrate on making Golden State Broadcasting something magnificent now. Samantha, you found the perfect place for our hero's base—it feels like where he should come from. I never doubted your desire but should have felt the same way about your ability. The Snow Queen saw something that I missed."

"That's because you're a man," she said to him but looking for a moment at me. "However, yes, it's perfect—exactly how I pictured it should be. That's how I found it—I just knew it was going to exist."

When the door closed, I walked around the apartment slowly, looking at the intricate maps of Hollywood the previous tenant had hand drawn. The guy who'd lived here no doubt spent a lot of time on his story and hiked many of the same paths Samantha and I had walked during our nights in the hills.

I checked out the maps and noticed that Astro Burger was only a block and half down from where we were. I wondered if, after we shot, Eliah would want to meet me down there. Was it too soon to start retracing all of the steps we'd taken together in the previous world?

I was tired of being brought back to memories that teased my present. I wanted that exact taste in my mouth, damn it, and I didn't care about morals or preconceived notions of what was right.

To get into the mind of the character, Samantha had started staying in the apartment—she'd set up shop in the old bedroom. She'd laid out the apartment just as Pace Skillman would have lived—a little writing desk, a record player, an old-school reel-to-reel voice recorder, and posters of all the revolutionaries I had trained to act like.

"I rewrote a bunch of the dialogue from our talks," she said. "I think you'll find it easier to believe the lines. There's more of you in this character now than what was on paper. I did my best to make it play perfectly for the camera. I wish I could write a scene where you'd actually call me back, though. I'm not expecting anything but for you to be decent—especially when we'd gotten so close."

"We can still be close," I said. "You've done so much for me—without you, none of this would have been possible. Look at what you created—I mean, even the maps on the wall look so much like our—"

The map of the benches that we'd drawn together had been put up on the wall in the middle of the ex-tenant's story.

"Yes," she said, backing away a bit. "I added it. I thought it was interesting that this guy and you might have walked the same path at one point, so I used it. That's the beauty of creating a character, Pace—you can keep moving the line between what's real and what's fiction. That's what we've been doing, anyway—just moving the line. And now, now we're close. The show's about to start, and you're going to become him. It's all happening. For all of us."

Samantha was always a bit more excited and enthusiastic than the rest of us—after all, she hadn't been in Hollywood anywhere near as long as Pete and I had—but she was creeping me out a little bit. Who was I to judge what was creepy, though, right? I mean, I was wearing a new face and trying to make an old love fall in love with me for a second time while starting work on something that would make me famous for not being myself.

Pace Skillman was the only identity I could hold on to.

Pete wanted to use mainly natural light for the interior shots, so the giant window that made up the back wall of the living room portion of the apartment was perfect because of the sunlight it allowed to flood the apartment. That era of *perfect* Hollywood was going to go the way of the man at the piano sitting in the front of the house playing songs for the moving pictures up on the screen.

My favorite part about the building that served as our studio was the small staircase that led to the rooftop, which had a magnificent view of the Hollywood Hills if you faced the back of the building. However, if you looked straight down from the backside, you'd see a dumpster that a number of newly homeless people would be going through, looking for materials to recycle to keep up their existence in the sun, which is one of the reasons why some people prefer looking at their reality on a screen.

We spent most of the day setting up a shot on the roof for when the sun was going to start going down. Pete loved to shoot during times of transition, either going night to day or day to night.

"You're not talking to me anymore," I said to Samantha, trying to break the tension. "Today is when everything you've done pays off. There's so much more for you than you realize. Take it from me—I've been here—waiting. Wishing. You'll move through this and come out with more power than you ever expected."

"I'm just here working," she said, trying to be confident. "Just like you, right? Take a look around—does this look like you envisioned it?"

No lighting crew, no food trucks downstairs—nothing like I'd envisioned a big budget production being. Hell, even the fact that Pete the Wolf was the one doing all of the camerawork seemed a bit odd to me.

"You're ready, though," she said. "Funny, for me, everything turned out looking exactly as I thought it would. Even you." She smiled even though she didn't want to and walked away in her cargo shorts and utility belt. Amazing how different this woman could look depending upon the occasion.

"We ready?" Pete said. "This is it. The beginning."

"Pete, you have a minute?" I asked. "Why is it that we have such a small crew? Isn't it against union rules? Don't we need some permits? I thought this was going to be a huge production."

"Remember, you're one man broadcasting out to the country with nothing but the belief that you are one hundred percent right. You're beautiful. We created you to look exactly like the leader they need. With your face and the words we've given you, it's a guaranteed hit. Don't think anymore—be it. Let me handle how we grow, okay? We're doing it this way because you are enough for now. It has to appear to be building from nothing. Are you ready to cross over?"

I was never so comfortable doing anything in my life than I was when Pace Skillman looked directly into the camera and into the hearts of all who were watching.

> You're out of work. The jobs you had aren't coming back. You fought wars. You paid taxes. You believed in their election speeches. Now what? Where is your bailout? Where is your story on the evening news? Can you even tell what's news and what's a commercial anymore?
>
> The American Dream you bought with your life is not coming true for you. So you can either wait for a return on your flag salutes, or you can do what is in the heart of every American out there. You can come to Hollywood and try to be a star.

I know you're out there, looking down on your phones and wondering where that connection is you've been looking for. It's not that you're looking for that connection. You want to be it. You're only pleased when more people follow you or like what you have to say. Do you check your phone in the morning before you talk to your husband or wife? What I'm here to say is that there's nothing wrong with that. We believe in your desire to be known—to be famous. In fact, I'm saying that the voice that keeps telling you to sit behind a desk or put on a uniform or put on a tie—that voice is un-American.

The true American Dream is the dream to become famous. Golden State Broadcasting can make that happen. We have bailed out the California government and are now partnering with them as special advisors to their budgetary process. We are looking for people out there who want a chance to be famous. We can't offer you any guarantees—this is Hollywood, after all. What we can offer you is a chance to be yourself and stop worrying about why your government doesn't understand you. Do you want to be forgotten and buried in the corner of an Excel spread sheet that determines who gets to have it easy and who has to stay buried in the system?

When people ask you who you are, you don't tell them you're an American—you talk to them about your state. Where you're from. I'm the same way. I'm from the great state of California. Golden State Broadcasting.

If you're looking for a job—if you're interested in working to build something for yourself, of yourself—there is a place for you on Golden State

Broadcasting. We can develop a show just for you. Thrillers, mysteries, love stories, educational—we know what people are waiting for, and we'll turn you into something they want to watch.

Log on to www.goldenstatebroadcasting.com and see how you can make a living—a real living—in Hollywood."

I looked over to Pete, and he was still rolling, even though I had finished. That's the way he was early on. He figured the more footage we had, the more we'd have to edit and piece together the story. Samantha was in tears.

"Did I do something wrong?" I asked her. "I've been practicing these lines for months."

"You didn't change a word. Not a word."

"That's because you wrote it perfectly."

Pete was shooting the sky and moved over to the elementary school across the street, where a few kids refused the oncoming darkness and continued chasing each other around for the sake of doing it. The sounds of children echoed throughout the shot, but I didn't realize that until I'd stopped talking. The sky faded to black.

Over the next few weeks, we shot at some of the local community colleges and office buildings downtown. Pete and Samantha would go into these offices with a small camera crew and ask the office managers if it was okay to shoot a small promo scene in there—explaining the concept of the show and that it was all in good fun despite its political nature. Anything to break up the day—and besides, in Los Angeles, most office workers have a headshot in their top drawers and are constantly looking at their phones to see if that big call came yet. If there was a camera rolling, you could get access to anywhere.

The setup of the scene would always be pretty much the same: People would be hard at work in the office, and I'd come in and give a speech to find out which of them wanted to stop working for someone else right there and start having their own shows.

We'd interview people like Alice Loopen, who had been working in the same place—an office that handled moving money from one 401K to another after an employee moved on to another job—since she'd finished college.

"What do you want to do with your life?" we asked her, cameras rolling. "It's okay—you're not going to get in trouble for telling us the truth. Would you mind sharing it for the show? It'll be fun."

"Yes, of course," she said, and then offered up her dream. "When I was in school, I had an idea to create a system of shoppers for the elderly. My grandmother had arthritis and had trouble at the market—you know, holding the bag and just getting money out of her purse. People would go crazy when she was in line in front of them at the market—so rude. Anyway, I wanted to start a nonprofit company of college students to go shopping for the elderly. Small idea, I know, but I thought it would make a difference."

"It's not a small idea," I said. "And I'll tell you what, Alice. I think you want to get up right now and walk out of this job and down to our development department and find out how to actually talk to people so they listen to you and you don't end up in a place like this for the rest of your life. At Golden State Broadcasting, we don't just create fictional worlds. We create reality programming that's worthy of the word *reality*. We'll create a station for you where you can reach thousands of students, develop followers, and get the leverage you need to take control in this new digital era. Independence is what you crave, and Goldenstatebroadcasting.com is the only place to be independent."

At this point with Alice, a guy named Richard Peevy stood up. Someone like Richard would always stand up and say something very much like what Richard said: "I've got to step in and defend the company on this one. We thought these were just standard interviews. You're fishing for a reaction."

"Look at your leader," I'd say to the sea of workers, some of whom might have been wondering if they should eat that special Tupperware treat squeezed into the company fridge full of others just like it now or wait until toward the end of the day. "He is coming to the defense of the company, not Alice Loopen over here. Alice Loopen, you deserve to do what makes you happy. At Golden State Broadcasting, you could have your own show, doing what you love. What you love needs to be shared with the world."

"I'm going to have to ask you to leave," Richard would say.

"Richard [or whoever it was acting like Richard]," I'd reply, putting my arm around him and saying so that only he could hear, "I think you could be a big help to us behind the scenes. Leadership is tough to find. How far can you go up in this company?"

And that would be it for Richard, because as soon as you ask people how far they can go in their jobs, the reality of those limitations comes on pretty quick.

With Richard trying to figure out why he couldn't find an answer in his employee handbook, Alice (or whoever) would say, "I don't know anything about running a show. Who would listen to me?"

"Don't you worry about that," I would tell her. "We have broadcasting executives with years of experience turning folks with far less talent than you have into successes. All you need to do is give up what you're doing now and join us."

Pete or Samantha would be holding the camera while making gestures for me to move in closer or to lead the one who decided to "join" us confidently down that aisle of desks. Leaving everything behind that she had pinned to her walls—those funny comic strips that had yellowed with age, the stuffed animals that some coworker had given her on her birthday—she would walk away and leave it all behind. Everyone around her, though they knew it was only a show, had these incredible looks on their faces, like they wanted to do the same thing in real life.

We'd film Pace speaking with every member of that office, and they would, unscripted, just tell me what they really wanted out of life, and in return, I'd tell them how Golden State Broadcasting could get them a show. After we were done shooting, it seemed like most of them didn't want us to leave—that we had touched something inside of them that made it hard for them to go back into their offices and do things that didn't matter to them. They promised to log on to Goldenstatebroadcasting.com and watch the show.

So many of them were ready to leave their jobs behind right then, but they settled for allowing us to use clips of what we shot to make fake news stories to promo the show. Pete and the Snow Queen seemed to have a magic formula to get directly at the viewer's heart.

When driving back to Hollywood that day after shooting the Alice Loopen promo, I turned to Pete and asked him if what we were doing in the name of entertainment was in any way cruel. I mean, I told him, we were poking these people and getting them excited—extracting their dreams from them and using them for our own gain.

"That's the point," he said. "Everyone in these offices wants what we shoot there to be true, right? How many folks are going to be sitting in offices all over America—all over the world—and hope some good-looking guy just like you walks through the door and offers them a TV show of exactly what their dreams are? They'll want it so bad they'll tune in.

"Samantha's scripts have data behind them," he said. "We purchased it from QUALITYMIND up in Fresno. They sell all kinds of information—what smells make you hungry, what color skin makes you horny. We'll get all that later, but for now, all we could afford on this round is, *What makes you question where you are in the world*? That's pretty good, isn't it?"

"Where do they get the data?"

"Credit card purchases. Social networking sites. Apps you've downloaded. All of that is valuable information, friend. That's gold these days. Don't think people are out there taking chances with entertainment. Investors want a sure thing."

And man, did Golden State Broadcasting have a sure thing. Each week, the people we interviewed watched their clips on our site and shared their brief fame with their friends. Soon, offices were begging us to come in. They logged in by the thousands so they could pitch their ideas for a show or see if we'd already made one of their ideas part of our show. An entire country filled with people not doing what they wanted with their lives started to live out their fantasies with us.

After some late-night editing sessions in the old apartment building, which we now had half of the apartments in and which served as the main studio and default headquarters for GSB (Pete had named the production company after the name of the show), we'd post new clips of the great movement of people coming to Hollywood to join us.

Almost immediately, people started posting their own audition tapes on the site. Golden State Broadcasting allowed users to create a profile and have a page where videos of their ideas for shows could be posted. We started holding contests, flying people out from wherever they were in the country to have them appear on the home page of the site with me for a show.

When Pete was asked for his grand plan by Naibe Rodriguez, who had finally found her sweet spot of politics and entertainment, he said: "To have every American be part of Golden State Broadcasting."

Our viewership went off any charts that had previously been created. We had advertisers calling in and begging to sponsor us—to have their products placed in a shot. Publishing companies were begging us to put their writers' books into my hands so I could be seen reading it during a broadcast.

Pete was selective about what he chose so that those people would feel like we were doing them a favor by putting their products on our show. It all looked authentic, though. For my ride, for instance, I had a Dodge Dart— kind of pimped out, but nothing flashy. We'd convinced Ford Motors that having an old car would make more sense because it proved that its engineering worked. It was a good foot in the door, as they wanted to give us more business and donate some other cars to any other productions we had—and even asked if we could create a show that made it look like Ford was opening up an auto factory in some of the prime open space in middle California.

At that point, we were just approaching half a million users. It was only the start.

Promotions were launched. Pete would hire out artists around the country to go out and do late-night graffiti campaigns and murals with my face on it saying, "Golden State Broadcasting Invites You to Join California."

The campaign looked absolutely real. Everything was being filmed and handled like it was really happening. And of course, I started to get a taste of fame. When I went out for whatever spare time I had when we weren't shooting, which wasn't all that much, I was mobbed by people wanting pictures of me, telling me how much Pace Skillman inspired them to go on their own. They had real love for me, even though I'd never met them.

On a rare night off, I took Eliah out to The Exclusive toward the end of the fancy part of Melrose. It was one of the few places where I could go out in public and still have a bit of a private space. There was a general dining area with tables and candles that allowed for a romantic first date or even a girls' night out to drink and forget about why they weren't on a romantic first date, but there was also a place toward the back where you could reserve a little wicker bungalow and enjoy some sense of seclusion.

"Pete was saying how good we looked together," I said, taking my scotch and her lychee martini off the waitress's tray and placing them on the table. "He wanted me to ask you if you'd be interested in being on the show as a love interest. Something about you giving me a compassionate side."

"The fact that my picture is being taken in public and people notice me for being your girlfriend is more than enough," she said, taking a sip of her martini. "Being on the show would take away any small amount of privacy I have left. Besides, my moments with you, I'd like them to be our moments. What business is it of anyone else's how we feel about each other? Don't ask for more, Pace; I may not be able to give it to you."

"For the first time in my life," I said, moving my hand over hers and tracing the space between her knuckles down the back of her hand, "I have everything I've ever wanted—and that's because of this role. I met you because of the show, Eliah. Without it—"

"Don't think about *without*," she said, looking away. "It's too empty."

Two girls popped in with their camera phones and begged for a picture. The security guard made a move to take them away, but I told him not to worry, that any fans of the revolution were friends of mine. They even asked Eliah to take the picture, which she did with a semi-pissed-off look on her face that still looked sexy to me. I made the foolish mistake of thinking it was jealousy that put it there. Men's egos are planets that need moons to revolve around them to give us some semblance of definition.

The two girls stood on either side of me and put their fists in the air.

"Oh my God!" the one on the left of me screamed. "I'm uploading it now with a GSB tag. You're so awesome. Sorry for breaking up your time."

They went away giggling, and the security guard promised not to let anyone like that over again.

"Starting to get pretty big, huh?" Eliah said. "I guess that's what everyone in this town wants—to get big."

"Not you, though? What's wrong with getting big?"

"It's not the getting big part that's a problem," she said, finishing her martini and playing with the lychee in her cheek. "It's finding a place that you fit into once you're too huge for the rest of the world."

"The rest of the world never had a place for me before."

We kissed one of those movie-moment kisses, and you could feel the camera and cell phones clicking all over the restaurant. Eliah moved to close the curtains on our bungalow, but I moved her hand away and kept them open.

"I don't want to share this with anyone," she said, forcing the curtains closed.

CHAPTER 15

Angel's

There weren't many diners like Angel's left in Hollywood—cheap places without much attention to modernization. Even the analog clock on the wall was actually backward, like you were looking at its reflection in the mirror. There weren't many owners like Angel Vasquez either: an owner who was also the line cook standing in front of the grill, which was in plain sight just behind the counter filled with lunchtime eaters looking for work or on their way to auditions or just sitting and waiting for the clock to move the right way.

Pete and I sat in a booth up against the window that separated us from the schoolgirls walking to class holding their books tight, followed by boys who didn't know how to talk yet. Sitting on the other side of the table was Dallas Curtis, an executive from one of the networks looking to bring us in under their control.

We talked small talk at first—the Dodgers' lack of hitting, global warming, how kids were on their cell phones too much, and how much better everything was when we were younger—the normal things people talk about before jumping into the real issues.

A few of the girls noticed me as they were walking by to school and showed me they had drawn our GSB logo on their notebooks. They smiled and walked away when I acknowledged them. When the young girls are going crazy for you, that's when you know you're Hollywood gold—which meant the networks had to have us. We were getting bigger than prime time, and the networks were dying because another formula for success was becoming more and more obvious, which is why Dallas Curtis was sitting in Angel's trying to woo us.

Dallas looked like he had just come out of the dry cleaners—pressed, lean, crisp-collared shirt and the right kind of watch, which Pete remarked how much he liked even though he knew the one he was wearing was better. Dallas drank grapefruit juice that came in one of those see-through cups with the yellow tint while picking at his plate of cottage cheese, melon slices, and rye bread—the only items he wanted from the "Healthy Side of Things" part of the menu.

"You've got a good thing going right now," Dallas said, sipping his juice and leaning out the window to watch the girls disappear down the street. "Don't you think it's time to have someone help you take it to another level? We'd like to bring GSB and run it on prime time—Thursday night. We'll do a national campaign, set up a tour. I've got a whole media plan. There'll be millions behind it to do it right and provide the help you no doubt need. You've had a good run, but there's no way you can keep it going all by yourself."

He slid his tablet across the table, and we swiped through the slide show of his presentation. One idea had girls dressed in revolutionary gear—form-fitting pants with a red sash cinched around the waist to accentuate but not completely give away their womanhood—set up in recruiting booths at Grauman's Chinese while protestors ("counter-revolutionaries") marched around chanting slogans about keeping California Golden. Plants would be in the crowd to start siding with our revolutionaries. Soon they would join our group and march mightily down Hollywood Boulevard carrying signs touting all the produce, manufacturing, and other jobs now available to those who'd move to California.

"We've already got millions behind our show, friend," Pete said, pushing the tablet back across the table until it clinked against Dallas's healthy plate. "What I do like is the thinking behind this. It's very creative and forward."

"Me and my team have ten more that are even better," he said, sitting back, pleased with himself. "But this is only the beginning of fantastic things. If you come in with us, there's no telling the level we can take it to."

"What about if you came in with us?" Pete countered, waving over the waitress to refresh his coffee. "What are you doing wasting your talent over at the network? You should be working with us. With a mind like yours, you could be running your own show instead of sitting in diners begging for your bosses. The fact they didn't come down here themselves is insulting—and it should be insulting for you to work for people like that. What would it take for you to come and join us?"

"I'm afraid you're misunderstanding why I'm here, Mr. Wolfson. You see, we want to bring you in. I'm authorized to offer you—can I talk freely here, around him?"

Pete looked at me and tapped me hard on the shoulder.

"Whatever you have to say, you can say around this man here. Without him, there is no show. He is the franchise—there's nothing he doesn't know."

"I'm prepared to offer you a five-year contract for three million dollars an episode and a thirty percent cut of the ad revenue. That's not counting what we can pull in with syndication. Rerun profits alone you can retire on."

A few more of the school kids had gathered around the window as we were talking. They were all throwing up their fists in a show of power and acknowledgment, which I returned with pleasure.

"See that?" asked Pete the Wolf. "I did that in about two months. Think of what happens when we expand on this. As we grow, as the show grows, these young folks are going to be looking at us. For direction. For entertainment. For education. We have the chance to shape their very thoughts. You think they're watching TV? Come on—their parents are watching TV in the living room while kids are up in their rooms with their doors closed. Nobody over seventeen has any idea what goes on in there. People are not sitting and watching anymore—at least, that's our belief. You see, son, we're going to erode the Hollywood system and make everyone else do it our way. You best jump ship now or risk being on the Titanic when it hits that iceberg that nobody saw coming.

"They're not tuning into NBC at eight o'clock anymore. That's old *Cosby Show* thinking. They don't care who's going to get off the island at seven on a Sunday. They're holding their TV in their hands twenty-four-seven. They're not interrupted by commercials and don't want to be a part of what their parents are a part of. That's what I think you don't understand. It would be in your interests to join us. Right now. We can start today."

"Are you seriously making me an offer?" Dallas said, then drained his grapefruit juice. "It would have to be better than what I have now, and what I have now is pretty amazing."

"Ask yourself this," Pete said, leaning in so nobody else could hear. "If you're so damn important, what are you doing in this diner in the middle of the day across from a couple of men who put up some videos on the Internet? Is your studio so desperate for creativity that you need to go searching for something that's already been created? Don't you want to be part of building something?"

"I'm here to make you an offer, Mr. Wolfson. Don't you want to even consider it? Don't you want to bring it back to your people? This is what people like you are waiting for, right? To be picked up. Well, here it is. I'm the dream."

Pete laughed. "That's the thing about all of this. You see, I don't have any people to bring it back to. There is no board I have to run my ideas past—it's only me and my crew. I have total control. Don't you want to be a part of something like that? You could be *known*, an innovator instead of another faceless piece of a puzzle that never gets completed."

"You are a very persuasive man," Dallas said, perhaps considering it behind his haircut. "But the only thing I'm authorized to do is make you an offer."

I saw Pete smile right there, knowing that this man could not see the vision. Not at that moment anyhow.

The sun came through the window, but we both already had our sunglasses on. The exec couldn't believe we were saying no, and what's more, couldn't believe that we were standing up and getting ready to leave. It was unheard of. Pete peeled off two twenties and a ten and left them on the table, even though we knew the bill wasn't going to be anywhere near that much. Taking care of the people who serve your food and host your events and then go home to rub their feet and soak their wrists is important, because at some point they are going to have the power to determine your success or failure.

"Mr. Curtis," Pete said, putting on his Brooklyn Dodgers fitted cap, "what you people fail to realize is that when the shit goes down, when what your movie execs refer to as the *apocalypse* changes everything, it's not going to look like one of your productions. There will not be burned-out buildings and people wandering around the streets looking for hope. On the outside, it will look exactly as it does today. The world is not going to fall apart; it's people's belief in your system that will. You're sitting in air-conditioned offices watching secretaries walking around and believing your own propaganda. My offer to you to join us is an open one. Whenever you decide to come aboard, I'd love to have you. There's talent inside of you—you just don't believe enough in yourself to trust it completely. For me, as you can see, talent is all I care about."

We walked out into the sunshine, and there, waiting for us at the end the block, was the group of little girls, all jumping and asking Pete if they could be in the next episode.

"You think I made the right move, holding onto everything?"

"Who can question you now?" I said, taking one of the few Vicodin I still had left from the operation and wondering when the pain was going to go away fully or even if it already had. "I'd love to go and visit the doc just to make sure everything is okay. I can wait until shooting stops, though. When do we wrap the first season?"

Pete pointed at all the girls clamoring for autographs.

"We're not stopping for a while. I'll make sure Dr. Addison comes and visits you on the set. Now, come on, there's audience building to do. I've got three more meetings like this today, but they should all be pretty much the same. Hopefully I can pick up some help. He was right about one thing, that's for sure: I can't do it alone."

CHAPTER 16

The Life

One of the best things about Pete shooting during the day to try to get the most of the natural light was that when the sun went down, work, for me at least, was over. He did love to get those sunset shots, so we all spent a lot of time up on the roof trying to make it happen. Pete would want to wait for the perfect amount of sunlight to be washing over the rooftop and capture that pink hue settling in over Southern California, a perfect postcard.

On this night, while Pete was setting up the sunset shot, Samantha sat on the edge of the building looking out, trying to capture that last piece of sunset for herself.

I walked over and sat next to her, offering her a bottle of water—the new ones that Pete had ordered with our logo on them. He was going to start pushing products by tossing the bottles up to the passing tour buses that made their way up and down Hollywood Boulevard.

"I remember when this was just a thought," she said, taking a long sip and doing her best not to look at me. "Just like you. You were once only a thought. Now, look: Pace Skillman, the star nobody saw coming."

It was the first time she had mentioned time before the operation. Hearing her talk about it worried me a bit, because hiding a lie is tough enough when only you know the lie, but knowing there were others out there who knew it had me just a bit on edge. I knew if it worried me, it probably worried Pete and everyone else.

"I've gotten everything I wanted," I said. "How many people can say that?"

"Not me," Samantha said. "I get to see it each week, but I don't go home with it. I don't wake up with it. I only get as much of you as your fans do. I don't understand why you turned off so quickly. We were so close, and then you just—"

She reached into her back pocket and pulled out a rolled-up *US Weekly* magazine with Eliah and me on one of the squares on the cover.

"Who's the New Girl?" the headline read. Photographers were starting to follow Eliah and me everywhere—and now everyone was a photographer. Publication was unfiltered, and experts and critics, though they had never held much weight in my book, were everywhere and spouting rhetoric with the tap of an Enter key.

History would decide whether this was advancement or decline.

"The Snow Queen wants me to write Eliah into the script," Samantha said. "A big love scene. Says that a revolution is always a good story, but there needs to be some love in between the struggle. That's the 'breath,' she says. How am I going to write a love story between the two of you? We were moments away from being a love story ourselves, until Pete rolled up blasting his music and took you away from me. You think I can write a damn love scene with the two of you in bed together? I can't give you those lines to say to her when it's me I'll be imagining you're speaking them to."

"How could you not?" I asked her, though wondering how I could convince Eliah to willingly move in front of the camera. "You wanted to be a writer—to be the creator of something. This show is as much yours as anyone's. Don't let it go because of something you might have felt for me. I had to go for a chance at love. You need to understand that. It's not that I don't feel for you—that we don't have something—but Eliah is the one I've been chasing. She—"

"You knew her from before, didn't you?"

I thought about lying to her, but that would have cheapened each of the moments we'd spent together, and I had hope that perhaps, when the anger and hurt had cleared, she'd realize the work she created from the pain.

She nodded, taking my silence as her answer. "I thought so. I told her I'd write the scenes, but know this: the lines I give to Eliah are the lines I'm going to be saying to you. The lines you say to her are what I wish you'd say to me. That you should be saying to me.

"It's not fair—I made you! I found you—maybe not first, but I looked at you through your soul, and I understood it. You think this girl feels the same? She's not in love with you—she's in love with your ability to take her away from whatever's haunting her. A man can't see that past his ego. I don't see what's so special about her anyway. Pete says the two of you look 'together' on film, and I think that's a bunch of bullshit."

She reached into the pouch of her hoodie and pulled out a nearly empty bottle of Vicodin, emptied it of its final two pills, and downed them with the bottle of water I'd handed her. "Looks like I'll have to head to the doc for more," she said. "Let me know if you want me to pick you up any."

She got up and walked slowly to the door leading to the stairs. I could feel her feet heavy as she marched away.

We were getting ready for the sunset shot. Every episode had to end with a sunset. "It's still Hollywood, after all," Pete would say. "You should be willing and charitable enough to give the public what they want."

We were ready for the last shot when the sky started thundering and then proceeded to open up with an unrelenting shower, cooling down months of squinting at the sun. Pete ran back downstairs into the apartment to keep himself and the camera dry, but I just stood there in the rain, letting it fall down on me. There was this magnificent silence that comes in Los Angeles when it rains. A smell rises from the cement, as if it's been beaten down for months by the sun, and now, finally, has its chance to move. That's the thing about living in this constructed city—you always forget that you exist in the rest of the world, but the rain, on the rare occasion that it comes down, allows everyone to remember.

I moved to the edge that looked out over Gardner Street and saw the actors and actresses; most sought shelter in doorways, but some just stayed out in the rare time of a natural set.

A blue umbrella against the stark grayness moved up the sidewalk below with little yellow rain boots sticking out from beneath its shelter. Eliah tipped the umbrella back a bit so that only her chin and mouth were exposed.

"It's the time of the non-drivers of the city," she yelled up, "so I figured you were the only one I could share it with!"

"What are you standing down there for? Everyone else is afraid of a little water. Come on up here, it's amazing—like wandering in the middle of a forest that's sprouted up out of nowhere."

She held out her hand and I dropped her the keys, which bounced off her umbrella and landed in a small puddle on the sidewalk. By the time she made it up to the roof, I was soaked and didn't need to share the umbrella with her, but she let me in anyway.

"People were taking pictures of me today—just me alone, out in the world, without you," she said. "That hasn't happened before. I don't like being captured by a camera. The whole world thinks I'm with you, thinks we're together."

"Aren't we?" I asked, grabbing her and pulling her close. "Can you think of one reason why we shouldn't be? Doesn't it just seem like the universe put us on each other's path? No matter what happens, no matter how big this thing gets, it all happens for a reason. You came into my life for a reason."

"Don't mistake our meeting each other for destiny," she said, talking loud over the raindrops. "That's a dangerous way to live life outside of Hollywood."

"Why would I want to leave Hollywood?" I asked, tilting her head up and looking down into her eyes. "Reality's too dangerous. I'm here because it's the only place I don't have to truly be me."

The rain refused to relent.

"That you isn't all that bad, is it?" she said. I watched the wetness take over the fabric covering her body, revealing curves that I'd only been seeing in my memory. "Don't you get tired of playing the same role over and over again?"

"I've only been this character for a short time," I said. "It takes a lifetime to get to know who we are inside."

"But you're not learning about yourself—right? It's false learning."

"I don't think any thoughts are false," I said, catching a few raindrops in my mouth. "I've given up trying to stop them from flooding my mind."

"How can you live so intense—" But I'd reached through the rain and placed my hands gently on either side of her face, feeling the rise of her cheeks against the underside of my hands, and kissed her. Tender. But that tenderness triggered a new rush of energy. I placed my hands on the collar of her shirt, and instead of going in gentle, like I had before in the hills, I ripped it open without a drop of patience left to wait for her. She stood, shocked at first, in only her bra and skirt to absorb the rain. She turned to go but then stopped, her stillness an invitation. She backed up on me and reached behind to me and moved one hand, trembling, down the front of my slacks, stroking me while I unbuckled.

I reached around her waist and under the top of her skirt, but just as my fingertips found the band of her panties, her hand reached down to stop me. Turning to look over her shoulder at me, she reached under her skirt and peeled them off slowly, followed by her bra and skirt.

I had matched her disrobing, and she rose and fell while backing up into me, rubbing herself up and down my shaft, testing the limits of its length.

The downpour made everything slippery and didn't allow for either of our touches to stay in one place—there was no center, no start, no end. I tried to turn her around so I could see her face, but she wouldn't let me—demanding that I enter her from behind by arching her backside up even more so that my dome piece barely glanced it as I hovered above her.

Slowly at first, rubbing my tip just above her lips, I moved it back and forth as her ass cheeks dipped down. Her backside was trembling, so I moved my fingers between her cheeks to calm her nerves and open her even more.

Finally, having enough of me arousing her, Eliah reached between her legs and grabbed my shaft and held it up to her lips, inserting the tip and pushing back so that the outer edges of my dome piece were resting on the inside of her. In that moment of knowing, I grabbed her waist and moved in slowly, so that I could watch my entire self disappear inside of her. Once fully in, I held it there and pushed even further, creating space to feel her even deeper.

As the speed of the rain increased, I pulled out slowly, keeping the tip of my head in, and then entered again, quickening my pace to the sounds of the rain hitting the roof. There were no cameras filming and no scripts to go from. Her thighs trembled, and the rest of her body let go, and I continued to move in and out from different angles, learning her insides with every new entry.

"Turn around," I said. "I want to see your face when I explode."

She turned her head and leaned it back, not letting me see her entire face. I grabbed her hair, which was done in two small ponytails, and went as hard as I could until the possibility of controlling myself was no longer there. She was screaming as if letting go of pain that had been trapped for so long and trying to replace it with me.

I pulled out just as I was about to give it away and spun her around so my cock was in her hand, and she dropped to her knees and made sure I emptied everything into her. The rain kept up its rhythm as we both crashed to the rooftop, breathing off of each other's inhales and exhales.

How many millions of drops of rain were coming down all over the city—and how many of them were finding our bodies there on the rooftop of my false life in Hollywood that I prayed to be real?

"It feels as if my body had been waiting for you," she whispered in between breaths. "I can't hold out any longer. There's something so familiar about you. You're full inside of me. I've been looking forever not to be the teacher. You came and found me. I guess I could take the cameras being on in exchange for that. I know that's what you want. I can't just take without giving something back in exchange. The time we spend together will be worth it. I trust you, Pace. It's my most valuable gift."

Our followers increased at exponential rates. People started flocking to Hollywood to be extras. Pete the Wolf's meetings with investors were increasing, as was the cost for advertising on the show. He raised my salary and increased the amount of money that was going to my mother. You'd think that I would have ached to see her, but knowing that I was doing something to take care of her—to set her up for life—was enough for me. That quiver in her voice that existed before I had taken care of her financial worries no longer haunted me at night.

The show had taken care of that, and now those executives who had been coming to us and asking us to join them were begging us for work. The networks, both broadcast and cable, were seeing viewership of their shows decline and were losing big-time ad dollars to our new production company as well as a few copycats that had sprung up in response to our success.

Pete the Wolf bought out the storefronts of the Gardner building downstairs and used them as offices so that people walking by on the streets could look through the glass at the constant buzz and motion we were generating.

Those giant red tour buses started driving past what was now known as the GSB studio, and people would scream for the buses to stop so they could come down and tell the people in the windowed offices their ideas for the show. All of America wanted to contribute. We'd touched some nerve in the public, fed up with working their entire lives for industries they had no vested interest in that would leave them exhausted and with nothing to show for a lifetime of labor.

Pete would welcome each one of them. They'd line up around the block, and the neighbors would call the police to move the droves from their front lawns, but the next day, a new bus with a fresh load would come by and it would start all over again. He filmed everything—whatever happened around the studio, he wanted to capture, use, and broadcast.

The ideas they found interesting, Samantha and the writers weaved into story. Those whose ideas were used on the show got mention on Goldenstatebroadcasting.com. We now had over 750,000 members and growing.

Pete hired more coders to work out an algorithm that transferred what people wanted to see and test it against the scripts Samantha wrote. When Pete went to the Snow Queen to tell her that the other two writers didn't like having their work checked by a computer, and that they'd quit if she continued doing so, she just shrugged. "Samantha's writing the whole show anyway," the Snow Queen said. "Who needs those two now? My girl can handle it."

Handle it and then some. That woman was amazing. She even tapped into the voice of the American farmer, who'd been screaming for years that he was being gutted. His voice came through loudest.

The question GSB always asked, part of the campaign Samantha initiated: "How would you be independent?"

It's been a while since I've checked, but I think even if you look today you'll find that the idea of Frank Hanson, of Sully, Iowa, is still the most viewed video on the site.

Here was Frank's take on his idea for a show: "Well, on those cooking channels, what if instead of having all those pretty-faced folks, you had farmers telling you what to cook with and what season to cook it in. Then, well, I suppose I could get Ellen to let go some of her mother's recipes that we use at our table. Kind of like—well, you would get to know the people who grow your food. It might get you thinking about where it comes from and how many hands have touched it just to get it to you.

"And, well, if you want another one, we could teach young folks how to tend the land a bit so they could be a part of it. Some countries have it where you have to join the military for two years. If I could say it, I would say that maybe we'd have these young kids get their hands in the soil before they sit down behind desks the rest of their lives and think that what they see on screen is real. That's not real. Hands in the soil, that's real.

"Of course, I'd be able to show you how to do it on my land here, if I hadn't sold it some years back to the same company that's bought up all the farms around me. So if California wants to give me some land to work, I'll do a show that does all I just told ya."

Frank got us a huge push in the Midwest, whose families might have been tired of those same twenty-two minutes of saccharine the networks were shoving down their throats. The idea of giving them land to work touched off a light that had been dim for too long.

Though Eliah didn't like the publicity, she started to love the actual work that went into acting. We stayed up into those late-night hours when the rest of the city was knocked out, and she would just stand there, naked, looking through the window with only the slightest amount of light trickling in through the door.

I remember seeing Eliah's breasts in that light and can still feel the coolness our bodies felt by escaping the heat and being awake at odd hours. We'd eat pomegranate blueberry sherbet with two spoons out of the tiny tub, laughing for no other reason than being with each other. She enjoyed the studying part of preparing for the next day's shoot, and I'd find her asleep on the big grandpa chair that I'd gotten from that old thrift store down Hollywood I'd pedaled past on my bike. Gotten the whole set, actually. I would stare at her and wonder what she was dreaming of before gently taking the script that was marked, highlighted, and broken into pieces she could remember for shooting.

We had all taken a lunch break before the first love scene I was supposed to do with Eliah, so to calm her down, I took her across the street and leaned up against the fence of the elementary school. I hadn't even realized it was Halloween until we saw all the kids come out in their costumes for their big parade. The teacher had set up a microphone in the middle of the schoolyard; each grade was announced and walked around the track that surrounded the assembled students.

Mrs. Lee's kindergarten!

The small team of vampires, ballerinas, and police officers walked around the track while marching music played. Across the street, grandparents and a few parents watched them go round and round in a circle. I rubbed Eliah's pinky from her hand that was gripping the chain-link fence.

"What was your favorite Halloween costume?" she asked, looking over at the group of parents and wincing a bit before she turned her attention back to the kids.

"Halloween was always a little rough for me," I said. "All I ever wanted was that store-bought costume—you know, the one that came in the little box—a Storm Trooper or something like that. But my mom, being the child of the sixties that she is, thought it would always be better if she made me one. I have some pictures of me that, man, I just can't even tell what I was."

Mr. Tortorice's first graders!

"I'd love to see what you looked like before."

"What about you?" I asked, changing the subject as a few ninjas and wizards rolled by us. "What would I have seen if little Eliah was walking around these school grounds? No doubt you were the star of the show."

"I never did Halloween," she said. "My parents—they passed when I was young, and though my aunt raised me as her own, she had her own children to take care of. I didn't feel right going out trick-or-treating without my parents. And to be truthful, I never liked dressing up as someone else either. So as soon as I was old enough to pull it off, on

Halloween, I was always absent. I would ditch school that day and go watch the scariest movie I could in the dark. Everyone thought it was a day to dress up and have fun—get candy or something. Myself, I figured that if I scared myself badly enough, I might have a heart attack and be able to talk with my parents. You know, when you're young like that, you put the world together as it makes the most sense to you."

Ms. Mazolla's second grade class!

A few pirates and cheerleaders walked by, looking as they went at the younger grades now sitting down before them and perhaps feeling for the first time that they were part of a progression—they very well could have realized their age right there. For me, Halloween was every day, but I loved my mask and was glad I could never take it off. Hell, in Hollywood, dressing up and playing make believe is something people want to do every day of their lives—at least, that's what they're striving for. Maybe we all should have just stayed kids.

"Come on, let's get something to eat," I said, peeling her hand away from the fence and walking her down to the In-N-Out Burger just off of Hollywood High School. The place was filled with skaters and teenagers from the high school who were allowed to take lunch across the street or just didn't care and went to go get a burger. I ordered one Animal Style for myself and a Double-Double for Eliah, who seemed to be able to eat those things and never gain any weight. Maybe she only ate them with me.

We took our number and grabbed a booth to wait. Right next to us, kids from a drama class all gathered around an order of French fries and talked while munching them down. The occasional tourist would come in and hold up the line and not know what to order—stunned that people would wait in line for a half an hour at a place where the menu was nothing but burgers, fries, and just variations of the same.

The high school boys had stopped dressing up for Halloween, confused enough to be in their own bodies that already didn't feel like the ones they'd grown up in, but the girls in their short skirts wore different variations of dead maids or dead fairies or haunted, indefinable creatures.

"Number eighty-eight!" the woman at the register called. "Eight-eight!"

I got up to grab the food, and though I had on an old LA Raiders hat and some very dark sunglasses, a few of the girls recognized me and started posing for pictures with me without asking. As I tried to get through them and bring Eliah our food, I could see the exasperated look on her face.

"The revolution needs to eat, don't you think?" I said to them after posing for a few shots before turning to Eliah.

They backed away with heads down at a zombie pace that matched their costumes, but still kept their cameras moving.

"Sorry about that," I said, putting down our food. "Maybe we can go away for a bit. Take a drive up the coast and just chill in a cabin up in Big Sur. I've seen pictures of that place and have always dreamed about spending time there. My dreams have been coming true lately."

"That's the law of attraction," she said, grabbing at a fry, still surprised at how good it tasted. "If you visualize something, it usually happens. Good and bad. It's not as if it's basic physics, but it doesn't have to be to make sense."

"These extra-crispy fries are basic physics," I said, "but the difference is the level of goodness that you taste can only be felt, not quantified."

"Your fry skills are more impressive than your ability to argue without a script," she said, grabbing her Double-Double and smiling at how familiar we were becoming. She took a bite and then washed it down with a Sprite after savoring the taste.

"Did you see that scene she wrote for us today?" she said then. "That woman's in love with you. Those things that she has me saying to you—no woman can write that kind of stuff if she doesn't mean it. Believe me. Did anything ever happen between the two of you?"

"Not really," I said, taking a bite of my burger, knowing that I couldn't tell Eliah about my recovery time with Samantha. "Could be she just wants me to fall deeper in love with your character. That's not that hard to do, though, know what I mean?"

"You can't see it? I think she's living that scene through me," Eliah said, looking up to the sky and sighing. "You know, it's been a while since I let any balloons go. Have to remember that. You're causing me to forget too many important parts of my life. You go over your lines—I've got some notes I need to write."

"To whom?"

"Never you mind whom—this is, well, personal, deep-down stuff. The last person I shared this with took it and then disappeared. I don't know why men always expect their desired results within a certain window." She gave her head a shake. "Sorry, old wound and nothing to do with you. Eat your burger, and study your lines. I don't want to feel guilty about you not being ready."

She opened her backpack and started writing out her note cards but scooted them over to herself like she was one of those high school kids sitting around us not wanting anyone to copy her work.

It was her moment of true vulnerability and sadness. I wanted so much to say something to her to comfort her, but I—the one who knew her darkest secrets—didn't exist to her.

"Come on," she said, jumping up from the table after a few minutes. "We need to find a balloon shop."

"Let me check Google Maps," I said, popping the last bite of burger in my mouth before taking out my phone.

"Don't," she said, putting her hand on mine and pushing it back into my pocket and then leaving her hand there. "We're going to search it out. Ask people. Every time you look something up on that thing, they're tracking more information on you. Before I started in on this contract—I guess it's a contract; who knows what it's turned in to—I was doing this kid's paper on the new trends in advertising, and it turns out that all of these social networking sites—all of this Google madness—is all just storing your information so they know how to market directly to you. They want to know your habits so they can feed you what makes you happy. They're getting to know what you need. You should stay off that thing if you know what's good for you."

"What's wrong with people knowing what I need? Who has time to go and search for things anymore in the real world? I like it right there for me. How many people have worked themselves to near death trying to get what they want—hell, even just what they need to survive?"

"That's a sad statement," Eliah said, still not moving her hand. "Isn't searching part of what makes us human?"

My pocket started vibrating right then, causing Eliah to jump back and remove her hand. I took it out and checked the caller ID.

"See?" said Eliah. "Never get to be alone with those things."

It was Pete on the other end. I'd never heard his voice that panicked before.

"Calm down, man," I said, worried. "What happened?"

"Samantha," he said, and then repeated. "Samantha. Samantha. She—just come on back, friend. It's not a good scene here, and I don't feel like walking through it alone. You should be here."

He hung up the phone, and somehow I knew—I'm not sure how I knew, but the truth was inside of me. I walked out silently, followed by Eliah. There was still a tray of fries left on the table.

A week later, we were back filming that love scene. I lay in bed with Eliah while the new camera crew shot us from every angle. She held me tight, trying to live the moment inside of me, since being filmed attempting intimacy in bed was near impossible for Eliah. She argued that she needed to at least be wearing a white tank top and not bare back with outlines of her breasts showing. I was moving in a fog, and I know Samantha's death shook Eliah, too. But there we were, as always, ready to work.

Perhaps it was her guilt over Samantha's suicide that allowed her to drop her inhibitions about being on camera. It was only a clip of what the full scene was going to be, but Pete knew by now to serve it out in small tastes.

INT. Bedroom—early morning. Eliah takes off PACE'S shirt that she's been sleeping in and puts on her own. Sunlight starts to flood the room. Eliah is doing her best not to look at him, but since it's the last time she'll ever see him, it's taking all of her strength.

ELIAH
I won't let our love stop the movement.

PACE
There's nothing to fight for without you.

A burst of sunlight takes over the shot.

After a few moments, when the light shifts back to normal, Pace reaches over and turns around, but she's gone. A note on the side of the bed asks him not to go looking for her, tells him she'll fade easier from his memory if he doesn't look. If he did look, the reality would be too harsh. There is a bottle of rye by the bed; leaned up against it is a pack of cigarettes. There's a sticky note on the bottle with these simple instructions: "Drink this. Smoke these. That's all the time you have to mourn. There are too many people waiting for you."

He, or I, pulled the cork from the bottle and started to drink, then lit up a smoke and just sat there, weeping, on the side of the bed. My tears were real on that. I couldn't be acting. Pete and Eliah stood by and watched, both of them doing their best to look tough for me. I drank in hopes of stopping the extreme beating of my heart. Now there was only one person in the world who knew who I really was.

I wanted to go out, but the streets were filled with people who loved me, and the last thing I felt I deserved was to be loved.

"Why did you push her to write me in as his lover?" Eliah asked. "It's obvious she was in into him. Nobody could write like that who didn't believe it."

"It wasn't me who pushed," Pete said, seeming to work to hold back his anger. "Hell, I didn't want her to write at all. The Queen wanted it. I liked it better when she was more by my side, actually."

Pete and Eliah moved to leave me alone with the bottle. Eliah walked through the door with the camera crew, but Pete took a moment before he left.

"You know," he said, "she made all of this happen. She gave you that side I could never even think was important or possible. The Snow Queen shouldn't have pushed her as hard as she did. I didn't help either. That's how I got here, though—I almost died a few times myself. That's what it takes, you know. That's why not that many people do it or even try more than once. Take your time to recover, but don't let it stop you. We've built something amazing here. She'd want it to go on."

"You're thinking about the damn show?" I screamed out. "Samantha jumped off the side of a building, and you're talking about a show? How can you even stand to be anywhere near here?" I'd stood up and gotten in his face, and he didn't move an inch.

"Don't think you're one bit different than me," he said. "I saw how that girl was looking at you. She was ready to give herself to you in every way. What did you do? You tossed it away for another piece of ass that will leave you when she moves on to her next distraction. Don't fool yourself on that. I may be a selfish asshole, but I know love when I see it—and this other one, that's not love she's looking at you with. That's escape. If you hadn't pushed Samantha away, she'd still be here with us. How can you live with that?"

"How the hell *can* I live with that?" I said, taking another swig from the bottle. "I'm done with this. We're done."

"You're going to go on," he said, grabbing the bottle from my hand and taking a swig for himself. "You're going to do what people have been doing forever—you're going to realize the ones you've hurt are gone and you're still here. That's the pain you walk with. There are other people worth fighting for, though—and you know it. Family. New loves. All of that can go away pretty quickly."

"What? You're going to expose who I really am?" I asked. "That might work out well for the both of us, you know. It would be a fitting way to end all of this—showing what a fraud it all is. You've been holding that card above me, and now you want to play it? Then play it already. The anticipation is killing me."

"If you think you can walk away, I want you to ponder what that new reality is going to look like. Where do you think you can go after all of this? There's no place to hide but right here. You and I are the same, friend. We're here because we no longer wanted to be ourselves. There's consequences for that. Feel them and move past them. It'll make you stronger."

He handed me the bottle, and I couldn't tell if he was going to hit me or hug me. He did neither—just walked out of the door and left me in the room where I'd just shot a good-bye scene for someone I never got to say good-bye to. I drank until it didn't hurt anymore and then stumbled out the door and onto Sunset Boulevard under the cover of a Saturday night.

CHAPTER 17

Stripped

I can't tell you how far I walked that night or even where I went. It seemed like the streets and sidewalks that I moved through were the same as they'd been my entire life. Had I ever changed? I wished the answer to that question was no. The hookers on Sunset and Hollywood Boulevards had been kicked off and replaced by pornos that played on a loop on the backs of headrests that sat comfortably in the newest rides that rolled up and down the Hollywood night.

Inside the car windows were fresh faces that were replicas of those I had seen a million times and that had passed me by just as many times. Nobody was looking for me in the one place I was most exposed: walking in Los Angeles.

At the Comedy Store just before the strip started up, some comics sat around a small table nursing their drink tickets and wondering why the public wasn't in the mood to laugh anymore.

Sunset was booming up in the distance, and there was something inside pushing me to that motion. I started to run—I think I was running, though I couldn't be sure of my pace at that moment. My heart was so far ahead of me—all over the place—smashed on the sidewalk that people were crawling over. It was a mess. The silence of being alone was rattling around in my head, so I ran faster until I finally made it to Rising Sushi at the top of the strip.

I had changed so much since I started the riot there that I thought maybe things there would've changed, but it was all the same. The crowd waiting to get in stretched up the little incline, while in the window above the servers in their uniforms and the busboys in theirs worked as they always had. The protesters were nowhere to be found—perhaps that was only done when the cameras were rolling. The line out front was huge, and Little Tom was letting in the girls while making the boys who had gone through so much trouble to mousse up their hair wait an extra half hour. By the time they got in, the girls would have handprints all over them.

Little Tom saw me and got excited.

"Oh yes! Pace Skillman! Come on in, man. What are you waiting out here for?"

He lifted up the velvet rope and let me in, but just before I walked through the door, I took a look at all the faces on the inside, then at his face, and then at the faces of those in line. None of them was what I was looking for. I turned away and shouted at him, "I'm looking for something obscene!"—slurring my words, I'm sure, though I can't recall the delivery. "That's some rip-off shit you have going on in there. Where is the nasty? I can't take what you're selling here. Someone take me to the nasty!"

I stumbled over to a Lincoln Navigator parked in front and blasting Odd Future.

The guy in the front seat reached for his waist and was about to tell me to the get hell out of his face when he noticed who I was and smiled.

"Hey, it's the leader of the revolution," he said, beaming. "We watch each week. Can't wait to see how it ends. You want to come in and get some of this? Think of it as our contribution!"

I looked around at the drugs and the porno playing on the tiny screens and wondered if the women and men behind those cameras—either the ones being filmed or the ones doing the filming—were after anything that much different from what I was after. How lucky I was to have only had to change my face to get paid for what I wanted to do. I could have just stayed with Samantha and been content, but it wasn't what I was after. I hated myself for the desire I had within to be greater and better—to have exactly what I wanted, how I wanted it. I couldn't find a normal place to breathe.

I spun away from the Navigator and headed down Sunset Boulevard, down the middle of the street—through the booming cars and celebrating folks. I was recognized each step I took—people cheering and screaming, no doubt thinking it was all part of the show. Maybe it was. There were cameras on all the stoplights, and they could have very well been filming everything for some grand movie at the end of this experiment we knew as Hollywood, to be shown at the Hollywood Bowl with a symphony playing twenty-four-hour stretches of uninterrupted comedies about humans trying to be better than they really are. Maybe the comics outside the Comedy Store might get some material.

I started to believe my own imagination and became paranoid that the cameras were all watching me, so I veered down a side street and made my way back toward Hollywood—taking shelter in the darkness of the streets below the strip. In the houses there, all the lights were out, and families, what was left of them, slept well. All I could think of was how to get to Eliah—how I could get to her and tell her who I really was. That was what I needed—to shed this mask and get back to my true self, but how was it possible to do that? How is that possible for any of us to do that? We've ended up at this point in our lives as the person we've become, not the person we thought we were.

I kept running up and down those side streets for hours, bolting up to Sunset to find a store open so I could down another energy drink to keep me going and moving through the world.

Down to Melrose, this time slower, running out of steam, with less anger and sadness fueling me. Everything shined here. It was Sunday morning—brunch time in Hollywood—with Sunday Riders and their Harley Davidsons leaned up in front of Johnny Rockets drinking Bloody Marys and eating omelets.

Everything was so clean and well put together, but the numbers on the license plates were kind of jumping around on me. I needed to get out of the heat, into some place cool, but wherever I stepped, I was noticed and mobbed.

Some little kid shoved a fanzine in my face that he'd made. It had a huge bear pushing California away from the rest of the country with the words *Golden State Broadcasting* done in graffiti on the state of California.

"Where can I submit this to get featured on the show?" he asked. "Could you be reading it casually while Eliah cooks you breakfast?"

The crowds started to gather. "Where's Eliah?" they said. "How's it going to end this season?"

"I came here to be part of whatever you're doing here, sir," said a girl no more than twenty-five, with that fresh-into-Los-Angeles look on her face that said she'd believe anything bursting from inside of her. "However I can help, please let me know. I can handle a gun plenty well. I got taught that young. You need a gunslinger?"

"It's a show, you know," I said. "None of this is real. You need to put your faith in something real. This isn't it."

I ran off down the street and didn't stop until I crossed Highland. Thank goodness I had all the green lights lined up, because had I run into a red light and someone handed me a jaywalking ticket, I would have ended up in jail for the rest of my life for assaulting a police officer.

My mind was splitting from the comedown from the energy drinks. I ducked into an old used bookstore on the other side of Highland. Across the street, there was a Hello Kitty art exhibition that people were waiting in line for, all dressed up in little Sanrio costumes.

There was a pair of girls in the bookstore going through old *Life* magazines, oohing and ahhing at how magnificent the old ads were just after the war. Both of the girls were wearing Hello Kitty shirts, though one of them was clearly homemade. Even in my crazed state, I had to admire the craftsmanship (or craftswomanship, in this case), and her courage for doing it on her own.

"You two should be in line over there with the rest of the Kitty crew," I said before turning to the small man who had to stand on his toes to see over the cat he was petting on the counter. "This here is a store for literature, right, sir? You should tell these two that they don't belong in here. Grab your cat because they might try to take it and dress it up in little clothes after making its head big. Hello Kitty *you*! That happens, you know. Don't think that it doesn't. Tell them that this is a place for literature—where people read and enjoy the books, and they don't need to tell people that they like them up on Facebook—just you and the book. Before movies. Right? Books were before movies! For sure before Hollywood. I'm sure even that damn cat would back me up on that one."

The man behind the counter wore a wrinkled, short-sleeved collared shirt, a thick leather pocket protector that housed his glasses and a pen, and a charcoal-colored cardigan sweater. As I was noticing his clothes and perhaps mumbling about what I was seeing, he grabbed his giant orange cat and moved toward the phone.

"Don't call the police!" I yelled. "Don't you dare call the police! I can't have that happen to me again. I am very close to getting my license back, and if you call them, what's going to happen to me? Now, tell these kind people what a good book for them to read in here is! Let's have some literature!"

"Sir, I don't want any trouble," he said, shaking and trying not to appear scared. "I've had this shop for twenty-six years. Things have come and gone around here, but I've managed to stay open because the landlord is kind enough not to raise the rent, and once in a while, people want to know about the history of the movies."

"Movies!"

"Yes, sir. This is a history of film bookstore. I am here to remind the young people about how glorious Hollywood once was. Now, you look very familiar, but I can't place you."

The two kids took the opportunity to run out of the store and get in line across the street. I ran to the door after them, standing and watching for the cop to come and hand them a ticket for crossing in the middle of the street, but it never happened.

I bolted out of the store after looking both ways and started to run up Highland. I needed to find Eliah—someone who knew me from before. Out the store and onto the street—that heat just wouldn't stop, and that damn sun wouldn't go down. Thing is, the sky was perfectly blue and clear—not a hint of cloud blemished the expanding blue canvas that seemed to stretch across the earth.

I looked up and saw these red dots against the perfect blue. One by one, following each other with some kind of hope that they might find comfort in their formation. I followed them to where they appeared to be big before rising up to the sky, leading me to Sunset and Highland, where Hollywood High School had set up one of those pop-up carnivals on their running track. I did my best to make myself look presentable. I'm not sure how good a job I could have done after being out all night and in the sun all afternoon—though I suppose it wasn't much different than most of the other folks in Hollywood walking around on a Sunday. My mind was moving in quick, frames-per-second twists like those crows that would sit on telephone wires all over the city even though nobody used the wires anymore. Quick glimpses of hand holding. Cotton candy licking. Face painting. Ring tossing onto old milk bottles.

Everything was still quick, even without the energy drinks fresh in my body. Blasting electro music was coming from one of the carnival tents. My heart was pounding, but I was looking for Eliah and trying not to be seen by any of the hundreds of faces that were looking to see if they knew me. One of the kids was selling these plastic masks. I handed him a five and took the mask—it might have been a Teenage Mutant Ninja Turtle—so I could walk through the crowd unnoticed. Only in Hollywood would you wear a turtle on your face so nobody could notice you.

Finally, in front of the game where you leaned up on the counter and shot a water gun into a clown's mouth until the balloon busted, I saw Eliah, holding a handful of balloons and letting them go one by one with her notes attached. I walked over to her, and she smiled but then had a strange, worried look on her face when she finally saw me coming toward her. Perhaps it was because she couldn't see me under the mask I was wearing and smiling beneath, so she was a bit freaked out and took a step back.

"Do I know you?" she said. "If you take one more step toward me, you'll find it very difficult to make any new little turtles in the future. Crazies like you need to stay away from carnivals and learn to be an adult."

"Says the girl sending balloons to people in the sky," I said, lifting up the Ninja Turtle mask to get some air. "I thought you'd be able to recognize me by my movements."

Still holding the balloons, she leaped on me and embraced me so that I tired for a minute, and all of that longing I was holding on to got squeezed away. I dropped the mask on the ground and hugged her back.

"I guess you picked up the walk of your character," she said. "Come on, I know a place where you might be able to sit for a bit and catch a breath. You didn't finish the bottle, did you? We need to get you some water."

She grabbed my hand with the hand she wasn't using to hold her balloons, and we went over to the bleachers just beyond the carnival and walked up to the top bench. There, you could see the entire carnival spread out on the football field; games are always played where games are played. She bought two bottles of water from a man in a straw cowboy hat selling drinks out of his cooler.

She continued with letting go of the balloons into the sky and then slowly started to tell me the story of why she did it. I listened as if I were hearing it for the first time. Only this time, she said she had added Samantha's name to the card.

"I feel like I took something from her that didn't belong to me," she said, looking at me with a bit of guilt. "You should have told me you were involved with her. I would have never started up with you in the first place. Why did you lie?"

"We were never intimate," I told her, watching the balloons go up. "Nothing ever happened. I never even kissed her."

"Physical," she huffed. "Men always think intimacy is about the physical. Did you tell her about your dreams? Your childhood? Did she tell you what she wanted out of life? You think a woman is just going to offer up that information to someone she doesn't care about? She loved you, but you didn't want it. Once love happens, there's nothing else. It's forever. Here, let one go."

She handed me a balloon and I let it go, watching it travel far into the sky, and wished for a moment that I could do the same. I took another sip of water, and when I looked down at the bottle, I laughed, seeing the GSB logo on it.

"Eliah," I said, moving my eyes from the balloon to her, "nothing in my life right now seems to be real. It's only you who knows me. I couldn't love Samantha because it's always been you."

"You've given my life such depth, such fun, and took control with me in a way that I've never experienced before," she said. She let go of the rest of her balloons, all except one. "When I'm with you, everything else crashes away. I wish I could tell you that I loved you as well, but I just can't. It's not in me."

"I don't understand," I said, feeling the weight of my crushing hurt fill up like a balloon inside of my throat. "I see the way you look at me. I know I give you everything you need. You're kidding yourself if you don't think that's love. When all of this is done, when the show is finished, it'll just be you and me. It'll be real."

"It's not that I don't feel for you," she said, handing me a balloon. "I've lost the one person I loved. Who knows, perhaps he was trying to be the man I always wanted him to be. Now—now I wish that I'd just let him be himself. I'll never have that now. I guess you and I are with each other because the people we really love are gone."

She got up and brushed off the bottom of her skirt, which had gotten a little dirty from the bleachers, and kissed me on the cheek.

"Be careful of Pete," she said, putting her sunglasses on. "He, like you, wants more than he can possibly handle."

As she walked toward the carnival crowd, I was cracking inside. I looked down at the card attached to the bottom of the balloon and saw the note:

Harold, when you're ready, I'm here.
Forever, Eliah

With Eliah about to disappear into the laughing crowd, my real self was pushing through my skin and tugging on my brain to say something in fear of losing her again.

"Eliah!" I screamed hoarsely. "It's me. It's Harold!"

She turned slowly, gathering herself in the crowd, and then walked calmly up to me before unleashing a slap so hard my face couldn't keep up with the impact.

"You're a lot of things, Pace," she said, "but I never would've thought a coward could be one of them. You think I'm going to go for some spiritual representation of the man I love? That you even have an ounce of his courage inside of you? Don't mistake what we have on-screen for what we have in real life. On-screen, it's love. Real life, you're just something to put inside of me. Half of the time I'm thinking of someone else."

"Eliah, I'm not sure how to explain it all to you—but it's me. Here. In front of you and telling you that I made a mistake. I became this. I like to think that I had no choice in becoming this, but it's not true. I'd be lying if I said that was true. I've been after it my whole life, but now, now we can finally be together. That fight we had on the rooftop, if I could take it back—"

"How the hell do you know about that fight?" she yelled, socking me in the chest, her face fuming with anger. "You went through my diary when I was sleeping?"

"It's me. Look at my eyes, Eliah. Think about how it feels when we kiss. It's the same, isn't it?"

"What about when you were first inside of me?" she said, testing me.

"I was only inside of you as...this."

She stood absolutely still—the carnival sounds all around us pausing for a moment too—frozen in acknowledgment of the truth.

Eliah walked close and touched my face, then looked into my eyes, searching for me.

"Why would you do this? I—I thought you would go out and find yourself, not become someone else. What have you done?"

"What do you mean? I'm famous. My mom's taken care of. I have more money than I know what to do with, and most of all, you still fell in love with me. That's everything."

"Are you insane? You must be. What we had wasn't love. I mean, yes, with you the first time, I loved you. I loved you so much I had to let you go out there in the world and make something of yourself. Why didn't you just turn around that night? This is how you've returned?"

"You were so sure about me that you went and slept with other people?"

"You were gone," she said, hanging her head. "At least I thought you were. I was running from regret. I feel like I'm going insane," she said. "I need some space. I—there's no way I can do any of this anymore. I need to get back to my life—enough time's been wasted. There's nothing left of me. There's nothing left of you, either."

She grabbed the last balloon out of my hand and squeezed it until it popped.

"I love you, though," I told her. "You can't deny that it's still me."

"There is no more you."

Suddenly, bursts of clapping sprang from the crowd. Folks had gathered and were filming us with their phones and cheering. They thought it was all part of the show. In some ways, I guess it was, just not the one that had been planned. I tried to run after Eliah but was surrounded by a bunch of fans seeking my autograph or to trying touch me or to be a part of whatever scene they thought was being filmed. They waved in the air at where they thought a camera might be filming from a plane or helicopter high above, but there was only us, on the ground.

About to walk away, my cell phone buzzed. Text from my mom.

Harold—surprise! I'm at Canter's in our booth. I need to see your face.

I should have vanished right there, but that would have meant leaving behind the last remaining piece of me. No matter how low you get, there's nothing that can fix it like Mom can.

CHAPTER 18

Mom

The inside of Canter's Deli never changes. Not even the woman who worked the register had changed; she moved at the pace of the antiquated machine she stood behind. The glass cases on the left held ten different kinds of cheesecakes, black-and-white cookies, and other treats I tasted in my childhood memories.

She was in a booth in the very back. I stood far away for as long as I could, just watching her munch on her bagel chips and sip on her Dr. Brown's Cream Soda. She was tan and thinner and glowing from her world travels. Still, she looked the same. It was the same face that read me Berenstain Bears stories to get me to go to sleep at night when I thought people would be coming to get me when the lights went out.

I walked slowly past the waitresses—both the ones who had been there for twenty-five years who thought it was a part-time gig and the new ones who had clean, pressed shirts and thought the same thing. Mounds of pastrami and potato pancakes zoomed past me on giant trays being delivered to eager eaters who seemed to blend in with the familiar colors of all the booths.

As I neared her table, she looked past me for a moment and then smiled kindly when she saw me looking at her. "Can I help you? If you don't mind, I'm waiting for my son, so please—you're blocking my view of the door."

I was sweating something fierce and looking down at the glass of water at the table.

"Do you mind?" I asked, not taking my eyes off the glass. "I'm in need of some water."

"That's not polite, to ask for things off of people's table," she said. "Someone should teach you some manners. You need to learn how to act in public. Some people. Jesus!"

"That's what Grammy used to say, Ma," I said, picking up the glass and drinking from it. I felt a bit more like myself after that sip. "Do you remember when she used to slap me in public for putting my hands in my mouth? You got so angry with her when she did that."

My mother looked up into my eyes and covered her mouth to stop the scream that she couldn't manage anyway. Her face looked like it was going to shake off. I slid right into the booth and put my hand on her shoulder.

"It's okay, Ma. It's me. Harold. It's me."

"What did you do to yourself?" she said. "Is it a mask?"

She reached for my face and tried to pull it off, and I let her try for a few seconds, hoping perhaps she might have some success. She moved back into the booth and froze.

"What have you done to my son?" she asked softly. "How could you, Harold?"

"I had to, Ma," I said. "The opportunity presented itself to me, and I took it. I've got my fame, and you're taken care of. It's all worth it, don't you see? We've made it now.

Nobody is ever going to take anything away from us again. I have a house for you in Malibu, and you can just be there. In peace. I've got this role to play, but it will end, eventually. Then my life will be my own. Then I can come visit." I stopped and thought about what that moment would look like. "We can visit."

"All I could think about," she said, gathering her strength. "All I could think about when I was going through the world was how I wished I was sharing it all with you. How I longed to see your face and just share a bowl of kreplach soup with you. Just look across the table and see my boy. I'll never have that again."

"But you'll have everything else."

"All you ever needed was yourself. Don't you see, Harold? The rest of it doesn't matter. You've taken away the only thing that matters. I have to go."

"Please don't," I said, reaching for her as she got up to leave. "I don't have anything left. I did it for you."

She sat back down, but I could tell she didn't know where she was anymore. Her eyes were lost, perhaps traveling back to our early days together. She was squinting at me, perhaps searching for that boy she used to reach across the car to when she stopped at a light.

She gathered herself.

"Harold, I love you, and one day—I might be able to look at you. But don't kid yourself about your intentions. You wanted everything this town could give you, and now you have it. The trade-off is that nobody else had the ability to match your fantasy expectations. I failed you, I think. Maybe I should have been more responsible. It's too far, Harold. Too far."

"You didn't fail me," I said. "You told me to go after my dreams."

"I told you to be yourself while chasing them," she said, standing and trying to only look at my eyes. "Now what do you have? I love you, son, but I can't look at you. Not now, not like this. What have you done to yourself? That's what you need to think about."

I tried to get up but had no more strength. She walked away through the passing trays and shuffling waitresses, off to the life I had created for her, while I tried to deal with the life I'd created for myself. The echoes of dishes dropping followed her out the door.

CHAPTER 19

Hollywood Endings

I made it back to Pace's apartment inside of the GSB studios on Gardner, the only place I had left to go. As I shut the doors to the world, the meaning of calendar days slipped away. The only contact I had with the outside was with various delivery people who knew that there was money under the mat and to leave the food after knocking. The AC stayed on full blast, my infinite iTunes list on loop, and the bamboo blinds rolled down in an attempt to block out the sun, but it was of little use. The tiny rays that managed to make it through the cracks were a just reminder of how impossible anything was to stop.

Remnants of takeout food were everywhere. My phone's battery had run down, allowing me to sit alone—unable to be contacted or send out updates on how I was doing. It's a haunting feeling to be alone in Hollywood during the middle of the day. Hell, maybe it's haunting to just be alone.

Perhaps Eliah was somewhere thinking of me. I tried to hold on to that possibility.

A knock at the door brought me out of my trance. I didn't make a sound. The knock came again, and then again, and I finally pushed myself out of that old dentist chair and stumbled to the door. Looking through the peephole, I saw Pete the Wolf, preparing himself to be seen at any angle, even through a distorted piece of glass. I checked to make sure the door was locked and walked back, looking over the maps on the wall that were created by and for me.

"Go away," I said, walking away from the door in hopes that I could move further away from my reality. "I'm finished with this. Take whatever legal action you want."

The sounds of a key turning the lock took a minute to process, but then the voice of reason came over me that of course Pete had a key. It was his set, after all. "Well, friend," he said, walking in the door and locking it behind him, "I wished you would invite me in, but I've never been one to stand on formalities."

I heard him moving across the room toward me, but I just slumped back into my chair without turning around.

"I figured you've been so into your movie-star tailspin that you might not have noticed what's been happening out there," he said. "It's beyond what we could have hoped for. We're more than just a hit, and we owe much of that to you and your passion for this role."

He moved into my line of sight, making room for himself at the old table near the bamboo-blinded window by clearing away some of the containers that lay about.

"Of course," he said, mostly smiles, "much of it is *also* due to my ability to pivot through the unforeseen, shall we say, obstacles that popped up during filming, as they always do. Still, even in my wildest dreams I never thought we'd reach this level—well, not like this, anyhow. The Snow Queen's doing backflips over Jupiter about it, too, friend, and would like to show her gratitude."

"All that's happened is I've lost everything," I said, looking away from him. "Nothing's been created. It'll all be forgotten soon enough. You can bet your life on that."

"But I have bet my life on it. We all have. Don't exclude yourself. God knows, you've lived your life without a safety net, just as we have, Pace."

"Stop calling me that. I'm Harold Hall. I won't give up any more of what little identity you've left me with."

"You say it like I took it from you, rather than you offering it to me," he said, cleaning his hands with a handkerchief that he left on the table instead of putting back in his pocket. "You know, friend, I drove out here from New York with nothing when I was eighteen. That's a thirty-year bid in Hollywood. Through all of the failed pilots, lost friends, self-pity, almost touches, and closed doors, I stayed here, trying to find someone who would let me create my vision. It wasn't until I met the Snow Queen that I realized nobody was going to give me anything—I had to take it. I had to make myself valuable. That's what we've been telling the American public, and they bought in more than we could have imagined.

"When the Snow Queen approached me about her Golden State Broadcasting idea, I told her I would only do it if I could make it my own—true to my own vision. She loved the fact that I had that passion to do it differently—that I wanted to be in control and not rely on how it had been done before. Of course, now I realize why she chose me. Why she surrounded herself with people like me—and you—to get this show going. We were meant to create, Pace, not join something that already exists. Why do you think the show has done as well as it has? Why, you don't even know what's been happening. See now, you've gone and distracted me from telling you what I came here to tell you."

"All that's happened is I've given away my identity for—for what? Fame? Money? Success? I have nothing left of myself—only my accomplishments. It all seems pretty pointless."

"Like most people focused on one vision, you're not even aware of what you're a part of," Pete said, rolling up the blinds to expose the sun actually going down and a few clouds starting to be illuminated from behind, giving off that odd pink tone. "Something magnificent has happened, friend, and it's going to continue to happen. We must first, however, complete the season. Everything is ready on the roof for the last scene of this season. All of the extras are in place, and we're just waiting for our star."

"What if I refuse?" I asked, noticing out the window the color of the sky and not feeling anything without someone to share that sight with. "You going to pull my mom's account or take me to court to make sure I hold up my contract? You can't strong-arm me, Pete. I don't believe in any of it anymore."

Pete the Wolf stood up and violently flipped the table over, sending my half-empty food spattering everywhere. The force with which the table flew shocked me, as I'd never seen him physically express himself.

Gathering control, he buttoned up his blazer and adjusted his collar. "Stop being such a nihilist," he said in an even-toned voice that didn't match his last actions. "You are nothing compared to the importance of the role you took on. Do you have any idea what's happened? You don't, because you're holed up in here feeling sorry for yourself. Out there, out there is the result of what you've done. What we've all done. We didn't even need to have the Snow Queen call in the military to execute. It just—it just happened."

"What are you talking about, Pete?" I said, getting irritated by his persistence. "Why don't you just let me be and find someone else to play the part?"

"That's rather impossible now, friend. There are too many eyes on us now. Just come with me up to the roof," he said, tossing me a pair of black sunglasses like the ones the Black Panthers used to wear. "Once you see what's happening, I'm confident that you'll feel like yourself again. Do put on the sunglasses, though—I think it will work better for both you and your character. I'll have someone take care of this mess in here."

Not having the strength or desire to argue, I put on the sunglasses and walked ahead of him out the door and into the hallway. I looked down the center stairs that led to the street. The two glass windows had been painted a black tint with red GSB logos (inverted from my perspective), blocking any possible view.

Up and down the hallway on my floor, carpenters were putting in new doors to all the apartments, and construction workers were underway laying new floors, painting, and putting GSB logos and position titles on each of the windows that led into the soon-to-be-offices. I had been yelling at my neighbors for making too much noise, but now I could see what was behind it. Funny how your imagination determines reality until your eyes actually see what's happening.

Pete was setting up his editing bay right across the hall from my apartment. Inside, a team of video directors stood glued in front of the twelve screens that showed various shots of huge, milling crowds. The large screen on the wall opposite the editing bay played the live stream being broadcast on Goldenstatebroadcasting.com.

In one of the shots, I caught a glimpse of a familiar building. Mine. "Are those crowds *outside*?" I asked. On another screen, a tighter shot, I saw something else I recognized: some of union organizers from Rising Sushi. I was sure it was them, though they were wearing GSB windbreakers now. "I think I know some of those people. What are they doing wearing the show's jacket?"

"It's what I've been trying to tell you," Pete said proudly as he motioned for me to go to the stairs that led to the roof. "We thought we were in control of entertainment, friend, but it's turned into something greater. America has responded with such support for us—don't ruin the surprise. Head up. I want to show you what you've helped to create."

We walked up the stairs and through the door that led to the roof, making our way over to the side that looked over Gardner with a hint of Sunset Boulevard. Even though the sun was starting to head down, it still taunted me with an overdose shot of vitamin D. The schoolyard was now filled with tour buses, overflowing with people getting off in droves, all unfurling signs and banners and filming themselves on their phones as they walked.

"What happened to the school? Did you kick the kids out?" I said, marveling at the sheer number of buses they'd managed to squeeze in there.

"It's Saturday," said Pete. "Lost track of your calendar, I imagine."

Everyone walking down Gardner Street was carrying a GSB water bottle, along with whatever kind of sign they'd put together (DAVID'S MANSCAPING, JACQUE'S TALENT MANAGEMENT FOR THE ODD, GOODMAN'S PAINLESS DENTAL, NIKKI'S BONDAGE BONANZA, VICTORIA'S HARLEY HOUSE) and filming themselves on their phones, heading down to

Sunset to join the procession. I remembered reading in the scripts a few weeks ago that the season finale would feature all of those who'd left their lives behind to join GSB to participate in some magnificent march down Sunset, all of them ready to start their own shows and take a shot at the Hollywood dream. There would be a romantic moment on the roof between Eliah and me to dilute the political nature of the scene.

I could swear Pete looked a little sad at the sight of all the people, which was strange to me, because it was his grand finale, and here it was unfolding before him.

"Aren't you happy?" I asked. "It's everything you asked for. I don't understand how you got so many extras—you must have hired every starving actor in the city—but still, this had to be the scene you envisioned."

"Very few of them are actors—well, very few *were* actors, I guess," Pete said, shaking his head and smiling a very humble smile, which just looked so odd on him. "It's incredible how it all turned out. They came, Pace. They really came."

"Who?"

"People from all around the country. People without hope. They picked up and came like it was another gold rush in California, only they came to be stars. Just for that possibility of making it. They didn't just watch, they actually came." He shook his head. "It's not my vision anymore, but that's fine. I was able to touch it."

An older restored tractor that I guessed to be from the 1950s rolled slowly down the street, ORGANIC ITALIAN WITH ZEEK GASPARRI III painted on the side. There was Dr. Addison, the man who'd carved Pace Skillman out of Harold Hall, along with his group of assistants, all wearing lab coasts and holding up signs that read: CREATION

NATION. One after another they moved down the boulevard. YOGA WITH YURI. EASY COMPUTER CODING. Each sign advertising a different show.

"I have to hand it to Dallas," Pete said, shaking his head.

"That TV exec we met at Angel's?"

Pete nodded. "He and Frank Hanson, our Sully farmer, made quite a team. Getting some of the farmers to throw in was key."

"You mean for the show, right? That's for next season or something?"

"There is no next season, friend," he said, still leaning over the edge and watching the procession. "That's the new GSB Farming Act that will be implemented. If your farm was individually owned, you keep it. The corporate farms in California are going to be broken up and owned by GSB, then redistributed to the farmers coming out here to work a piece of land they can call their own."

"If you think those corporations are just going to hand you over their land, you've been in the sun too long." I knew the voice, but it took me a minute to believe it. "Nobody just gives away power like that."

Seeing Eliah again filled my emptiness like cool water poured into a glass. I had to grip the edge of the building to keep my feet. She was standing next to a man it took me another minute to remember. Then I looked at his side and saw him holding the leash of his red-nosed pit bull. Eliah was holding a plain paper shopping bag from Trader Joe's by its handles.

I was so focused on her that I nearly didn't see the Snow Queen walk through the door that led to the roof. She was just suddenly there, shielding herself from the sun with a parasol.

"I found her up some trail in Runyon Canyon," said the man with the dog. "Thought I might find her up there. She was just lying under a tree—no idea what was happening in the city below. When I told her, though, well, I guess the lady had to come and see for herself."

"I knew what was happening in the city," she said. "What I needed was some space so I could figure out what was causing it. I think I have some idea now."

"Are you okay?" I asked as quietly as I could, wanting to run to her but too shaky to do it, still trying to figure out what was happening. She nodded.

"You're wrong about the corporations' cooperation, my dear," the Snow Queen said to Eliah. "You see, this show that you've all been engaged in—the plan all along was for it to be real. We were putting everything in place under the cover of entertainment. All of the information we gathered from the viewers—information of unprecedented depth and breadth about what they were watching, when and how long they watched, what they 'liked' or shared or blocked, and what that all told us about what they desired and feared and would or would not do—all of that was to leave those in power—you can call it government or corporations, take your pick—no choice but to allow us to take control. Why would they resist? Siding with us and making California its own entity would be more profitable.

"What so many people fail to realize or remember is that currency needs to have something behind it to be worth anything. These days, it is information that moves money. California had fallen behind and needed a savior. Who else but Hollywood could do it? Only this time, we weren't going to send some politician up to Sacramento to take power. It was time to move the capital."

Eliah looked at her like she was crazy. "You think these people are going to let you control them when they find out about what you have planned? When they find out that all of this is really happening?"

"That's the funny thing, my dear. You see, our plan—to partner with the state to control the people—never needed to be executed. First, the people never needed to be tricked or forced—they just came, because of the possibilities the show inspired. Who else was giving them hope? Politicians on the campaign trail? They all just started coming here, willingly, to be a part of Golden State Broadcasting. The people made the concept real and are now taking control of the storyline. Well, they think they are. Everyone wants to be a star. Even those little men and women sitting in corner offices with views of the people they control, there is something inside them that makes them want fame. They'd trade it all in a minute just to be recognized and taste the Hollywood life. Of course, Pace, we all know what that life really tastes like."

Eliah had moved next to me, now not saying a word, just watching and listening. Pete was looking over at a camera set up across the roof, pointing off into the distance.

"Are we filming right now?" I said, beyond confused. "Is the Snow Queen going to be in the final scene? This is off script."

"You're goddamn right it's off script," the Snow Queen yelled, then recoiled when she moved over to the edge with us to see the crowds of people marching past.

Eliah caught my eye and nodded toward the hills, where a row of ten military helicopters hovered.

"It was so close to happening for real," the Snow Queen said. "Those helicopters? They're mine. Those tanks on Sunset Boulevard as well. If you were anywhere near the beach, you'd see those battleships on the horizon. It was all set. Today was going to be a very rough day for those who didn't believe in what Golden State Broadcasting was doing. Sacramento had already accepted our demands. I'd just started explaining to them how it was in their best interest to turn it all over to us, just got to the part where I showed them how we'd balance their budget within ten years—and that was it. The magic words: 'balance' and 'budget.'

"There were some holdouts, of course—but only until I convinced them of our military connections' ability to field a significant army to deal with the reaction of the rest of the country—as well as any adverse internal reaction. We were ready to throw down!

"But as it turned out, none of those precautions were necessary. We've had to turn to our military friends once or twice, but only for crowd control during marches. People just kept signing onto the site. One hundred million followers and growing. And they started coming and *kept* coming. All willing, all *pleading* to be taken under Hollywood as their government."

She looked out over the surging tide of people below us and shook her head in wonder. "Our propaganda was so good, they bought it. The people simply chose media over government. Just show the revolution as entertainment and they'll beg for more. Occupy Your Minds, 2013."

The Snow Queen handed me a picture of Eliah and me on our date in the hills, when I was still Harold, sitting on that bench looking over the city as the sun set. The man with the dog had been sent to see how I looked in my natural state by the Snow Queen after the audition.

"That's the memory I want to hold on to," I said softly to Eliah. "We're still those same people."

Eliah shook her head. "But we're not, Pace," she said, looking at the Snow Queen now. "You can never be who you were in the past. These people came and stole that moment from us, but you can't expect things to be perfect. Expecting that clouds your vision. That's why I hate pictures. They paint a certain image of yourself that people can't get out of their heads." Her eyes still steady on the Snow Queen, she said, "We should look, as much as possible, at what is real."

Jumping into our moment, the Snow Queen said to me, "I had to see what you looked like when you weren't auditioning. The leader I needed would be a natural. He wouldn't need to act like anyone but himself. And then I saw the two of you together. If I hadn't seen your chemistry with this woman, I'd never have brought her back to you." She sighed. "It was unfortunate that Samantha fell in love with you. Tragic, as it turned out."

Then, after one more tender moment, she straightened—full-blown Snow Queen once again. "But we have to look at the big picture. We've managed to create a hit that has brought us what we wanted, more than we wanted, regardless of the journey each of us took."

"Well," Eliah said, "that's great for you, but I can't see the benefit of me staying. What are you prepared to offer?" She was talking to the Snow Queen like I'd heard her talk when she'd negotiated with her clients—clear, firm, fearless.

The Snow Queen nodded as if she'd expected this. "It's true, Eliah, that you have more to gain than most. You are in the unique position of being able to give us your demands—though I can't imagine we'll have any problem meeting them. What is your fallback, after all—to return to your previous position?"

"That's right. I liked the boss."

The Snow Queen laughed. "Yes, there's something to be said for being one's own boss, I'll agree. But still, you must see the benefits of helping us grow. Our growth certainly won't hurt yours."

Eliah shrugged. "I still don't see what I stand to gain from joining you, though. My whole life I've been against people like you—systems like yours. I've made my own way."

"That's true, my dear. Only, you never existed outside of the system—even in your independence. You needed the running water, electricity, police—all of the workings that make society, well, social. Now that's just all provided by a different system. You can still exist inside of it and be independent. Why, that's why everyone else is coming here."

"I'm not like anyone else though, am I?" Eliah said, matching the Snow Queen's coolness. "My only recorded existence is on Golden State Broadcasting. You've made an ideal of me, and that's hard to replace. I'm going to need something substantial to stay on."

"Well, I'm waiting, dear," answered the Snow Queen, smiling confidently. "What is it that you want?"

"Total autonomy," she said. "I have my own show and no one touches my show but me; I'm on the front page of Goldenstatebroadcasting.com each time I have a new episode and have all the access I need to your production capabilities. Free of charge, of course. I'd also like control over all libraries and the resources and personnel to keep them full so that young people under your system have a place to get away from screens. There will be no shows allowed in there, and they will be blocked of all Internet connections. You can put me in charge of that, and I'll do it as I choose. I'll still do GSB though, as, strangely enough, I've come to like working on it. Besides, I need to see firsthand what's happening. So my request to you is that your government, whatever it turns out to be, does not interfere with my plans to subvert it."

"That seems like a lot to make up on the spot," the Snow Queen said, smiling at Eliah's negotiating skills. "A little subversion always makes for good viewing, though."

"I had some time to think up in the hills," Eliah responded. "One of the many benefits of not being where everyone else is."

The Snow Queen reached out her hand, and the two of them sealed the deal when Eliah shook it, each moving the same amount of space toward the other.

"Good," said the Snow Queen, turning her attention to Pete the Wolf. "As long as we have the helicopters here for a full shot, let's talk about positioning." Pete the Wolf and the Snow Queen wandered off toward the side of the roof closest to the hills.

"That was amazing," I said to Eliah, remembering more of what had made me fall so hard for her. "Some of the reason you came back had to have been for me, Eliah. For us. You can't tell me what you've felt for us is completely gone."

"I can't exist from what once was," she said, shaking her head. "I'm sorry, Pace—Harold—but love? It's just not there anymore. How could our love ever be clean? You made love to me as someone else. You sold me away to your character." She looked away from me, down to the flowing crowds on the streets. Something seemed to shift in her. "And that's who I belong to now—it's still on my terms, within this new framework. It's going to have to be enough. That's the trick, isn't it? To make your own reality inside of you that nobody can touch."

"But you came back," I said loudly, looking around to everyone else, as if they could help me. "She came back, right?" I turned back to Eliah. "The camera is ready—are you sure you still want to do the scene?"

"Of course I came back. There's no escaping reality," Eliah told me, starting to edge me over to where the camera was positioned. "I'm still me. It's not like I was forced to become someone else." She drew up, realizing how that sounded. "I'm sorry, Harold—Pace—I didn't mean to—"

"It's fine," I said, feeling the reality. "I wasn't forced either. It was my choice. This is everything I ever wanted."

We'd stopped halfway across the roof. She nodded, looking at me deeply. "There's nothing to do now but live life," she said at last. "Maybe it's not ideal. There may not ever be an ideal. This is what life is—not your projections of what you think it should be. This is it. This is real.

"Look at the world around us now," she said. "They're starting to see that they can create their own reality without asking anyone's permission to do so. I think this show you've helped to create has given them that knowledge." She took a deep breath, looking off past the cameras to the hills. "What I never realized before now is that when you escape one system, there's just another one waiting for you. This one, though—at least it allows me to exist how I want to inside it. That's not something you just hand over. You have to negotiate until you get life on your terms." She turned to me. "That's what I've always wanted you to realize. Look at what you've done just by being you. You've become the most important person in Hollywood and made this city the home of independence in the process. It's time to do the same for yourself."

Still scrambling to wrap my head around it all, I asked, "You really want to continue with the show? With me?"

"Why not?" she said, smiling slightly and winking, as if she had planned to join in all along. "If the new currency of California is information, I might be the richest person in the state. The reality is I could never go back to my old way of living—I'm too well known now. Both the Snow Queen and I knew it. I just had to make sure I wasn't giving up my way of life."

"I want you to tell me you love me," I said. "That's all I care about."

"If that's all you wanted, Pace," she said, looking deep into my eyes, "you would have had that. But it's not. You wanted exactly what you have. Don't be so down—you've done something incredible with your life. You've shown people how to make something of themselves." When she saw how little that meant to me at that moment, she said, "How about I tell you I love you when the cameras are rolling? Would that be enough? You'll be able to hear it as long as we're broadcasting."

I turned to Pete and the Snow Queen. Pete was already standing behind the camera and talking on a walkie-talkie to the helicopter circling above. The Snow Queen smiled at me.

"This is what it feels like to get what you want, dear," she said. "I hope it's enough, for all of us."

I nodded. What else was I going to do? I'd given my whole life to be part of what was happening in Hollywood, and now I'd spend the foreseeable future living it, leading people from all over the country to try and do the same.

Pete the Wolf yelled action and started filming Eliah and me against the Hollywood Hills, now nearly covered by a cloud bank, lit bright pink by the sunset. The sounds of helicopters above would be pushed back a bit in the editing, and we'd bring up some dubbed-over songs supposedly being sung by the marchers below. The country was descending on Hollywood, and we were now its center. Eliah was still holding that Trader Joe's bag, from which she pulled out a single small potted flower.

She held it in her hands, rose up on her toes, and sniffed me at the base of the neck. Just as she was about to pull away, she whispered to me so that only I could hear, "It's the only one that survived."

She placed the flower behind our feet, away from the shot, and leaned back to look lovingly at me.

I braced myself, and Eliah too, in my arms. Her eyes looked like they did in the photo of us, but she was doing it on purpose, not naturally. Her lips smiled tenderly. All I had to do was slip into character along with her—and I did it. No matter how the universe handed her to me, I was willing to accept it.

After making sure we were backlit by the day's last drop of light, Pete the Wolf nodded with great satisfaction at the picture we made in his lens, then stood up confused, realizing we—and it seemed to me, all of Hollywood—had fallen silent.

"Lines!" he yelled.

The End

ACKNOWLEDGMENTS

To the amazing city of Los Angeles, who guided me through my youth and another bid as a young adult. You are a gem that must be studied to find your beauty—you carry characters on your sidewalks and buses, providing treasure hunts on every inch of your stretched-out landscape. I thank you for providing a canvas on which this story could be told.

For those in the trenches with me during the edits of this book, Terry Goodman and David Downing, I thank you for believing that something out of the ordinary is worthy of construction. To Carissa Bluestone, for making sure the patient never left the operating table until truly ready for the world.

To my friends who provided me love and companionship through the madness of Los Angeles. Zaron, Dave, Pesc, Langston, Jeff, Danny B., Todd, and Tommy—you always allowed for the unreal. Much love and respect.

For my wife Saruul, without whom I would only be half a person, you are the reason I move through the world with a smile on my face.

ABOUT THE AUTHOR

Photo © Mingus, 2012

After working in the New York advertising world and seeing the possibilities that social media and the digital revolution held for writers, Christopher Herz fully went after his dream of writing novels and took to selling copies of his first book, *The Last Block in Harlem*, on the streets of New York. His unorthodox efforts and fresh contemporary prose garnered the attention of media outlets everywhere, earning him an early spot on the AmazonEncore roster. AmazonEncore then republished the book to critical acclaim, and his novel *Pharmacology* was released a year later. Herz is a graduate of the San Francisco State University creative writing program and a regular contributor to the *Huffington Post*, where he writes extensively on art and culture. Born in New York City, Herz grew up in California, the setting for his searing portrait of American life, *Hollywood Forever*.

Made in the USA
Charleston, SC
24 December 2012